A MONSTROUS TOAD-LIKE THING SQUATTED ON TOP OF THE MONOLITH

I saw its bloated, repulsive and unstable outline against the moonlight. Set in what would have been the face of a natural creature, its huge, blinking eyes reflected all the lust, abysmal greed, obscene cruelty and monstrous evil that has stalked the sons of men since their ancestors moved hairless in the tree-tops. In those grisly eyes were mirrored all the unholy things and vile secrets that sleep in the cities under the sea. And so that ghastly thing that the unhallowed ritual and sadism and blood had evoked from the silence of the hills leered and blinked down on its bestial worshippers, who groveled in abhorrent abasement before it.

Now the beast-masked priest lifted the bound and weakly writhing girl in his brutish hands and held her up toward that horror on the monolith. And as that monstrosity sucked in its breath, lustfully and slobberingly, something snapped in my brain . . .

CTHULHU

THE MYTHOS AND KINDRED HORRORS

ROBERT E. HOWARD

Edited by David Drake

CTHULHU

A Baen Books Original

Baen Publishing Enterprises
P.O. Box 1403
Riverdale, N.Y. 10471

ISBN: 0-671-65641-4

Cover art by Steve Hickman

First printing, May 1987
Second printing, September 1989
Third printing, March 1992

Distributed by
SIMON & SCHUSTER
1230 Avenue of the Americas
New York, N.Y. 10020

Printed in the United States of America

CONTENTS

INTRODUCTION by David Drake   1
ARKHAM   5
THE BLACK STONE   7
THE FIRE OF ASSHURBANIPAL   29
THE THING ON THE ROOF   59
DIG ME NO GRAVE   71
SILENCE FALLS ON MECCA'S WALLS   89
THE VALLEY OF THE WORM   91
THE SHADOW OF THE BEAST   119
OLD GARFIELD'S HEART   133
PEOPLE OF THE DARK   145
WORMS OF THE EARTH   169
PIGEONS FROM HELL   209
AN OPEN WINDOW   247

ACKNOWLEDGMENTS

These stories have appeared previously, in a somewhat different form, as follows:

"Arkham," *Weird Tales*, August 1932. Copyright 1932 by Popular Fiction Publishing Co.

"The Black Stone," *Weird Tales*, November 1931. Copyright 1931 by Popular Fiction Publishing Co.

"The Fire of Asshurbanipal," *Weird Tales*, December 1936. Copyright 1936 by Popular Fiction Publishing Co.

"The Thing on the Roof," *Weird Tales*, February 1932. Copyright 1932 by Popular Fiction Publishing Co.

"Dig Me No Grave," *Weird Tales*, February 1937. Copyright 1937 by Popular Fiction Publishing Co.

"Silence Falls on Mecca's Walls," copyright 1987 by Alla Ray Kuykendall and Alla Ray Morris.

"The Valley of the Worm," *Weird Tales*, February 1934. Copyright 1934 by Popular Fiction Publishing Co.

"The Shadow of the Beast," *The Shadow of the Beast*. Copyright 1977 by Glenn Lord.

"Old Garfield's Heart," *Weird Tales*, December 1933. Copyright 1933 by Popular Fiction Publishing Co.

"People of the Dark," *Strange Tales*, June 1932. Copyright 1932 by The Clayton Magazines, Inc.

"Worms of the Earth," *Weird Tales*, November 1932. Copyright 1932 by Popular Fiction Publishing Co.

"Pigeons From Hell," *Weird Tales*, May 1938. Copyright 1938 by Popular Fiction Publishing Co.

"An Open Window," *Weird Tales*, September 1932. Copyright 1932 by Popular Fiction Publishing Co.

INTRODUCTION

David Drake

Robert E. Howard had the personal misfortune to spend most of his life in a place where black hatreds ruled everyone; where currents of violence so closely underlay the surface of ordinary existence that a snub, a woman, or the ethnic background of a chance acquaintance was apt to bring a lethal outburst; where a man's only path to respect was through strength and his willingness to use that strength.

I don't mean Peaster, in the post-oak country of Texas where Howard was born in 1906, nor Cross Plains, where his family settled a few years later. Rural Texas had its share of color and violence, certainly—cattle ranches, oil rigs, and men who could remember the Comanches. But residents of small towns in West Texas had small-town virtues, of which respectability was probably the most prominent. Other writers of the Prohibition Era, living in the low-rent districts of major cities, were in a far more violent milieu than was Robert E. Howard.

But we humans don't live in geographical locations; we live in our minds. Everything we see, everything that happens to us, is filtered through our perceptions, and the world beyond the immediate range of our senses is *wholly* a mental construct. Our beliefs are more important than our memories, and memory is selective even when it isn't false.

The world—the scheme of belief, expectation, and selected facts—within the mind of Robert E. Howard was a grim, dark place; and it killed him before he was thirty-one.

Although Howard's worldview a bleak and ultimately destructive one, he was neither stupid nor ill-educated. He graduated from high school in Brownswood, Texas, and later took business courses at Howard Payne College in the same town. This record of formal education compares favorably with that of many writers who were his contemporaries. For example, H. P. Lovecraft failed to graduate from high school (Lovecraft's statements to the contrary are not supported by school records).

Besides formal schooling, Howard was an enthusiastic reader who continued to learn and use his learning throughout his life. His sources were frequently stories written by other authors. I suspect most of what Howard "knew" about the Picts who figure largely in his fiction came from *Puck of Pook's Hill*, for instance. Nonetheless, Howard showed good judgment in the choice of writers whose work he cannibalized for backgrounds. Kipling, Harold Lamb, and Robert W. Chambers aren't bad windows into past times.

It was Howard's intention from his early youth to become a professional writer. He proceeded toward that goal with skill and determination. He sold his first story when he was 18, young even for that period when pulp magazines provided far more outlets for new writers than exist today.

Howard continued to better himself in his profession after his first successes. He rose to being (with Seabury Quinn) one of the two most popular writers in *Weird Tales*, his primary market. Furthermore, though Quinn's work is relatively little known today, Howard's writing retains popularity and commercial value at least equal to that of his great contemporary, H. P. Lovecraft. Without suggesting that Howard wrote for the ages, I would expect his stories to see popular publication well into the next century—unlike, for instance, those of Ben Hecht or many others of high literary reputation in the '20s and '30s.

Weird Tales was never financially secure during its long career. Sales there could not be expected to put food on the table until years later, and even then payment was not certain. Howard therefore worked to expand his markets into genres other than fantasy. His intention was professional and (to my mind) laudable, though it sometimes took him into fields for which he had no discernible aptitude.

But he persevered and at last found a genre in which he could equal his previous success with heroic fantasy: western stories whose humorous exaggeration made them almost tall tales. By 1936, Howard was selling regularly to *Argosy*, one of the top three pulp markets of the day. Robert E. Howard was thirty years old, and his career was about to take off.

Then he shot himself in the head.

The immediate impetus for Howard's suicide was the fact that his mother had slipped into her final coma, but the root cause was deeper than the relationship between mother and son. Mrs. Howard was certainly over-protective, doing her best to cut Robert off from women of his own age. Robert was certainly over-solicitous, performing menial tasks for his mother and bowing to her whims instead of living an adult life of his own.

But Howard had nearly commited suicide earlier, when his twelve-year-old dog died.

Howard's success and continuing popularity stems from the way he really believed in—*lived* in—the black, violent world of which he wrote. Not the ghosts and the monsters, of course, but the passions that drive men to death and bloody triumph. He had friends, largely though not entirely by correspondence, but Howard's family and his dog were the only things that he could fully trust not somehow to betray him.

Then his dog died; and his mother, too, was preparing to abandon him.

The place in which Robert E. Howard spent his life was a personal misfortune for him; but if he had lived in a brighter world, you and I as readers would have been the poorer for it.

ARKHAM

Drowsy and dull with age the houses blink
On aimless streets the rat-gnawed years forget
But what inhuman figures leer and slink
Down the old alleys when the moon has set?

THE BLACK STONE

They say foul things of Old Times still lurk
In dark forgotten corners of the world,
And Gates still gape to loose, on certain nights,
Shapes pent in Hell.

—JUSTIN GEOFFREY

I READ of it first in the strange book of Von Junzt,
the German eccentric who lived so curiously and died
in such grisly and mysterious fashion. It was my fortune
to have access to his Nameless Cults in the original
edition, the so-called Black Book, published in Dusseldorf in 1839, shortly before a hounding doom overtook
the author. Collectors of rare literature were familiar
with Nameless Cults mainly through the cheap and
faulty translation which was pirated in London by
Bridewall in 1845, and the carefully expurgated edition
put out by the Golden Goblin Press of New York, 1909.
But the volume I stumbled upon was one of the unex-
purgated German copies, with heavy leather covers
and rusty iron hasps. I doubt if there are more than
half a dozen such volumes in the entire world today,
for the quantity issued was not great, and when the
manner of the author's demise was bruited about, many
possessors of the book burned their volumes in panic.

Von Junzt spent his entire life (1795-1840) delving into forbidden subjects; he traveled in all parts of the world, gained entrance into innumerable secret societies, and read countless little-known and esoteric books and manuscripts in the original; and in the chapters of the Black Book, which range from startling clarity of exposition to murky ambiguity, there are statements and hints to freeze the blood of a thinking man. Reading what Von Junzt dared put in print arouses uneasy speculations as to what it was that he dared not tell. What dark matters, for instance, were contained in those closely written pages that formed the unpublished manuscript on which he worked unceasingly for months before his death, and which lay torn and scattered all over the floor of the locked and bolted chamber in which Von Junzt was found dead with the marks of taloned fingers on his throat? It will never be known, for the author's closest friend, the Frenchman Alexis Ladeau, after having spent a whole night piecing the fragments together and reading what was written, burnt them to ashes and cut his own throat with a razor.

But the contents of the published matter are shuddersome enough, even if one accepts the general view that they but represent the ravings of a madman. There among many strange things I found mention of the Black Stone, that curious, sinister monolith that broods among the mountains of Hungary, and about which so many dark legends cluster. Von Junzt did not devote much space to it—the bulk of his grim work concerns cults and objects of dark worship which he maintained existed in his day, and it would seem that the Black Stone represents some order or being lost and forgotten centuries ago. But he spoke of it as one of the keys—a phrase used many times by him, in various relations, and constituting one of the obscurities of his work. And he hinted briefly at curious sights to be seen about the monolith on midsummer's night. He mentioned Otto Dostmann's theory that this monolith was a remnant of the Hunnish invasion and had been erected to commemorate a victory of Attila over the Goths. Von Junzt contradicted this assertion without giving any refutory facts, merely remarking that to attribute the origin of the Black Stone to the Huns was as logical as assuming that William the Conqueror reared Stonehenge.

This implication of enormous antiquity piqued my interest immensely and after some difficulty I succeeded in locating a rat-eaten and moldering copy of Dostmann's *Remnants of Lost Empires* (Berlin, 1809, "Der Drachenhaus" Press). I was disappointed to find that Dostmann referred to the Black Stone even more briefly than had Von Junzt, dismissing it with a few lines as an artifact comparatively modern in contrast with the Greco-Roman ruins of Asia Minor which were his pet theme. He admitted his inability to make out the defaced characters on the monolith but pronounced them unmistakably Mongoloid. However, little as I learned from Dostmann, he did mention the name of the village adjacent to the Black Stone— Stregoicavar—an ominous name, meaning something like Witch-Town.

A close scrutiny of guidebooks and travel articles gave me no further information—Stregoicavar, not on any map that I could find, lay in a wild, little-frequented region, out of the path of casual tourists. But I did find subject for thought in Dornly's *Magyar Folklore*. In his chapter on dream myths he mentions the Black Stone and tells of some curious superstitions regarding it—especially the belief that if anyone sleeps in the vicinity of the monolith, that person will be haunted by monstrous nightmares for ever after; and he cited tales of the peasants regarding too-curious people who ventured to visit the

Stone on Midsummer Night and who died raving mad because of something they saw there.

That was all I could gleam from Dornly, but my interest was even more intensely roused as I sensed a distinctly sinister aura about the Stone. The suggestion of dark antiquity, the recurrent hint of unnatural events on Midsummer Night, touched some slumbering instinct in my being, as one senses, rather than hears, the flowing of some dark subterraneous river in the night.

And I suddenly saw a connection between this Stone and a certain weird and fantastic poem written by the mad poet, Justin Geoffrey: "The People of the Monolith." Inquiries led to the information that Geoffrey had indeed written that poem while traveling in Hungary, and I could not doubt that the Black Stone was the very monolith to which he referred in his strange verse. Reading his stanzas again, I felt once more the strange dim stirrings of subconscious promptings that I had noticed when first reading of the Stone.

I had been casting about for a place to spend a short vacation and I made up my mind. I went to Stregoicavar. A train of obsolete style carried me from Temesvar to within striking distance, at least, of my objective, and a three days' ride in a jouncing coach brought me to the little village which lay in a fertile valley high up in the fir-clad mountains.

The journey itself was uneventful, but during the first day we passed the old battlefield of Schomvaal where the brave Polish-Hungarian knight, Count Boris Vladinoff, made his gallant and futile stand against the victorious hosts of Suleiman the Magnificent, when the Grand Turk swept over eastern Europe in 1526.

The driver of the coach pointed out to me a great heap of crumbling stones on a hill nearby, under which, he said, the bones of the brave Count lay. I remembered a passage from Larson's *Turkish Wars*. "After the skirmish" (in which the Count with his small army had beaten back the Turkish advance-guard) "the Count was standing beneath the half-ruined walls of the old castle on the hill, giving orders as to the disposition of his forces, when an aide brought to him a small lacquered case which had been taken from the body of the famous Turkish scribe and historian, Selim Bahadur, who had fallen in the fight. The Count took therefrom a roll of parchment and began to read, but he had not read far before he turned very pale and without saying a word, replaced the parchment in the case and thrust the case into his cloak. At that very instant a hidden Turkish battery suddenly opened fire, and the balls striking the old castle, the Hungarians were horrified to see the walls crash down in ruin, completely covering the brave Count. Without a leader the gallant little army was cut to pieces, and in the warswept years which followed, the bones of the noblemen were never recovered. Today the natives point out a huge and moldering pile of ruins near Schomvaal beneath which, they say, still rests all that the centuries have left of Count Boris Vladinoff."

I found the village of Stregoicavar a dreamy, drowsy little village that apparently belied its sinister cognomen—a forgotten back-eddy that Progress had passed by. The quaint houses and the quainter dress and manners of the people were those of an earlier century. They were friendly, mildly curious but not inquisitive, though visitors from the outside world were extremely rare.

"Ten years ago another American came here and stayed a few days in the village," said the owner of the tavern where I had put up, "a young fellow and queer-acting—mumbled to himself—a poet, I think."

I knew he must mean Justin Geoffrey.

"Yes, he was a poet," I answered, "and he wrote a poem about a bit of scenery near this very village."

"Indeed?" Mine host's interest was aroused. "Then, since all great poets are strange in their speech and actions, he must have achieved great fame, for his actions and conversations were the strangest of any man I ever knew."

"As is usual with artists," I answered, "most of his recognition has come since his death."

"He is dead, then?"

"He died screaming in a madhouse five years ago."

"Too bad, too bad," sighed mine host sympathetically. "Poor lad—he looked too long at the Black Stone."

My heart gave a leap, but I masked my keen interest and said casually. "I have heard something of this Black Stone; somewhere near this village, is it not?"

"Nearer than Christian folk wish," he responded. "Look!" He drew me to a latticed window and pointed up at the fir-clad slopes of the brooding blue mountains. "There beyond where you see the bare face of that jutting cliff stands that accursed Stone. Would that it were ground to powder and the powder flung into the Danube to be carried to the deepest ocean! Once men tried to destroy the thing, but each man who laid hammer or maul against it came to an evil end.

"So now the people shun it."

"What is there so evil about it," I asked curiously.

"It is a demon-haunted thing," he answered uneasily and with the suggestion of a shudder. "In my childhood I knew a young man who came up from below and laughed at our traditions—in his foolhardiness he went to the Stone on Midsummer Night and at dawn stumbled into the village again, stricken dumb and mad. Something had shattered his brain and sealed his lips, for until the day of his death, which came soon after, he spoke only to utter terrible blasphemies or to slaver gibberish.

"My own nephew when very small was lost in the mountains and slept in the woods near the Stone, and now in his manhood he is tortured by foul dreams so that at times he makes the night hideous with his screams and wakes with cold sweat upon him.

"But let us talk of something else, Herr; it is not good to dwell upon such things."

I remarked on the evident age of the tavern and he answered with pride. "The foundations are more than four hundred years old; the original house was the only one in the village which was not burned to the ground when Suleiman's devil swept through the mountains. Here, in the house that then stood on these same foundations, it is said, the scribe Selim Bahadur had his headquarters while ravaging the country hereabouts."

I learned then that the present inhabitants of Stregoicavar are not descendants of the people who dwelt there before the Turkish raid of 1526. The victorious Moslems left no living human in the village or the vicinity thereabouts when they passed over. Men, women and children they wiped out in one red holocaust of murder, leaving a vast stretch of country silent and utterly deserted. The present people of Stregoicavar are descended from hardy settlers from the lower valleys who came into the ruined village after the Turk was thrust back.

Mine host did not speak of the extermination of the original inhabitants with any great resentment and I learned that his ancestors in the lower levels had looked on the mountaineers with even more hatred and aversion than they regarded the Turks. He was rather vague regarding the causes of this feud, but said that the original inhabitants of Stregoicavar had been in the habit of making stealthy raids on the lowlands and stealing girls and children. Moreover, he said that they were not exactly of the same blood as his own people; the sturdy, original Magyar-Slavic stock had mixed and intermarried with a degraded aboriginal race until the breeds had blended; producing an unsavory amalgamation. Who these aborigines were, he had not the slightest idea, but maintained that they were "pagans" and had dwelt in the mountains since time immemorial, before the coming of the conquering peoples.

I attached little importance to this tale; seeing in it merely a parallel to the amalgamation of Celtic tribes with Mediterrean aborigines in the Galloway hills, with the resultant mixed race which, as Picts, has such an extensive part in Scotch legendary. Time has a curious foreshortening effect on folklore, and just as tales of the Picts became intertwined with legends of an older Mongoloid race, so that eventually the Picts were ascribed the repulsive appearance of the squat primitives, whose individuality merged, in the telling, into Pictish tales, and was forgotten; so, I felt, the supposed inhuman attributes of the first villages of Stregoicavar could be traced to older, outworn myths with invading Huns and Mongols.

The morning after my arrival I received directions from mine host, who gave them worriedly, and set out to find the Black Stone. A few hours' tramp up the fir-covered slopes brought me to the face of the rugged, solid stone cliff which jutted boldly from the mountainside. A narrow trail wound up it, and mounting this, I looked out over the peaceful valley of Stregoicavar, which seemed to drowse, guarded on either hand by the great blue mountains. No huts or any sign of human tenancy showed between the cliff whereon I stood and the village. I saw numbers of scattering farms in the valley but all lay on the other side of Stregoicavar, which itself seemed to shrink from the brooding slopes which masked the Black Stone.

The summit of the cliffs proved to be a sort of thickly wooded plateau. I made my way through the dense growth for a short distance and came into a wide glade; and in the center of the glade reared a gaunt figure of black stone.

It was octagonal in shape, some sixteen feet in height and about a foot and a half thick. It had once evidently been highly polished, but now the surface was thickly dinted as if savage efforts had been made to demolish it; but the hammers had done little more than to flake off small bits of stone and mutilate the characters which once had evidently marched in a spiraling line round and round the shaft to the top. Up to ten feet from the base these characters were almost completely blotted out, so that it was very difficult to trace their direction. Higher up they were plainer, and I managed to squirm part of the way up the shaft and scan them at close range. All were more or less defaced, but I was positive that they symbolized no language now remembered on the face of the earth. I am fairly familiar with all hieroglyphics known to researchers and philologists and I can say, with certainty, that those characters were like nothing of which I have ever read or heard. The nearest approach to them that I ever saw were some crude scratches on a gigantic and strangely symmetrical rock in a lost valley of the Yucatan. I remember that when I pointed out these marks to the archeologist who was my companion, he maintained that they either represented natural weathering or the idle scratching of some Indian. To my theory that the rock was really the base of a long-vanished column, he merely laughed, calling my attention to the dimensions of it, which suggested, if it were built with any natural rules of architectural symmetry, a column a thousand feet high. But I was not convinced.

I will not say that the characters on the Black Stone were similar to those on that colossal rock in the Yucatan; but one suggested the other. As to the substance of the monolith, again I was baffled. The stone of which it was composed was a dully gleaming black, whose surface, where it was not dinted and roughened, created a curious illusion of semitransparency.

I spent most of the morning there and came away baffled. No connection of the Stone with any other artifact in the world suggested itself to me. It was as if the monolith had been reared by alien hands, in an age distant and apart from human ken.

I returned to the village with my interest in no way abated. Now that I had seen the curious thing, my desire was still more keenly whetted to investigate the matter further and seek to learn by what strange hands and for what strange purpose the Black Stone had been reared in the long ago.

I sought out the tavernkeeper's nephew and questioned him in regard to his dreams, but he was vague, though willing to oblige. He did not mind discussing them, but was unable to describe them with any clarity. Though he dreamed the same dreams repeatedly, and though they were hideously vivid at the time, they left no distinct impression on his waking mind. He remembered them only as chaotic nightmares through which huge whirling fires shot lurid tongues of flames and a black drum bellowed incessantly. One thing only he had seen the Black Stone, not on a mountain slope but set like a spire on a colossal black castle.

As for the rest of the villagers I found them not inclined to talk about the Stone, with the exception of the schoolmaster, a man of surprising education, who spent much more of his time out in the world than any of the rest.

He was much interested in what I told him of Von Junzt's remarks about the Stone, and warmly agreed with the German author in the alleged age of the monolith. He believed that a coven had once existed in the vicinity and that possibly all of the original villagers had been members of that fertility cult which once threatened to undermine European civilization and gave rise to the tales of witchcraft. He cited the very name of the village to prove his point; it had not been originally named Stregoicavar, he said; according to legends the builders had called it Xuthltan, which was the aboriginal name of the site on which the village had been built many centuries ago.

This fact roused again an indescribable feeling of uneasiness. The barbarous name did not suggest connection with any Scythic, Slavic or Mongolian race to which an aboriginal people of these mountains would, under natural circumstances, have belonged.

That the Magyars and Slavs of the lower valleys believed the original inhabitants of the village to be members of the witchcraft cult was evident, the schoolmaster said, by the name they gave it, which name continued to be used even after the older settlers had been massacred by the Turks, and the village rebuilt by a cleaner and more wholesome breed.

He did not believe that the members of the cult erected the monolith but he did believe that they used it as a center of their activities, and repeating vague legends which had been handed down since before the Turkish invasion, he advanced the theory that the degenerate villagers had used it as a sort of altar on which they offered human sacrifices, using as victims the girls and babies stolen from his own ancestors in the lower valleys.

He discounted the myths of weird events on Midsummer Night, as well as a curious legend of a strange deity which the witch-people of Xuthltan were said to have invoked with chants and wild rituals of flagellation and slaughter.

He had never visited the Stone on Midsummer Night, he said, but he would not fear to do so; whatever had existed or taken place there in the past, had been long engulfed in the mists of time and oblivion. The Black Stone had lost its meaning save as a link to a dead and dusty past.

It was while returning from a visit with his schoolmaster one night about a week after my arrival at Stregoicavar that a sudden recollection struck me—it was Midsummer Night! The very time that the legends linked with grisly implications to the Black Stone. I turned away from the tavern and strode swiftly through the village. Stregoicavar lay silent; the villagers retired early. I saw no one as I passed rapidly out of the village and up into the firs which masked the mountains slopes with whispering darkness. A broad silver moon hung above the valley, flooding the crags and slopes in a weird light and etching the shadows blackly. No wind blew through the firs, but a mysterious, intangible rustling and whispering was abroad. Surely on such nights in past centuries, my whimsical imagination told me, naked witches on magic broomsticks had flown across the valley, pursued by jeering demoniac familiars.

I came to the cliffs and was somewhat disquieted to note that the illusive moonlight lent them a subtle appearance I had not noticed before—in the weird light they appeared less like natural cliffs and more like the ruins of cyclopean and Titan-reared battlements jutting from the mountain-slope.

Shaking off this hallucination with difficulty I came upon the plateau and hesitated a moment before I plunged into the brooding darkness of the woods. A sort of breathless tenseness hung over the shadows, like an unseen monster holding its breath lest it scare away its prey.

I shook off the sensation—a natural one, considering the eeriness of the place and its evil reputation—and made my way through the wood, experiencing a most unpleasant sensation that I was being followed, and halting once, sure that something clammy and unstable had brushed against my face in the darkness.

I came out into the glade and saw the tall monolith rearing its gaunt height above the sward. At the edge of the woods on the side toward the cliffs was a stone which formed a sort of natural seat. I sat down, reflecting that it was probably while there that the mad poet, Justin Geoffrey, had written his fantastic "People of the Monolith." Mine host thought that it was the Stone which had caused Geoffrey's insanity, but the seeds of madness had been sown in the poet's brain long before he ever came to Stregoicavar.

A glance at my watch showed that the hour of midnight was close at hand. I leaned back, waiting whatever ghostly demonstration might appear. A thin night wind started up among the branches of the firs, with an uncanny suggestion of faint, unseen pipes whispering an eerie and evil tune. The monotony of the sound and my steady gazing at the monolith produced a sort of self-hypnosis upon me; I grew drowsy. I fought this feeling, but sleep stole on me in spite of myself; the monolith seemed to sway and dance, strangely distorted to my gaze, and then I slept.

I opened my eyes and sought to rise, but lay still, as if an icy hand gripped me helpless. Cold terror stole over me. The glade was no longer deserted. It was thronged by a silent crowd of strange people, and my distended eyes took in strange barbaric details of costume which my reason told me were archaic and forgotten even in this backward land. Surely,

I thought, these are villagers who have come here to hold some fantastic conclave—but another glance told me that these people were not the folk of Stregoicavar. They were a shorter, more squat race, whose brows were lower, whose faces were broader and duller. Some had Slavic or Magyar features, but those features were degraded as from a mixture of some baser, alien strain I could not classify. Many wore the hides of wild beasts, and their whole appearance, both men and women, was one of sensual brutishness. They terrified and repelled me, but they gave me no heed. They formed in a vast half-circle in front of the monolith and began a sort of chant, flinging their arms in unison and weaving their bodies rhythmically from the waist upward. All eyes were fixed on the top of the Stone which they seemed to be invoking. But the strangest of all was the dimness of their voices; not fifty yards from me hundreds of men and women were unmistakably lifting their voices in a wild chant, yet those voices came to me as a faint indistinguishable murmur as if from across vast leagues of Space—or time.

Before the monolith stood a sort of brazier from which a vile, nauseous yellow smoke billowed upward, curling curiously in a swaying spiral around the black shaft, like a vast unstable snake.

On one side of this brazier lay two figures—a young girl, stark naked and bound hand and foot, and an infant, apparently only a few months old. On the other side of the brazier squatted a hideous old hag with a queer sort of black drum on her lap; this drum she beat with slow, light blows of her open palms, but I could not hear the sound.

The rhythm of the swaying bodies grew faster and into the space between the people and the monolith sprang a naked young woman, her eyes blazing, her long black hair flying loose. Spinning dizzily on her toes, she whirled across the open space and fell prostrate before the Stone, where she lay motionless. The next instant a fantastic figure followed her—a man from whose waist hung a goatskin, and whose features were entirely hidden by a sort of mask made from a huge wolf's head, so that he looked like a monstrous, nightmare being, horribly compounded of elements both human and bestial. In his hand he held a bunch of long fir switches bound together at the larger ends, and the moonlight glinted on a chain of heavy gold looped about his neck.

A smaller chain depending from it suggested a pendant of some sort, but this was missing.

The people tossed their arms violently and seemed to redouble their shouts as this grotesque creature loped across the open space with many a fantastic leap and caper. Coming to the woman who lay before the monolith, he began to lash her with the switches he bore, and she leaped up and spun into the wild steps of the most incredible dance I have ever seen. And her tormentor danced with her, keeping the wild rhythm, matching her every shirl and bound, while incessantly raining cruel blows on her naked body. And at every blow he shouted a single word, over and over, and all the people shouted it back. I could see the working of their lips, and now the faint far-off murmur of their voices merged and blended into one distant shout, repeated over and over with slobbering ecstasy. But what that one word was, I could not make out.

In dizzy whirls spun the wild dancers, while the lookers-on, standing still in their tracks, followed the rhythm of their dance with swaying bodies and weaving arms. Madness grew in the eyes of the capering votaress and was reflected in the eyes of the watchers. Wilder and more extravagant grew the whirling frenzy of that mad dance—it became a bestial and obscene thing, while the old hag howled and battered the drum like a crazy woman, and the switches cracked out a devil's tune.

Blood trickled down the dancer's limbs but she seemed not to feel the lashing save as a stimulus for further enormities of outrageous motion; bounding into the midst of the yellow smoke which now spread out tenuous tentacles to embrace both flying figures, she seemed to merge with that foul fog and veil herself with it. Then emerging into plain view, closely followed by the beast-thing that flogged her, she shot into an indescribable, explosive burst of dynamic mad motion, and on the very crest of that mad wave, she dropped suddenly to the sward, quivering and panting as if completely overcome by her frenzied exertions. The lashing continued with unabated violence and intensity and she began to wiggle toward the monolith on her belly. The priest—or such I will call him—followed, lashing her unprotected body with all the power of his arm as she writhed along, leaving a heavy track of blood on the trampled earth. She reached the monolith, and gasping and panting, flung both arms about it and covered the cold stone with fierce hot kisses, as in frenzied and unholy adoration.

The fantastic priest bounded high in the air, flinging away the red-dabbled switches, and the worshippers, howling and foaming at the mouths, turned on each other with tooth and nail, rendering one another's garments and flesh in a blind passion of bestiality. The priest swept up the infant with a long arm, and shouting again that Name, whirled the wailing babe high in the air and dashed its brains out against the monolith, leaving a ghastly stain on the black surface. Cold with horror I saw him rip the tiny body open with his bare brutish fingers and fling handfuls of blood on the shaft, then toss the red and torn shape into the brazier, extinguishing flame and smoke in a crimson rain, while the maddened brutes behind him howled over and over the Name. Then suddenly they all fell prostrate, writhing like snakes, while the priest flung wide his gory hands as in triumph. I opened my mouth to scream my horror and loathing, but only a dry rattle sounded; a huge monstrous toadlike thing squatted on the top of the monolith!

I saw its bloated, repulsive and unstable outline against the moonlight and set in what would have been the face of a natural creature, its huge, blinking eyes which reflected all the lust, abysmal greed, obscene cruelty and monstrous evil that has stalked the sons of men since their ancestors moved blind and hairless in the tree-tops. In those grisly eyes were mirrored all the unholy things and vile secrets that sleep in the cities under the sea, and that skulk from the light of day in the blackness of primordial caverns. And so that ghastly thing that the unhallowed ritual and sadism and blood had evoked from the silence of the hills, leered and blinked down on its bestial worshippers, who groveled in abhorrent abasement before it.

Now the beast-masked priest lifted the bound and weakly writhing girl in his brutish hands and held her up toward that horror on the monolith. And as that monstrosity sucked in its breath, lustfully and slobberingly, something snapped in my brain and I fell into a merciful faint.

I opened my eyes on a still white dawn. All the events of the night rushed back on me and I sprang up, then stared about me in amazement. The monolith brooded gaunt and silent above the sward which waved, green and untrampled, in the morning breeze. A few quick strides took me across the glade; here had the dancers leaped and bounded until the ground should have been trampled bare, and here had the votaress wriggled her painful way to the Stone, streaming blood on the earth. But no drop of crimson showed on the uncrushed sward. I looked, shud-

deringly, at the side of the monolith against which
the bestial priest had brained the stolen baby—but
no dark stain nor grisly clot showed there.

A dream! It had been a wild nightmare—or else—I
shrugged my shoulders. What a vivid clarity for a
dream!

I returned quietly to the village and entered the
inn without being seen. And there I sat meditating
over the strange events of the night. More and more
was I prone to discard the dream-theory. That what I
had seen was illusion and without material substance,
was evident. But I believed that I had looked on the
mirrored shadow of a deed perpetrated in ghastly
actuality in bygone days. But how was I to know?
What proof to show that my vision had been a gathering of foul specters rather than a nightmare origi-
nating in my brain?

As if for answer a name flashed into my mind—
Selim Bahadur! According to legend this man, who
had been a soldier as well as a scribe, had commanded that part of Suleiman's army which had dev-
astated Stregoicavar; it seemed logical enough; and
if so, he had gone straight from the blotted-out countryside to the bloody field of Schomvaal, and his
doom. I sprang up with a sudden shout—that manuscript which was taken from the Turk's body, and
which Count Boris shuddered over—might it not
contain some narration of what the conquering Turks
found in Stregoicavar? What else could have shaken
the iron nerves of the Polish adventurer? And since
the bones of the Count had never been recovered,
what more certain than that the lacquered case, with
its mysterious contents, still lay hidden beneath the
ruins that covered Boris Vladinoff? I began packing
my bag with fierce haste.

Three days later found me esconced in a little
village a few miles from the old battlefield, and when

the moon rose I was working with savage intensity
on the great pile of crumbling stone that crowned
the hill. It was back-breaking toil—looking back now
I cannot see how I accomplished it, though I labored
without a pause from moonrise to dawn. Just as the
sun was coming up I tore aside the last tangle of
stones and looked on all that was mortal of Count
Boris Vladinoff—only a few pitiful fragments of crumbling bone—and among them, crushed out of all original shape, lay a case whose lacquered surface had
kept it from complete decay through the centuries.

I seized it with frenzied eagerness, and back in my
tavern chamber I opened the case and found the
parchment comparatively intact; and there was something else in the case—a small squat object wrapped
in silk. I was wild to plumb the secrets of those
yellowed pages, but weariness forbade me. Since leaving Stregoicavar I had hardly slept at all, and the
terrific exertions of the previous night combined to
overcome me. In spite of myself I was forced to
stretch myself on my bed, nor did I awake until
sundown.

I snatched a hasty supper, and then in the light of
a flickering candle, I set myself to read the near
Turkish characters that covered the parchment. It
was difficult work, for I am not deeply versed in the
language and the archaic style of the narrative baffled
me. But as I toiled through it a word or a phrase
here and there leaped at me and a dimly growing
horror shook me in its grip. I bent my energies
fiercely to the task, and as the tale grew clearer and
took more tangible form my blood chilled in my
veins, my hair stood up and my tongue clove to my
mouth.

At last when gray dawn was stealing through the
latticed window, I laid down the manuscript and
took up and unwrapped the thing in the bit of silk.
Staring at it with haggard eyes I knew the truth of

the matter was clinched, even had it been possible to doubt the veracity of that terrible manuscript.

And I replaced both obscene things in the case, nor did I rest or sleep or eat until the case containing them had been weighted with stones and flung into the deepest current of the Danube which, God grant, carried them back into the Hell from which they came.

It was no dream I dreamed on Midsummer Midnight in the hills above Stregoicavar. Well for Justin Geoffrey that he tarried there only in the sunlight and went his way, for had he gazed upon that ghastly conclave, his mad brain would have snapped before it did. How my own reason held, I do not know.

No—it was no dream—I gazed upon a foul rout of votaries long dead, come up from Hell to worship as of old; ghosts that bowed before a ghost. For Hell has long claimed their hideous god.

By what foul alchemy or godless sorcery the Gates of Hell are opened on that one eery night I do not know, but mine own eyes have seen. And I know I look on no living thing that night, for the manuscript written in the careful hand of Selim Bahadur narrated at length what he and his raiders found in the valley of Stregoicavar; and I read, set down in detail, the blasphemous obscenities that torture wrung from the lips of screaming worshippers; and I read, too, of the lost, grim black cavern high in the hills where the horrified Turks hemmed a monstrous, bloated, wallowing toad-like being and slew it with flame and ancient steel blessed in old times by Muhammad, and with incantations that were old when Arabia was young. And even staunch old Selim's hand shook as he recorded the cataclysmic, earth-shaking death-howls of the monstrosity, which died not alone; for half-score of his slayers perished with him, in ways that Selim would not or could not describe.

And that squat idol carved of gold and wrapped in

silk was an image of himself, and Selim tore it from the golden chain that looped the neck of the slain high priest of the mask.

Well that the Turks swept out that foul valley with torch and cleanly steel! Such sights as those brooding mountains have looked on belong to the darkness and abysses of lost eons. No—it is not fear of the toad-thing that makes me shudder in the night. He is made fast in Hell with his nauseous horde, freed only for an hour on the most weird night of the year, as I have seen. And of his worshippers, none remains.

But it is the realization that such things once crouched beastlike above the souls of men which bring cold sweat to my brow; and I fear to peer again into the leaves of Von Junzt's abomination. For now I understand his repeated phrase of keys!— aye! Keys to Outer Doors—links with an abhorrent past and—who knows?—of abhorrent spheres of the present. And I understand why the tavernkeeper's nightmare-haunted nephew saw in his dream, the Black Stone like a spire on a cyclopean black castle. If men ever excavate among those mountains they may find incredible things below those masking slopes. For the cave wherein the Turks trapped the—thing— was not truly a cavern, and I shudder to contemplate the gigantic gulf of eons which must stretch between this age and the time when the earth shook herself and reared up, like a wave, those blue mountains that, rising, enveloped unthinkable things. May no man ever seek to uproot that ghastly spire men call the Black Stone!

A Key! Aye, it is a Key, symbol of a forgotten horror. That horror has faded into the limbo from which it crawled, loathsomely, in the black dawn of the earth. But what of the other fiendish possibilities hinted at by Von Junzt—what of the monstrous hand which strangled out his life? Since reading what Selim

Bahadur wrote, I can no longer doubt anything in the Black Book. Man was not always master of the earth—and is he now? What nameless shapes may even now lurk in the dark places of the world?

THE FIRE OF ASSHURBANIPAL

YAR ALI squinted carefully down the blue barrel of his Lee-Enfield, called devoutly on Allah and sent a bullet through the brain of a flying rider.

"*Allaho akbar!*"

The big Afghan shouted in glee, waving his weapon above his head, "God is great! By Allah, *sahib*, I have sent another one of the dogs to Hell!"

His companion peered cautiously over the rim of the sand-pit they had scooped with their hands. He was a lean and wiry American, Steve Clarney by name.

"Good work, old horse," said this person. "Four left. Look—they're drawing off."

The white-robed horsemen were indeed reining away, clustering together just out of accurate rifle-range, as if in council. There had been seven when they had first swooped down on the comrades, but the fire from the two rifles in the sand-pit had been deadly.

"Look, *sahib*—they abandon the fray!"

Yar Ali stood up boldly and shouted taunts at the departing riders, one of whom whirled and sent a bullet that kicked up sand thirty feet in front of the pit.

"They shoot like the sons of dogs," said Yar Ali in complacent self-esteem. "By Allah, did you see that rogue plunge from his saddle as my lead went home? Up, *sahib*; let us run after them and cut them down!"

Paying no attention to this outrageous proposal—for he knew it was but one of the gestures Afghan nature continually demands—Steve rose, dusted off his breeches and gazing after the riders, now white specks far out on the desert, said musingly: "Those fellows ride as if they had some set purpose in mind—not a bit like men running from a licking."

"Aye," agreed Yar Ali promptly and seeing nothing inconsistent with his present attitude and recent blood-thirsty suggestion, "they ride after more of their kind—they are hawks who give up their prey not quickly. We had best move our position quickly, Steve *sahib*. They will come back—maybe in a few hours, maybe in a few days—it all depends on how far away lies the oasis of their tribe. But they will be back. We have guns and lives—they want both. And behold."

The Afghan levered out the empty shell and slipped a single cartridge into the breech of his rifle.

"My last bullet, *sahib*."

Steve nodded. "I've got three left."

The raiders whom their bullets had knocked from the saddle had been looted by their own comrades. No use searching the bodies which lay in the sand for ammunition. Steve lifted his canteen and shook it. Not much water remained. He knew that Yar Ali had only a little more than he, though the big Afridi, bred in a barren land, had used and needed less water than did the American; although the latter, judged from a white man's standards, was hard and tough as a wolf. As Steve unscrewed the canteen cap and drank very sparingly, he mentally reviewed the chain of events that had led them to their present position.

Wanderers, soldiers of fortune, thrown together
by chance and attracted to each other by mutual
admiration, he and Yar Ali had wandered from India
up through Turkistan and down through Persia, an
oddly assorted but highly capable pair. Driven by
the restless urge of inherent wanderlust, their avowed
purpose—which they swore to and sometimes believed themselves—was the accumulation of some
vague and undiscovered treasure, some pot of gold at
the foot of some yet unborn rainbow.

Then in ancient Shiraz they had heard of the Fire
of Asshurbanipal. From the lips of an ancient Persian
trader, who only half believed what he repeated to
them, they heard the tale that he in turn had heard
from the babbling lips of delirium, in his distant
youth. He had been a member of a caravan, fifty
years before, which, wandering far on the southern
shore of the Persian Gulf trading for pearls, had
followed the tale of a rare pearl far into the desert.

The pearl, rumored found by a diver and stolen by
a shaykh of the interior, they did not find, but they
did pick up a Turk who was dying of starvation, thirst
and a bullet wound in the thigh. As he died in
delirium, he babbled a wild tale of a silent dead city
of black stone set in the drifting sands of the desert
far to the westward, and of a flaming gem clutched in
the bony fingers of a skeleton on an ancient throne.

He had not dared bring it away with him, because
of an overpowering brooding horror that haunted the
place, and thirst had driven him into the desert
again, where Bedouins had pursued and wounded him.
Yet he had escaped, riding hard until his horse fell
under him. He died without telling how he had
reached the mythical city in the first place, but the
old trader thought he must have come from the
northwest—a deserter from the Turkish army, making a desperate attempt to reach the Gulf.

The men of the caravan had made no attempt to plunge still further into the desert in search of the city; for, said the old trader, they believed it to be the ancient, ancient City of Evil spoken of in the *Necronomicon* of the mad Arab Alhazred—the city of the dead on which an ancient curse rested. Legends named it vaguely: the Arabs called it *Beled-el Djinn*, the City of Devils, and the Turks, *Kara-Shehr*, the Black City. And the gem was that ancient and accursed jewel belonging to a king of long ago, whom the Grecians called Sardanapalus and the Semitic peoples Asshurbanipal.

Steve had been fascinated by the tale. Admitting to himself that it was doubtless one of the ten thousand cock-and-bull myths booted about the East, still there was a possibility that he and Yar Ali had stumbled onto a trace of that pot of rainbow gold for which they searched. And Yar Ali had heard hints before of a silent city of the sands; tales had followed the eastbound caravans over the high Persian uplands and across the sands of Turkistan, into the mountain country and beyond—vague tales, whispers of a black city of the djinn, deep in the hazes of a haunted desert.

So, following the trail of the legand, the companions had come from Shiraz to a village on the Arabian shore of the Persian Gulf, and there had heard more from an old man who had been a pearl-diver in his youth. The loquacity of age was on him and he told tales repeated to him by wandering tribesmen who had them in turn from the wild nomads of the deep interior; and again Steve and Yar Ali heard of the still black city with giant beasts carved of stone, and the skeleton sultan who held the blazing gem.

And so, mentally swearing at himself for a fool, Steve had made the plunge, and Yar Ali, secure in the knowledge that all things lay on the lap of Allah, had come with him. Their scanty supply of money had been just sufficient to provide riding-camels and provisions for a bold flying invasion of the unknown. Their only chart had been the vague rumors that placed the supposed location of Kara-Shehr.

There had been days of hard travel, pushing the beasts and conserving water and food. Then, deep in the desert they invaded, they had encountered a blinding sand-wind in which they had lost the camels. After that came long miles of staggering through the sands, battered by a flaming sun, subsisting on rapidly dwindling water from their canteens, and food Yar Ali had in a pouch. No thought of finding the mythical city now. They pushed on blindly, in hope of stumbling upon a spring; they knew that behind them no oases lay within a distance they could hope to cover on foot. It was a desperate chance, but their only one.

Then white-clad hawks had swooped down on them, out of the haze of the skyline, and from a shallow and hastily scooped trench the adventurers had exchanged shots with the wild riders who circled them at top speed. The bullets of the Bedouins had skipped through their makeshift fortifications, knocking dust into their eyes and flicking bits of cloth from their garments, but by good chance neither had been hit.

Their one bit of luck, reflected Clarney, as he cursed himself for a fool. What a mad venture it had been anyway! To think that two men could so dare the desert and live, much less wrest from its abysmal bosom the secrets of the ages! And that crazy tale of a skeleton hand gripping a flaming jewel in a dead city—bosh! What utter rot! He must have been crazy himself to credit it, the American decided with the clarity of view that suffering and danger bring.

"Well, old horse," said Steve, lifting his rifle, "let's get going. It's a toss-up if we die of thirst or get sniped off by the desert-brothers. Anyway, we're doin' no good here."

"God gives," agreed Yar Ali cheerfully. "The sun sinks westward. Soon the coolness of night will be upon us. Perhaps we shall find water yet, *sahib*. Look, the terrain changes to the south."

Clarney shaded his eyes against the dying sun. Beyond a level, barren expanse of several miles width, the land did indeed become more broken; aborted hills were in evidence. The American slung his rifle over his arm and sighed.

"Heave ahead; we're food for the buzzards anyhow."

The sun sank and the moon rose, flooding the desert with weird silver light. Drifted and glimmered in long ripples, as if a sea had suddenly been frozen into immobility. Steve, parched fiercely by a thirst he dared not fully quench, cursed beneath his breath. The desert was beautiful beneath the moon, with the beauty of a cold marble lorelei to lure men to destruction. What a mad quest! his weary brain reiterated; the Fire of Asshurbanipal retreated into the mazes of unreality with each dragging step. The desert became not merely a material wasteland, but the gray mists of the lost eons, in whose depths dreamed sunken things.

Clarney stumbled and swore; was he failing already? Yar Ali swung along with the easy, tireless stride of the mountain man, and Steve set his teeth, nerving himself to greater effort. They were entering the broken country at last, and the going became harder. Shallow gullies and narrow ravines knifed the earth with wavering patterns. Most of them were nearly filled with sand, and there was no trace of water.

"This country was once oasis country," commented Yar Ali. "Allah knows how many centuries ago the sand took it, as the sand has taken so many cities in Turkistan."

They swung on like dead men in a gray land of death. The moon grew red and sinister as she sank, and shadowy darkness settled over the desert before they had reached a point where they could see what lay beyond the broken belt. Even the big Afghan's feet began to drag, and Steve kept himself erect only by a savage effort of will. At last they toiled up a sort of ridge, on the southern side of which the land sloped downward.

"We rest," declared Steve. "There's no water in this hellish country. No use in goin' on forever. My legs are stiff as gun-barrels. I couldn't take another step to save my neck. Here's a kind of stunted cliff, about as high as a man's shoulder, facing south. We'll sleep in the lee of it."

"And shall we not keep watch, Steve *sahib*?"

"We don't," answered Steve. "If the Arabs cut our throats while we're asleep, so much the better. We're goners anyhow."

With which optimistic observation Clarney lay down stiffly in the deep sand. But Yar Ali stood, leaning forward, straining his eyes into the elusive darkness that turned the star-flecked horizons to murky wells of shadow.

"Something lies on the skyline to the south," he muttered uneasily. "A hill? I cannot tell, or even be sure that I see anything at all."

"You're seeing mirages already," said Steve irritably. "Lie down and sleep."

And so saying Steve slumbered.

The sun in his eyes awoke him. He sat up, yawning, and his first sensation was that of thirst. He lifted his canteen and wet his lips. One drink left. Yar Ali still slept. Steve's eyes wandered over the southern horizon and he started. He kicked the recumbent Afghan.

"Hey, wake up, Ali. I reckon you weren't seeing

things after all. There's your hill—and a queer-lookin' one, too."

The Afridi woke as a wild thing wakes, instantly and completely, his hand leaping to his long knife as he glared about for enemies. His gaze followed Steve's pointing fingers and his eyes widened.

"By Allah and by Allah!'" he swore. "We have come into a land of djinn! That is no hill—it is a city of stone in the midst of the sands!"

Steve bounded to his feet like a steel spring released. As he gazed with bated breath, a fierce shout escaped his lips. At his feet the slope of the ridge ran down into a wide and level expanse of sand that stretched away southward. And far away, across those sands, to his straining sight the "hill" slowly took shape, like a mirage growing from the drifting sands.

He saw great uneven walls, massive battlements; all about crawled the sands like a living, sensate thing, drifted high about the walls, softening the rugged outlines. No wonder that at first glance the whole had appeared like a hill.

"Kara-Shehr!" Clarney exclaimed fiercely. "Beledel-Djinn! The city of the dead! It wasn't a pipe dream after all! We've found it—by Heaven, we've found it! Come on! Let's go!"

Yar Ali shook his head uncertainly and muttered something about evil djinn under his breath, but he followed. The sight of the ruins had swept from Steve his thirst and hunger, and the fatigue that a few hours' sleep had not fully overcome. He trudged on swiftly, oblivious to the rising heat, his eyes gleaming with the lust of the explorer. It was not altogether greed for the fabled gem that had prompted Steve Clarney to risk his life in that grim wilderness; deep in his soul lurked the age-old heritage of the white man, the urge to seek out the hidden places of

the world, and that urge had been stirred to the
depths by the ancient tales.

Now as they crossed the level wastes that separated the broken land from the city, they saw the
shattered walls take clearer form and shape, as if
they grew out of the morning sky. The city seemed
built of huge blocks of black stone, but how high the
walls had been there was no telling because of the
sand that drifted high about their base; in many
places they had fallen away and the sand hid the
fragments entirely.

The sun reached her zenith and thirst intruded
itself in spite of zeal and enthusiasm, but Steve fiercely
mastered his suffering. His lips were parched and
swollen, but he would not take that last drink until
he had reached the ruined city. Yar Ali wet his lips
from his own canteen and tried to share the remain-
der with his friend. Steve shook his head and plod-
ded on.

In the ferocious heat of the desert afternoon they
reached the ruin, and passing through a wide breach
in the crumbling wall, gazed on the dead city. Sand
choked the ancient streets and lent fantastic form to
huge, fallen and half-hidden columns. So crumbled
into decay and so covered with sand was the whole
that the explorers could make out little of the original plan of the city; now it was but a waste of drifted
sand and crumbling stone over which brooded, like
an invisible cloud, an aura of unspeakable antiquity.

But directly in front of them ran a broad avenue,
the outline of which not even the ravaging sands and
winds of time had been able to efface. On either side
of the wide way were ranged huge columns, not
unusually tall, even allowing for the sand that hid
their bases, but incredibly massive. On the top of
each column stood a figure carved from solid stone—
great, somber images, half human, half bestial, par-

taking of the brooding brutishness of the whole city.
Steve cried out in amazement.

"The winged bulls of Nineveh! The bulls with
men's heads! By the saints, Ali, the old tales are
true! The Assyrians did build this city! The whole
tale's true! They must have come here when the
Babylonians destroyed Assyria—why, this scene's a
dead ringer for pictures I've seen—reconstructed
scenes of Old Nineveh! And look!"

He pointed down the broad street to the great
building which reared at the other end, a colossal,
brooding edifice whose columns and walls of solid
black stone blocks defied the winds and sands of
time. The drifting, obliterating sea washed about its
foundations, overflowing into its doorways, but it
would require a thousand years to inundate the
whole structure.

"An abode of devils!" muttered Yar Ali, uneasily.

"The temple of Baal!" exclaimed Steve. "Come on!
I was afraid we'd find all the palaces and temples
hidden by the sand and have to dig for the gem."

"Little good it will do us," muttered Yar Ali. "Here
we die."

"I reckon so." Steve unscrewed the cap of his
canteen. "Let's take our last drink. Anyway, we're
safe from the Arabs. They'd never dare come here,
with their superstitions. We'll drink and then we'll
die, I reckon, but first we'll find the jewel. When I
pass out, I want to have it in my hand. Maybe a few
centuries later some lucky son-of-a-gun will find our
skeletons—and the gem. Here's to him, whoever he
is!"

With which grim jest Clarney drained his canteen
and Yar Ali followed suit. They had played their last
ace; the rest lay on the lap of Allah.

They strode up the broad way, and Yar Ali, utterly
fearless in the face of human foes, glanced nervously

to right and left, half expecting to see a horned and fantastic face leering at him from behind a column. Steve himself felt the somber antiquity of the place, and almost found himself fearing a rush of bronze war chariots down the forgotten streets, or to hear the sudden menacing flare of bronze trumpets. The silence in dead cities was so much more intense, he reflected, than that on the open desert.

They came to the portals of the great temple. Rows of immense columns flanked the wide doorway, which was ankle-deep in sand, and from which sagged massive bronze frameworks that had once braced mighty doors, whose polished woodwork had rotted away centuries ago. They passed into a mighty hall of misty twilight, whose shadowy stone roof was upheld by columns like the trunks of forest trees. The whole effect of the architecture was one of awesome magnitude and sullen, breathtaking splendor, like a temple built by somber giants for the abode of dark gods.

Yar Ali walked fearfully, as if he expected to awake sleeping gods, and Steve, without the Afridi's superstitions, yet felt the gloomy majesty of the place lay somber hands on his soul.

No trace of a footprint showed in the deep dust on the floor; half a century had passed since the affrighted and devil-ridden Turk had fled these silent halls. As for the Bedouins, it was easy to see why those superstitious sons of the desert shunned this haunted city— and haunted it was, not by actual ghosts, perhaps, but by the shadows of lost splendors.

As they trod the sands of the hall, which seemed endless, Steve pondered many questions: How did these fugitives from the wrath of frenzied rebels build this city? How did they pass through the country of their foes,—for Babylonia lay between Assyria and the Arabian desert. Yet there had been no other place for them to go; westward lay Syria and the sea, and north and east swarmed the "dangerous Medes," those fierce Aryans whose aid had stiffened the arm of Babylon to smite her foe to the dust.

Possibly, thought Steve, Kara Shehr—whatever its name had been in those dim days—had been built as an outpost border city before the fall of the Assyrian empire, whither survivals of that overthrow fled. At any rate it was possible that Kara-Shehr had outlasted Nineveh by some centuries—a strange, hermit city, no doubt, cut off from the rest of the world.

Surely, as Yar Ali had said, this was once fertile country, watered by oases; and doubtless in the broken country they had passed over the night before, there had been quarries that furnished the stone for the building of the city.

Then what caused its downfall? Did the encroachment of the sands and the filling up of the springs cause the people to abandon it, or was Kara-Shehr a city of silence before the sands crept over the walls? Did the downfall come from within or without? Did civil war blot out the inhabitants, or were they slaughtered by some powerful foe from the desert? Clarney shook his head in baffled chagrin. The answers to those questions were lost in the maze of forgotten ages.

"*Allaho akbar!*" They had traversed the great shadowy hall and at its further end they came upon a hideous black stone altar, behind which loomed an ancient god, bestial and horrific. Steve shrugged his shoulders as he recognized the monstrous aspect of the image—aye, that was Baal, on whose black altar in other ages many a screaming, writhing, naked victim had offered up its naked soul. The idol embodied in its utter, abysmal and sullen bestiality the whole soul of this demoniac city. Surely, thought Steve, the builders of Nineveh and Kara-Shehr were cast in another mold from the people of today. Their art and culture were too ponderous, too grimly barren of the lighter aspects of humanity, to be wholly human, as modern man understands humanity. Their architecture was repellent; of high skill, yet so massive, sullen and brutish in effect as to be almost beyond the comprehension of moderns.

The adventurers passed through a narrow door which opened in the end of the hall close to the idol, and came into a series of wide, dim, dusty chambers connected by column-flanked corridors. Along these they strode in the gray ghostly light, and came at last to a wide stair, whose massive stone steps led upward and vanished in the gloom. Here Yar Ali halted.

"We have dared much, *sahib*," he muttered. "Is it wise to dare more?"

Steve, aquiver with eagerness, yet understood the Afghan's mind. "You mean we shouldn't go up those stairs?"

"They have an evil look. To what chambers of silence and horror may they lead? When djinn haunt deserted buildings, they lurk in the upper chambers. At any moment a demon may bite off our heads."

"We're dead men anyhow," grunted Steve. "But I tell you—you go on back through the hall and watch for the Arabs while I go upstairs."

"Watch for a wind on the horizon," responded the Afghan gloomily, shifting his rifle and loosening his long knife in its scabbard. "No Bedouin comes here. Lead on, *sahib*. Thou'rt mad after the manner of all Franks, but I would not leave thee to face the djinn alone."

So the companions mounted the massive stairs, their feet sinking deep into the accumulated dust of centuries at each step. Up and up they went, to an incredible height until the depths below merged into a vague gloom.

"We walk blind to our doom, *sahib*," muttered Yar Ali. "*Allah il allah*—and Muhammad is his Prophet! Nevertheless, I feel the presence of slumbering Evil and never again shall I hear the wind blowing up the Khyber Pass."

Steve made no reply. He did not like the breathless silence that brooded over the ancient temple, nor the grisly gray light that filtered from some hidden source.

Now above them the gloom lightened somewhat and they emerged into a vast circular chamber, grayly illuminated by light that filtered in through the high, pierced ceiling. But another radiance lent itself to the illumination. A cry burst from Steve's lips, echoed by Yar Ali.

Standing on the top step of the broad stone stair, they looked directly across the broad chamber, with its dust-covered heavy tile floor and bare black stone walls. From above the center of the chamber, massive steps led up to a stone dais, and on this dais stood a marble throne. About this throne glowed and shimmered an uncanny light, and the awe-struck adventurers gasped as they saw its source. On the throne slumped a human skeleton, an almost shapeless mass of moldering bones. A fleshless hand sagged outstretched upon the broad marble throne-arm, and in its grisly clasp there pulsed and throbbed like a living thing, a great crimson stone.

The Fire of Asshurbanipal! Even after they had found the lost city Steve had not really allowed himself to believe that they would find the gem, or that it even existed in reality. Yet he could not doubt the evidence of his eyes, dazzled by that evil, incredible glow. With a fierce shout he sprang across the chamber and up the steps. Yar Ali was at his heels, but when Steve would have seized the gem, the Afghan laid a hand on his arm.

"Wait!" exclaimed the big Muhammadan. "Touch it not yet, *sahib!* A curse lies on ancient things—and surely this is a thing triply accursed! Else why has it lain here untouched in a country of thieves for so many centuries? It is not well to disturb the possessions of the dead."

"Bosh!" snorted the American. "Superstitions! The Bedouins were scared by the tales that have come down to 'em from their ancestors. Being desert-dwellers they mistrust cities anyway, and no doubt this one had an evil reputation in its lifetime. And nobody except Bedouins have seen this place before, except that Turk, who was probably half demented with suffering.

"These bones may be those of the king mentioned in the legend—the dry desert air preserves such things indefinitely—but I doubt it. May be Assyrian—most likely Arab—some beggar that got the gem and then died on that throne for some reason or other."

The Afghan scarcely heard him. He was gazing in fearful fascination at the great stone, as a hypnotized bird stares into a serpent's eye.

"Look at it, *sahib!*" he whispered. "What is it? No such gem as this was ever cut by mortal hands! Look how it throbs and pulses like the heart of a cobra!"

Steve was looking, and he was aware of a strange undefined feeling of uneasiness. Well versed in the knowledge of precious stones, he had never seen a stone like this. At first glance he had supposed it to be a monster ruby, as told in the legends. Now he was not sure, and he had a nervous feeling that Yar Ali was right, that this was no natural, normal gem. He could not classify the style in which it was cut, and such was the power of its lurid radiance that he found it difficult to gaze at it closely for any length of time. The whole setting was not one calculated to soothe restless nerves. The deep dust on the floor suggested an unwholesome antiquity; the gray light evoked a sense of unreality, and the heavy black walls towered grimly, hinting at hidden things.

"Let's take the stone and go!" muttered Steve, an unaccustomed panicky dread rising in his bosom.

"Wait!" Yar Ali's eyes were blazing, and he gazed, not at the gem, but at the sullen stone walls. "We are flies in the lair of the spider! *Sahib*, as Allah lives, it is more than the ghosts of old fears that lurk over this city of horror! I feel the presence of peril, as I have felt it before—as I felt it in a jungle cavern where a python lurked unseen in the darkness—as I felt it in the temple of Thuggee where the hidden stranglers of Siva crouched to spring upon us—as I feel it now, tenfold!"

Steve's hair prickled. He knew that Yar Ali was a grim veteran, not to be stampeded by silly fear or senseless panic; he well remembered the incidents referred to by the Afghan, as he remembered other occasions upon which Yar Ali's Oriental telepathic instinct had warned him of danger before that danger was seen or heard.

"What is it, Yar Ali?" he whispered.

The Afghan shook his head, his eyes filled with a weird mysterious light as he listened to the dim occult promptings of his subconsciousness.

"I know not; I know it is close to us, and that it is very ancient and very evil. I think——" Suddenly he halted and wheeled, the eery light vanishing from his eyes to be replaced by a glare of wolf-like fear and suspicion.

"Hark, *sahib!*" he snapped. "Ghosts or dead men mount the stair!"

Steve stiffened as the stealthy pad of soft sandals on stone reached his ear.

"By Judas, Ali!" he rapped; "something's out there——"

The ancient walls re-echoed to a chorus of wild yells as a horde of savage figures flooded the chamber. For one dazed insane instant Steve believed wildly that they were being attacked by re-embodied

warriors of a vanished age; then the spiteful crack of
a bullet past his ear and the acrid smell of powder
told him that their foes were material enough. Clarney
cursed; in their fancied security they had been caught
like rats in a trap by the pursing Arabs.

Even as the American threw up his rifle, Yar Ali
fired point-blank from the hip with deadly effect,
hurled his empty rifle into the horde and went down
the steps like a hurricane, his three-foot Khyber
knife shimmering in his hairy hand. Into his gusto for
battle went real relief that his foes were human. A
bullet ripped the turban from his head, but an Arab
went down with a split skull beneath the hillman's
first, shearing stroke.

A tall Bedouin clapped his gun-muzzle to the Afghan's side, but before he could pull the trigger,
Clarney's bullet scattered his brains. The very num-
ber of the attackers hindered their onslaught on the
big Afridi, whose tigerish quickness made shooting
as dangerous to themselves as to him. The bulk of
them swarmed about him, striking with scimitar and
rifle-stock while others charged up the steps after
Steve. At that range there was no missing; the American simply thrust his rifle muzzle into a bearded
face and blasted it into a ghostly ruin. The others
came on, screaming like panthers.

And now as he prepared to expend his last cartridge, Clarney saw two things in one flashing
instant—a wild warrior who, with froth on his beard
and a heavy scimitar uplifted, was almost upon him,
and another who knelt on the floor drawing a careful
bead on the plunging Yar Ali. Steve made an instant
choice and fired over the shoulder of the charging
swordsman, killing the rifleman—and voluntarily of-
fering his own life for his friend's; for the scimitar
was swinging at his own head. But even as the Arab
swung, grunting with the force of the blow, his sandaled foot slipped on the marble steps and the curved

blade, veering erratically from its arc, clashed on Steve's rifle-barrel. In an instant the American clubbed his rifle, and as the Bedouin recovered his balance and again heaved up the scimitar, Clarney struck with all his rangy power, and stock and skull shattered together.

Then a heavy ball smacked into his shoulder, sickening him with the shock.

As he staggered dizzily, a Bedouin whipped a turban-cloth about his feet and jerked viciously. Clarney pitched headlong down the steps, to strike with stunning force. A gun-stock in a brown hand went up to dash out his brains, but an imperious command halted the blow.

"Slay him not, but bind him hand and foot."

As Steve struggled dazedly against many gripping hands, it seemed to him that somewhere he had heard that imperious voice before.

The American's downfall had occurred in a matter of seconds. Even as Steve's second shot had cracked, Yar Ali had half severed a raider's arm and himself received a numbing blow from a rifle-stock on his left shoulder. His sheepskin coat, worn despite the desert heat, saved his hide from half a dozen slashing knives. A rifle was discharged so close to his face that the powder burnt him fiercely, bringing a bloodthirsty yell from the maddened Afghan. As Yar Ali swung up his dripping blade the rifleman, ashyfaced, lifted his rifle above his head in both hands to parry the downward blow, whereat the Afridi, with a yelp of ferocious exultation, shifted as a jungle-cat strikes and plunged his long knife into the Arab's belly. But at that instant a rifle-stock, swung with all the hearty ill-will its wielder could evoke, crashed against the giant's head, laying open the scalp and dashing him to his knees.

With the dogged and silent ferocity of his breed,

Yar Ali staggered blindly up again, slashing at foes he could scarcely see, but a storm of blows battered him down again, nor did his attackers cease beating him until he lay still. They would have finished him in short order then but for another peremptory order from their chief; whereupon they bound the senseless knife-man and flung him down alongside Steve, who was fully conscious and aware of the savage hurt of the bullet in his shoulder.

He glared up at the tall Arab who stood looking down at him.

"Well, *sahib*," said this one—and Steve saw he was no Bedouin—"do you not remember me?"

Steve scowled; a bullet-wound is no aid to concentration.

"You look familiar—by Judas!—you are! Nureddin El Mekru!"

"I am honored! The *sahib* remembers!" Nureddin salaamed mockingly. "And you remember, no doubt, the occasion on which you made me a present of—this?"

The dark eyes shadowed with bitter menace and the shaykh indicated a thin white scar on the angle of his jaw.

"I remember," snarled Clarney, whom pain and anger did not tend to make docile. "It was in Somaliland, years ago. You were in the slave-trade then. A wretch of a nigger escaped from you and took refuge with me. You walked into my camp one night in your high-handed way, started a row and in the ensuing scrap you got a butcher-knife across your face. I wish I'd cut your lousy throat."

"You had your chance," answered the Arab. "Now the tables are turned."

"I thought your stamping-ground lay west," growled Clarney; "Yemen and the Somali country."

"I quit the slave-trade long ago," answered the shaykh. "It is an outworn game. I led a band of thieves in Yemen for a time; then again I was forced to change my location. I came here with a few faithful followers, and by Allah, those wild men nearly slit my throat at first. But I overcame their suspicions, and now I lead more men than have followed me in years.

"They whom you fought off yesterday were my men—scouts I had sent out ahead. My oasis lies far to the west. We have ridden for many days, for I was on my way to this very city. When my scouts rode in and told me of two wanderers, I did not alter my course, for I had business first in Beled-el-Djinn. We rode into the city from the west and saw your tracks in the sand. We followed them, and you were blind buffalo who heard not our coming.

Steve snarled. "You wouldn't have caught us so easy, only we thought no Bedouin would dare come into Kara-Shehr."

Nureddin nodded. "But I am no Bedouin. I have traveled far and seen many lands and many races, and I have read many books. I know that fear is smoke, that the dead are dead, and that djinn and ghosts and curses are mists that the wind blows away. It was because of the tales of the red stone that I came into this forsaken desert. But it has taken months to persuade my men to ride with me here.

"But—I am here! And your presence is a delightful surprise. Doubtless you have guessed why I had you taken alive; I have more elaborate entertainment planned for you and that Pathan swine. Now—I take the Fire of Asshurbanipal and we will go."

He turned toward the dais, and one of his men, a bearded one-eyed giant, exclaimed, "Hold, my lord! Ancient evil reigned here before the days of Muhammad! The djinn howl through these halls when the winds blow, and men have seen ghosts dancing on the walls beneath the moon. No man of mortals has dared this black city for a thousand years—save one, half a century ago, who fled shrieking.

"You have come here from Yemen; you do not know the ancient curse on this foul city, and this evil stone, which pulses like the red heart of Satan! We have followed you here against our judgment, because you have proven yourself a strong man, and have said you hold a charm against all evil beings. You said you but wished to look on this mysterious gem, but now we see it is your intention to take it for yourself. Do not offend the djinn!"

"Nay, Nureddin, do not offend the djinn!" chorused the other Bedouins. The shaykh's own hard-bitten ruffians, standing in a compact group somewhat apart from the Bedouins, said nothing; hardened to crimes and deeds of impiety, they were less affected by the superstitions of the desert men, to whom the dread tale of the accursed city had been repeated for centuries. Steve, even while hating Nureddin with concentrated venom, realized the magnetic power of the man, the innate leadership that had enabled him to overcome thus far the fears and traditions of ages.

"The curse is laid on infidels who invade the city," answered Nureddin, "not on the Faithful. See, in this chamber have we overcome our *kafar* foes!"

A white-bearded desert hawk shook his head.

"The curse is more ancient than Muhammad, and recks not of race or creed. Evil men reared this black city in the dawn of the Beginnings of Days. They oppressed our ancestors of the black tents, and warred among themselves; aye, the black walls of this foul city were stained with blood, and echoed to the shouts of unholy revel and the whispers of dark intrigues.

"Thus came the stone to the city; there dwelt a magician at the court of Asshurbanipal, and the black wisdom of ages was not denied to him. To gain honor and power for himself, he dared the horrors of a nameless vast cavern in a dark, untraveled land, and from those fiend-haunted depths he brought that blazing gem, which is carved of the frozen flames of Hell! By reason of his fearful power in black magic, he put a spell on the demon which guarded the ancient gem, and so stole away the stone. And the demon slept in the cavern unknowing.

"So this magician—Xuthltan, by name—dwelt in the court of the sultan Asshurbanipal and did magic and forecast events by scanning the lurid deeps of the stone, into which no eyes but his could look unblinded. And men called the stone the Fire of Asshurbanipal, in honor of the king.

"But evil came upon the kingdom and men cried out that it was the curse of the djinn, and the sultan in great fear bade Xuthltan take the gem and cast it into the cavern from which he had taken it, lest worse ill befall them.

"Yet it was not the magician's will to give up the gem wherein he read strange secrets of pre-Adamite days, and he fled to the rebel city of Kara-Shehr, where soon civil war broke out and men strove with one another to possess the gem. Then the king who ruled the city, coveting the stone, seized the magician and put him to death by torture, and in this very room he watched him die; with the gem in his hand the king sat upon the throne—even as he has sat upon the throne—even as he has sat throughout the centuries—even as now he sits!"

The Arab's finger stabbed at the moldering bones on the marble throne, and the wild desert men blenched; even Nureddin's own scoundrels recoiled, catching their breath, but the shaykh showed no sign of perturbation.

"As Xuthltan died," continued the old Bedouin, "he cursed the stone whose magic had not saved him, and he shrieked aloud the fearful words which undid the spell he had put upon the demon in the cavern, and set the monster free. And crying out on the forgotten gods, Cthulhu and Koth and Yog-Sothoth, and all the pre-Adamite Dwellers in the black cities under the sea and the caverns of the earth, he called upon them to take back that which was theirs, and with his dying breath pronounced doom on the false king, and that doom was that the king should sit on his throne holding in his hand the Fire of Asshurbanipal until the thunder of Judgment Day.

"Thereat the great stone cried out as a live thing cries, and the king and his soldiers saw a black cloud spinning up from the floor, and out of the cloud blew a fetid wind, and out of the wind came a grisly shape which stretched forth fearsome paws and laid them on the king, who shriveled and died at their touch. And the soldiers fled screaming, and all the people of the city ran forth wailing into the desert, where they perished or gained through the wastes to the far oasis towns. Kara-Shehr lay silent and deserted, the haunt of the lizard and the jackal. And when some of the desert-people ventured into the city they found the king dead on his throne, clutching the blazing gem, but they dared not lay hand upon it, for they knew the demon lurked near to guard it through all the ages—as he lurks near even as we stand here.

The warriors shuddered involuntarily and glanced about, and Nureddin said, "Why did he not come forth when the Franks entered the chamber? Is he deaf, that the sound of the combat has not awakened him?"

"We have not touched the gem," answered the old Bedouin, "nor had the Franks molested it. Men have looked on it and lived; but no mortal may touch it and survive."

Nureddin started to speak, gazed at the stubborn, uneasy faces and realized the futility of argument. His attitude changed abruptly.

"I am master here," he snapped, dropping a hand to his holster. "I have not sweat and bled for this gem to be balked at the last by groundless fears! Stand back, all! Let any man cross me at the peril of his head!"

He faced them, his eyes blazing, and they fell back, cowed up the force of his ruthless personality. He strode boldly by the marble steps, and the Arabs caught their breath, recoiling toward the door; Yar Ali, conscious at last, groaned dismally. God! thought Steve, what a barbaric scene!—bound captives on the dust-heaped floor, wild warriors clustered about, gripping their weapons, the raw acid scent of blood and burnt powder still fouling the air, corpses strewn in horrid welter of blood, brains and entrails—and on the dais, the hawk-faced shaykh, oblivious to all except the evil crimson glow in the skeleton fingers that rested on the marble throne.

A tense silence gripped all as Nureddin stretched forth his hand slowly, as if hypnotized by the throbbing crimson light. And in Steve's subconsciousness there shuddered a dim echo, as of something vast and loathsome waking suddenly from an age-long slumber. The American's eyes moved instinctively toward the grim cyclopean walls. The jewel's glow had altered strangely; it burned a deeper, darker red, angry and menacing.

"Heart of all evil," murmured the shaykh, "how many princes died for thee in the Beginnings of Happenings? Surely the blood of kings throbs in thee. The sultans and the princesses and the generals who wore thee, they are dust and are forgotten, but thou blazest with majesty undimmed, fire of the world——"

Nureddin seized the stone. A shuddery wail broke from the Arabs, cut through by a sharp inhuman cry. To Steve it seemed, horribly, that the great jewel had cried out like a living thing! The stone slipped from the shaykh's hand. Nureddin might have dropped it; to Steve it looked as though it leaped convulsively, as a live thing might leap. It rolled from the dais, bounding from step to step, with Nureddin springing after it, cursing as his clutching hand missed it. It struck the floor, veered sharply, and despite the deep dust, rolled like a revolving ball of fire toward the back wall. Nureddin was close upon it—it struck the wall—the shaykh's hand reached for it.

A scream of mortal fear ripped the tense silence. Without warning the solid wall had opened. Out of the black wall that gaped there, a tentacle shot and gripped the shaykh's body as a python girdles its victim, and jerked him headlong into the darkness. And then the wall showed blank and solid once more; only from within sounded a hideous, high-pitched, muffled screaming that chilled the blood of the listeners. Howling wordlessly, the Arabs stampeded, jammed in a battling, screeching mass in the doorway, tore through and raced madly down the wide stairs.

Steve and Yar Ali, lying helplessly, heard the frenzied clamor of their flight fade away into the distance, and gazed in dumb horror at the grim wall. The shrieks had faded into a more horrific silence. Holding their breath, they heard suddenly a sound that froze the blood in their veins—the soft sliding of metal or stone in a groove. At the same time the hidden door began to open, and Steve caught a glimmer in the blackness that might have been the glitter of monstrous eyes. He closed his own eyes; he dared not look upon whatever horror slunk from that hideous black well. He knew that there are strains the human brain cannot stand, and every primitive instinct in his soul cried out to him that this thing was nightmare and lunacy. He sensed that Yar Ali likewise closed his eyes, and the two lay like dead men.

* * *

Clarney heard no sound, but he sensed the presence of a horrific evil too grisly for human comprehension—of an Invader from Outer Gulfs and far black reaches of cosmic being. A deadly cold pervaded the chamber, and Steve felt the glare of inhuman eyes sear through his closed lids and freeze his consciousness. If he looked, if he opened his eyes, he knew stark black madness would be his instant lot.

He felt a soul-shakingly foul breath against his face and knew that the monster was bending close above him, but he lay like a man frozen in a nightmare. He clung to one thought: neither he nor Yar Ali had touched the jewel this horror guarded.

Then he no longer smelled the foul odor, the coldness in the air grew appreciably less, and he heard again the secret door slide in its groove. The fiend was returning to its hiding-place. Not all the legions of Hell could have prevented Steve's eyes from opening a trifle. He had only a glimpse as the hidden door slid to—and that one glimpse was enough to drive all consciousness from his brain. Steve Clarney, iron-nerved adventurer, fainted for the only time in his checkered life.

How long he lay there Steve never knew, but it could not have been long, for he was roused by Yar Ali's whisper, "Lie still, *sahib*, a little shifting of my body and I can reach thy cords with my teeth."

"Steve felt the Afghan's powerful teeth at work on his bonds, and as he lay with his face jammed into the thick dust, and his wounded shoulder began to throb agonizingly—he had forgotten it until now—he began to gather the wandering threads of his consciousness, and it all came back to him. How much, he wondered dazedly, had been the nightmares of delirium, born from suffering and the thirst that caked his throat? The fight with the Arabs had been real—the bonds and the wounds showed that—but the grisly doom of the shaykh—the thing that had crept out of the black entrance in the wall—surely that had been a figment of delirium. Nureddin had fallen into a well or pit of some sort—Steve felt his hands were free and he rose to a sitting posture, fumbling for a pocket-knife the Arabs had overlooked. He did not look up or about the chamber as he slashed the cords that bound his ankles, and then freed Yar Ali, working awkwardly because his left arm was stiff and useless.

"Where are the Bedouins?" he asked, as the Afghan rose, lifting him to his feet.

"Allah, *sahib*," whispered Yar Ali, "are you mad? Have you forgotten? Let us go quickly before the djinn returns!"

"It was a nightmare," muttered Steve. "Look—the jewel is back on the throne——" His voice died out. Again that red glow throbbed about the ancient throne, reflecting from the moldering skull; again in the outstretched finger-bones pulsed the Fire of Asshurbanipal. But at the foot of the throne lay another object that had not been there before—the severed head of Nureddin El Mekru stared sightlessly up at the gray light filtering through the stone ceiling. The bloodless lips were drawn back from the teeth in a ghastly grin, the staring eyes mirrored an intolerable horror. In the thick dust of the floor three spoors showed—one of the shaykh's where he had followed the red jewel as it rolled to the wall, and above it two other sets of tracks, coming to the throne and returning to the wall—vast, shapeless tracks, as of splayed feet, taloned and gigantic, neither human nor animal.

"My God!" choked Steve. "It was true—and the Thing—the Thing I saw——"

* * *

Steve remembered the flight from that chamber as a rushing nightmare, in which he and his companion hurtled headlong down an endless stair that was a gray well of fear, raced blindly through dusty silent chambers, past the glowering idol in the mighty hall and into the blazing light of the desert sun, where they fell slavering, fighting for breath.

Again Steve was roused by the Afrida's voice: "*Sahib, sahib*, in the Name of Allah the Compassionate, our luck has turned!"

Steve looked at this companion as a man might look in a trance. The big Afghan's garments were in tatters, and blood-soaked. He was stained with dust and caked with blood, and his voice was a croak. But his eyes were alight with hope and he pointed with a trembling finger.

"In the shade of yon ruined wall!" he croaked, striving to moisten his blackened lips. "*Allah il allah!* The horses of the men we killed! With canteens and food-pouches at the saddle-horns! Those dogs fled without halting for the steeds of their comrades!"

New life surged up into Steve's bosom and he rose, staggering.

"Out of here," he mumbled. "Out of here quick!"

Like dying men they stumbled to the horses, tore them loose and climbed fumblingly into the saddles.

"We'll lead the spare mounts," croaked Steve, and Yar Ali nodded emphatic agreement.

"Belike we shall need them ere we sight the coast."

Though their tortured nerves screamed for the water that swung in canteens at the saddle-horns, they turned the mounts aside and, swaying in the saddle, rode like flying corpses down the long sandy street of Kara-Shehr, between the ruined palaces and the crumbling columns, crossed the fallen wall and swept out into the desert. Not once did either glance back toward that black pile of ancient horror, nor did either speak until the ruins faded into the hazy distance. Then and only then did they draw rein and ease their thirst.

"*Allah il allah!*" said Yar Ali piously. "Those dogs have beaten me until it is as though every bone in my body were broken. Dismount, I beg thee, *sahib*, and let me probe for that accursed bullet, and dress thy shoulder to the best of my meager ability."

While this was going on, Yar Ali spoke, avoiding his friend's eye. "You said, *sahib*, you said something about—about seeing? What saw ye, in Allah's name?"

A strong shudder shook the American's steely frame.

"You didn't look when—when the—the Thing put back the jewel in the skeleton's hand and left Nureddin's head on the dais?"

"By Allah, not I!" swore Yar Ali. "My eyes were as closed as if they had been welded together by the molten irons of Satan!"

Steve made no reply until the comrades had once more swung into the saddle and started on their long trek for the coast, which, with spare horses, food, water and weapons, they had a good chance to reach.

"I looked," the American said somberly. "I wish I had not; I know I'll dream about it for the rest of my life. I had only a glance; I couldn't describe it as a man describes an earthly thing. God help me, it wasn't earthly or sane either. Mankind isn't the first owner of the earth; there were Beings here before his coming—and now, survivals of hideously ancient epochs. Maybe spheres of alien dimensions press unseen on this material universe today. Sorcerers have called up sleeping devils before now and controlled them with magic. It is not unreasonable to suppose an Assyrian magician could invoke an elemental demon out of the earth to avenge him and guard something that must have come out of Hell in the first place.

"I'll try to tell you what I glimpsed; then we'll never speak of it again. It was gigantic and black and shadowy; it was a hulking monstrosity that walked upright like a man, but it was like a toad, too, and it was winged and tentacled. I saw only its back; if I'd seen the front of it—its face—I'd have undoubtedly lost my mind. The old Arab was right; God help us, it was the monster that Xuthltan called up out of the dark blind caverns of the earth to guard the Fire of Asshurbanipal!"

THE THING ON THE ROOF

They lumber through the night
  With their elephantine tread;
I shudder in affright
  As I cower in my bed
They lift colossal wings
  On the high gable roofs
Which tremble to the trample
  On their mastodonic hoofs.

—Justin Geoffrey: *Out of the Old Land.*

LET ME begin by saying that I was surprised when Tussmann called on me. We had never been close friends; the man's mercenary instincts repelled me; and since our bitter controversy of three years before, when he attempted to discredit my *Evidences of Nahua Culture in Yucatan*, which was the result of years of careful research, our relations had been anything but cordial. However, I received him and found his manner hasty and abrupt, but rather abstracted, as if his dislike for me had been thrust aside in some driving passion that had hold of him.

His errand was quickly stated. He wished my aid in obtaining a volume in the first edition of Von

Junzt's *Nameless Cults*—the edition known as the Black Book, not from its color, but because of its dark contents. He might almost as well have asked me for the original Greek translation of the *Necronomicon*. Though since my return from the Yucatan I had devoted practically all my time to my avocation of book collecting, I had not stumbled on to any hint that the book in the Dusseldorf edition was still in existence.

A word as to this rare work. Its extreme ambiguity in spots, coupled with its incredible subject matter, has caused it long to be regarded as the ravings of a maniac and the author was damned with the brand of insanity. But the fact remains that much of his assertions are unanswerable, and that he spent the full forty-five years of his life prying into strange places and discovering secret and abysmal things. Not a great many volumes were printed in the first edition and many of these were burned by their frightened owners when Von Junzt was found strangled in a mysterious manner, in his barred and bolted chamber one night in 1840, six months after he had returned from a mysterious journey to Mongolia.

Five years later a London printer, one Bridewall, pirated the work, and issued a cheap translation for sensational effect, full of grotesque wood-cuts, and riddled with misspellings, faulty translations and the usual errors of a cheap and unscholarly printing. This still further discredited the original work, and publishers and public forgot about the book until 1909 when the Golden Goblin Press of New York brought out an edition.

Their production was so carefully expurgated that fully a fourth of the original matter was cut out; the book was handsomely bound and decorated with the exquisite and weirdly imaginative illustrations of Diego Vasquez. The edition was intended for popular consumption but the artistic instinct of the publishers defeated that end, since the cost of issuing the book was so great that they were forced to cite it at a prohibitive price.

I was explaining all this to Tussmann when he interrupted bruskly to say that he was not utterly ignorant in such matters. One of the Golden Goblin books ornamented his library, he said, and it was in it that he found a certain line which aroused his interest. If I could procure him a copy of the original 1839 edition, he would make it worth my while; knowing, he added, that it would be useless to offer me money, he would, instead, in return for my trouble in his behalf, make a full retraction of his former accusations in regard to my Yucatan researches, and offer a complete apology in *The Scientific News*.

I will admit that I was astounded at this, and realized that if the matter meant so much to Tussmann that he was willing to make such concessions, it must indeed be of the utmost importance. I answered that I considered that I had sufficiently refuted his charges in the eyes of the world and had no desire to put him in a humiliating position, but that I would make the utmost efforts to procure him what he wanted.

He thanked me abruptly and took his leave, saying rather vaguely that he hoped to find a complete exposition of something in the Black Book which had evidently been slighted in the later edition.

I set to work, writing letters to friends, colleagues and bookdealers all over the world, and soon discovered that I had assumed a task of no small magnitude. Three months elapsed before my efforts were crowned with success, but at last, through the aid of Professor James Clement of Richmond, Virginia, I was able to obtain what I wished.

I notified Tussmann and he came to London by the next train. His eyes burned avidly as he gazed at the thick, dusty volume with its heavy leather covers and rusty iron hasps, and his fingers quivered with eagerness as he thumbed the time-yellowed pages.

And when he cried out fiercely and smashed his clenched fist down on the table I knew that he had found what he hunted.

"Listen!" he commanded, and he read to me a passage that spoke of an old, old temple in a Honduras Jungle where a strange god was worshipped by an ancient tribe which became extinct before the coming of the Spaniards. And Tussmann read aloud of the mummy that had been, in life, the last high priest of that vanished people, and which now lay in a chamber hewn in the solid rock of the cliff against which the temple was built. About that mummy's withered neck was a copper chain, and on that chain a great red jewel carved in the form of a toad. This jewel was a key, Von Junzt went on to say, to the treasure of the temple which lay hidden in a subterranean crypt far below the temple's altar.

Tussmann's eyes blazed.

"I have seen that temple! I have stood before the altar. I have seen the sealed-up entrance of the chamber in which, the natives say, lies the mummy of the priest. It is a very curious temple, no more like the ruins of the prehistoric Indians than it is like the buildings of the modern Latin-Americans. The Indians in the vicinity disclaim any former connection with the place; they say that the people who built that temple were a different race from themselves, and were there when their own ancestors came into the country. I believe it to be a remnant of some long-vanished civilization which began to decay thousands of years before the Spaniards came.

"I would have liked to have broken into the sealed-up chamber, but I had neither the time nor the tools for the task. I was hurrying to the coast, having been wounded by an accidental gunshot in the foot, and I stumbled on to the place purely by chance.

"I have been planning to have another look at it, but circumstances have prevented—now I intend to let nothing stand in my way! By chance I came upon a passage in the Golden Goblin edition of this book, describing the temple. But that was all; the mummy was only briefly mentioned. Interested, I obtained one of Bridewall's translations but ran up against a blank wall of baffling blunders. By some irritating mischance the translator had even mistaken the location of the Temple of the Toad, as Von Junzt calls it, and has it in Guatemala instead of Honduras. The general description is faulty, the jewel is mentioned and the fact that it is a 'key'. But a key to what, Bridewall's book does not state. I now felt that I was on the track of a real discovery, unless Von Junzt *was*, as many maintain, a madman. But that the man was actually in Honduras at one time is well attested, and no one could so vividly describe the temple—as he does in the Black Book—unless he had seen it himself. How he learned of the jewel is more than I can say. The Indians who told me of the mummy said nothing of any jewel. I can only believe that Von Junzt found his way into the sealed crypt somehow—the man had uncanny ways of learning hidden things.

"To the best of my knowledge only one other white man has seen the Temple of the Toad besides Von Junzt and myself—the Spanish traveller Juan Gonzalles, who made a partial exploration of that country in 1793. He mentioned, briefly, a curious fane that differed from most Indian ruins, and spoke skeptically of a legend current among the natives that there was 'something unusual' hidden under the temple. I feel certain that he was referring to the Temple of the Toad.

"Tomorrow I sail for Central America. Keep the

book; I have no more use for it. This time I am going fully prepared and I intend to find what is hidden in that temple, if I have to demolish it. It can be nothing less than a great store of gold! The Spaniards missed it, somehow; when they arrived in Central America, the Temple of the Toad was deserted; they were searching for living Indians from whom torture could wring gold; not for mummies of lost peoples. But I mean to have that treasure."

So saying Tussman took his departure. I sat down and opened the book at the place where he had left off reading, and I sat until midnight, wrapt in Von Junzt's curious, wild and at times, utterly vague expoundings. And I found pertaining to the Temple of the Toad certain things which disquieted me so much that the next morning I attempted to get in touch with Tussmann, only to find that he had already sailed.

Several months passed and then I received a letter from Tussmann, asking me to come and spend a few days with him at his estate in Sussex; he also requested me to bring the Black Book with me.

I arrived at Tussmann's rather isolated estate just after nightfall. He lived in almost feudal state, his great ivy-grown house and broad lawns surrounded by high stone walls. As I went up the hedge-bordered way from the gate to the house, I noted that the place had not been well kept in its master's absence. Weeds grew rank among the trees, almost choking out the grass. Among some unkempt bushes over against the outer wall, I heard what appeared to be a horse or an ox blundering and lumbering about. I distinctly heard the clink of its hoof on a stone.

A servant who eyed me suspiciously admitted me and I found Tussmann pacing to and fro in his study like a caged lion. His giant frame was leaner, harder than when I had last seen him; his face was bronzed by a tropic sun. There were more and harsher lines in his strong face and his eyes burned more intensely than ever. A smoldering, baffled anger seemed to underlie his manner.

"Well, Tussmann," I greeted him, "what success? Did you find the gold?"

"I found not an ounce of gold," he growled. "The whole thing was a hoax—well, not all of it. I broke into the sealed chamber and found the mummy—"

"And the jewel?" I exclaimed.

He drew something from his pocket and handed it to me.

I gazed curiously at the thing I held. It was a great jewel, clear and transparent as crystal, but of a sinister crimson, carved, as Von Junzt had declared, in the shape of a toad. I shuddered involuntarily; the image was peculiarly repulsive. I turned my attention to the heavy and curiously wrought copper chain which supported it.

"What are these characters carved on the chain?" I asked curiously.

"I can not say," Tussmann replied. "I had thought perhaps you might know. I find a faint resemblance between them and certain partly defaced hieroglyphics on a monolith known as the Black Stone in the mountains of Hungary. I have been unable to decipher them."

"Tell me of your trip," I urged, and over our whiskey-and-sodas he began, as if with a strange reluctance.

"I found the temple again with no great difficulty, though it lies in a lonely and little-frequented region. The temple is built against a sheer stone cliff in a deserted valley unknown to maps and explorers. I would not endeavor to make an estimate of its antiquity, but it is built of a sort of unusually hard basalt, such as I have never seen anywhere else, and its extreme weathering suggests incredible age.

"Most of the columns which form its facade are in

ruins, thrusting up shattered stumps from worn bases, like the scattered and broken teeth of some grinning hag. The outer walls are crumbling, but the inner walls and the columns which support such of the roof as remains intact, seem good for another thousand years, as well as the walls of the inner chamber.

"The main chamber is a large circular affair with a floor composed of great squares of stone. In the center stands the altar, merely a huge, round, curiously carved block of the same material. Directly behind the altar, in the solid stone cliff which forms the rear wall of the chamber, is the sealed and hewn-out chamber wherein lay the mummy of the temple's last priest.

"I broke into the crypt with not too much difficulty and found the mummy exactly as is stated in the Black Book. Though it was in a remarkable state of preservation, I was unable to classify it. The withered features and general contour of the skull suggested certain degraded and mongrel peoples of lower Egypt, and I feel certain that the priest was a member of a race more akin to the Caucasian than the Indian. Beyond this, I can not make any positive statement.

"But the jewel was there, the chain looped about the dried-up neck."

From this point Tussmann's narrative became so vague that I had some difficulty in following him and wondered if the tropic sun had affected his mind. He had opened a hidden door in the altar somehow with the jewel—just how, he did not plainly say, and it struck me that he did not clearly understand himself the action of the jewel-key. But the opening of the secret door had had a bad effect on the hardy rogues in his employ. They had refused point-blank to follow him through that gaping black opening which had appeared so mysteriously when the gem was touched to the altar.

Tussmann entered alone with his pistol and electric torch, finding a narrow stone stair that wound down into the bowels of the earth, apparently. He followed this and presently came into a broad corridor, in the blackness of which his tiny beam of light was almost engulfed. As he told this he spoke with strange annoyance of a toad which hopped ahead of him, just beyond the circle of light, all the time he was below ground.

Making his way along dank tunnels and stairways that were wells of solid blackness, he at last came to a heavy door fantastically carved, which he felt must be the crypt wherein was secreted the gold of the ancient worshippers. He pressed the toad-jewel against it at several places and finally the door gaped wide.

"And the treasure?" I broke in eagerly.

He laughed in savage self-mockery.

"There was no gold there, no precious gems—nothing"—he hesitated—"nothing that I could bring away."

Again his tale lapsed into vagueness. I gathered that he had left the temple rather hurriedly without searching any further for the supposed treasure. He had intended bringing the mummy away with him, he said, to present to some museum, but when he came up out of the pits, it could not be found and he believed that his men, in superstitious aversion to having such a companion on their road to the coast had thrown it into some well or cavern.

"And so," he concluded, "I am in England again no richer than when I left."

"You have the jewel," I reminded him. "Surely it is valuable."

He eyed it without favor, but with a sort of fierce avidness almost obsessional.

"Would you say that it is a ruby?" he asked.

I shook my head. "I am unable to classify it."

"And I. But let me see the book."

He slowly turned the heavy pages, his lips moving as he read. Sometimes he shook his head as if puzzled, and I noticed him dwell long over a certain line.

"This man dipped so deeply into forbidden things," said he. "I can not wonder that his fate was so strange and mysterious. He must have had some foreboding of his end—here he warns men not to disturb sleeping things."

Tussmann seemed lost in thought for some moments.

"Aye, sleeping things," he muttered, "that seem dead, but only lie waiting for some blind fool to awake them—I should have read further in the Black Book—and I should have shut the door when I left the crypt—but I have the key and I'll keep it in spite of hell."

He roused himself from his reveries and was about to speak when he stopped short. From somewhere upstairs had come a peculiar sound.

"What was that?" he glared at me. I shook my head and he ran to the door and shouted for a servant. The man entered a few moments later and he was rather pale.

"You were upstairs?" growled Tussmann.

"Yes, sir."

"Did you hear anything?" asked Tussmann harshly and in a manner almost threatening and accusing.

"I did, sir," the man answered with a puzzled look on his face.

"What did you hear?" The question was fairly snarled.

"Well, sir," the man laughed apologetically, "you'll say I'm a bit off, I fear, but to tell you the truth, sir, it sounded like a horse stamping around on the roof!"

A blaze of absolute madness leaped into Tussmann's eyes.

"You fool!" he screamed. "Get out of here!" The

man shrank back in amazement and Tussmann snatched up the gleaming toad-carved jewel.

"I've been a fool!" he raved. "I didn't read far enough—and I should have shut the door—but by heaven, the key is mine and I'll keep it in spite of man or devil."

And with these strange words he turned and fled upstairs. A moment later his door slammed heavily and a servant, knocking timidly, brought forth only a blasphemous order to retire and a luridly worded threat to shoot any one who tried to obtain entrance into the room.

Had it not been so late I would have left the house, for I was certain that Tussmann was stark mad. As it was, I retired to the room a frightened servant showed me, but I did not go to bed. I opened the pages of the Black Book at the place where Tussmann had been reading.

This much was evident, unless the man was utterly insane: he had stumbled upon something unexpected in the Temple of the Toad. Something unnatural about the opening of the altar door had frightened his men, and in the subterraneous crypt Tussmann had found *something* that he had not thought to find. And I believed that he had been followed from Central America, and that the reason for his persecution was the jewel he called the Key.

Seeking some clue in Von Junzt's volume, I read again of the Temple of the Toad, of the strange pre-Indian people who worshipped there, and of the huge, tittering, tentacled, hoofed monstrosity that they worshipped.

Tussmann had said that he had not read far enough when he had first seen the book. Puzzling over this cryptic phrase I came upon the line he had pored over—marked by his thumb nail. It seemed to me to be another of Von Junzt's many ambiguities, for it merely stated that a temple's god was the temple's treasure. Then the dark implication of the hint struck me and cold sweat beaded my forehead.

The Key to the Treasure! And the temple's treasure was the temple's god! And sleeping Things might awaken on the opening of their prison door! I sprang up, unnerved by the intolerable suggestion, and at that moment something crashed in the stillness and the death-scream of a human being burst upon my ears.

In an instant I was out of the room, and as I dashed up the stairs I heard sounds that have made me doubt my sanity ever since. At Tussmann's door I halted, essaying with shaking hand to turn the knob. The door was locked, and as I hesitated I heard from within a hideous high-pitched tittering and then the disgusting squashy sound as if a great, jelly-like bulk was being forced through the window. The sound ceased and I could have sworn I heard a faint swish of gigantic wings. Then silence.

Gathering my shattered nerves, I broke down the door. A foul and overpowering stench billowed out like a yellow mist. Gasping in nausea I entered. The room was in ruins, but nothing was missing except that crimson toad-carved jewel Tussmann called the Key, and that was never found. A foul, unspeakable slime smeared the window-sill, and in the center of the room lay Tussmann, his head crushed and flattened and on the red ruin of skull and face, the plain print of an enormous hoof.

DIG ME NO GRAVE

THE THUNDER of my old-fashioned door-knocker, reverberating eerily through the house, roused me from a restless and nightmare-haunted sleep. I looked out the window. In the last light of the sinking moon, the white face of my friend John Conrad looked up at me.

"May I come up, Kirowan?" His voice was shaky and strained.

"Certainly!" I sprang out of bed and pulled on a bathrobe as I heard him enter the front door and ascend the stairs.

A moment later he stood before me, and in the light which I had turned on I saw his hands tremble and noticed the unnatural pallor of his face.

"Old John Grimlan died an hour ago," he said abruptly.

"Indeed? I had not known that he was ill."

"It was a sudden, virulent attack of peculiar nature, a sort of seizure somewhat akin to epilepsy. He had been subject to such spells of late years, you know."

I nodded. I knew something of the old hermit-like man who had lived in his great dark house on the hill; indeed, I had once witnessed one of his strange

71

seizures, and I had been appalled at the writhings, howlings and yammerings of the wretch, who had groveled on the earth like a wounded snake gibbering terrible curses and black blasphemies until his voice broke in a wordless screaming which spattered his lips with foam. Seeing this, I understood why people in old times looked on such victims as men possessed by demons.

"—some hereditary trait," Conrad was saying. "Old John doubtless fell heir to some ingrown weakness brought on by some loathsome disease, which was his heritage from perhaps a remote ancestor—such things occasionally happen. Or else—well, you know old John himself pried about in the mysterious parts of the earth, and wandered all over the East in his younger days. It is quite possible that he was infected with some obscure malady in his wanderings. There are still many unclassified diseases in Africa and the Orient."

"But," said I, "you have not told me the reason for this sudden visit at this unearthly hour—for I notice that it is past midnight."

My friend seemed rather confused.

"Well, the fact is that John Grimlan died alone, except for myself. He refused to receive any medical aid of any sort, and in the last few moments when it was evident that he was dying, and I was prepared to go for some sort of help in spite of him, he set up such a howling and screaming that I could not refuse his passionate pleas—which were that he should not be left to die alone.

"I have seen men die," added Conrad, wiping the perspiration from his pale brow, "but the death of John Grimlan was the most fearful I have ever seen."

"He suffered a great deal?"

"He appeared to be in much physical agony, but this was mostly submerged by some monstrous mental or psychic suffering. The fear in his distended eyes and his screams transcended any conceivable earthly terror. I tell you, Kirowan, Grimlan's fright was greater and deeper than the ordinary fear of the Beyond shown by a man of ordinarily evil life."

I shifted restlessly. The dark implications of this statement sent a chill of nameless apprehension trickling down my spine.

"I know the country people always claimed that in his youth he sold his soul to the Devil, and that his sudden epileptic attacks were merely a visible sign of the Fiend's power over him; but such talk is foolish, of course, and belongs in the Dark Ages. We all know that John Grimlan's life was a peculiarly evil and vicious one, even toward his last days. With good reason he was universally detested and feared, for I never heard of his doing a single good act. You were his only friend."

"And that was a strange friendship," said Conrad. "I was attracted to him by his unusual powers, for despite his bestial nature, John Grimlan was a highly educated man, a deeply cultured man. He had dipped deep into occult studies, and I first met him in this manner; for as you know, I have always been strongly interested in these lines of research myself.

"But, in this as in all other things, Grimlan was evil and perverse. He had ignored the white side of the occult and delved into the darker, grimmer phases of it—into devil-worship and voodoo and Shintoism. His knowledge of these foul arts and sciences was immense and unholy. And to hear him tell of his researches and experiments was to know such horror and repulsion as a venomous reptile might inspire. For there had been no depths to which he had not sunk, and some things he only hinted at, even to me. I tell you, Kirowan, it is easy to laugh at tales of the black world of the unknown, when one is in pleasant company under the bright sunlight, but had you sat at ungodly hours in the silent bizarre library of John Grimlan and looked on the ancient musty volumes and listened to his grisly talk as I did, your tongue would have cloven to your palate with sheer horror as mine did, and the supernatural would have seemed very real to you—as it seemed to me!"

"But in God's name, man!" I cried, for the tension was growing unbearable; "come to the point and tell me what you want of me."

"I want you to come with me to John Grimlan's house and help carry out his outlandish instructions in regard to his body."

I had no liking for the adventure, but I dressed hurriedly, an occasional shudder of premonition shaking me. Once fully clad, I followed Conrad out of the house and up the silent road which led to the house of John Grimlan. The road wound uphill, and all the way, looking upward and forward, I could see that great grim house perched like a bird of evil on the crest of the hill, bulking back and stark against the stars. In the west pulsed a single dull red smear where the young moon had just sunk from view behind the low black hills. The whole night seemed full of brooding evil, and the persistent swishing of a bat's wings somewhere overhead caused my taut nerves to jerk and thrum. To drown the quick pounding of my own heart, I said:

"Do you share the belief so many hold, that John Grimlan was mad?"

We strode on several paces before Conrad answered, seemingly with a strange reluctance, "But of one incident, I would say no man was ever saner. But one night in his study, he seemed suddenly to break all bonds of reason.

"He had discoursed for hours on his favorite subject—black magic—when suddenly he cried, as his face lit with a weird unholy glow: 'Why should I sit here babbling such child's prattle to you? These voodoo rituals—these Shinto sacrifices—feathered

snakes—goats without horns—black leopard cults—
bah! Filth and dust that the wind blows away! Dregs
of the real Unknown—the deep mysteries! Mere ech-
oes from the Abyss!

" 'I could tell you things that would shatter your
paltry brain! I could breathe into your ear names that
would wither you like a burnt weed! What do you
know of Yog-Sathoth, of Kathulos and the sunken
cities? None of these names is even included in your
mythologies. Not even in your dreams have you
glimpsed the black cyclopean walls of Koth, or shriveled before the noxious winds that blow from Yuggoth!

" 'But I will not blast you lifeless with my black
wisdom! I cannot expect your infantile brain to bear
what mine holds. Were you as old as I—had you
seen, as I have see, kingdoms crumple and generations pass away—had you gathered as ripe grain the
dark secrets of the centuries—'

"He was raving away, his wildly lit face scarcely
human in appearance, and suddenly, noticing my
evident bewilderment, he burst into a horrible cackling laugh.

" 'Gad!' he cried in a voice and accent strange to
me, "methinks I've frighted ye, and certes, it is
not to be marveled at, sith ye be but a naked savage
in the arts of life, after all. Ye think I be old, eh?
Why, ye gaping lout, ye'd drop dead were I to
divulge the generations of men I've known—'

"But at this point such horror overcame me that I
fled from him as from an adder, and his high-pitched,
diabolical laughter followed me out of the shadowy
house. Some days later I received a letter apologiz-
ing for his manner and ascribing it candidly— too
candidly—to drugs. I did not believe it, but I re-
newed our relations, after some hesitation."

"It sounds like utter madness," I muttered.

"Yes," admitted Conrad, hesitantly. "But—Kirowan, have you ever seen anyone who knew John Grimlan in his youth?"

I shook my head.

"I have been at pains to inquire about him discreetly," said Conrad. "He has lived here—with the exception of mysterious absences often for months at a time—for twenty years. The older villagers remember distinctly when he first came and took over that old house on the hill, and they all say that in the intervening years he seems not to have aged perceptibly. When he came here he looked just as he does now—or did, up to the moment of his death—of the appearance of a man about fifty.

"I met old Von Boehnk in Vienna, who said he knew Grimlan when a very young man studying in Berlin, fifty years ago, and he expressed astonishment that the old man was still living; for he said at that time Grimlan seemed to be about fifty years of age."

I gave an incredulous exclamation, seeing the implication toward which the conversation was trending.

"Nonsense! Professor Von Boehnk is past eighty himself, and liable to the errors of extreme age. He confused this man with another." Yet as I spoke, my flesh crawled unpleasantly and the hairs on my neck prickled.

"Well," shrugged Conrad, "here we are at the house."

The huge pile reared up menacingly before us, and as we reached the front door a vagrant wind moaned through the nearby trees and I started foolishly as I again heard the ghostly beat of the bat's wings. Conrad turned a large key in the antique lock, and as we entered, a cold draft swept across us like a breath from the grave—moldy and cold. I shuddered.

We groped our way through a black hallway and into a study, and here Conrad lighted a candle, for no gas lights or electric lights were to be found in the house. I looked about me, dreading what the light might disclose, but the room, heavily tapestried and bizarrely furnished, was empty save for us two.

"Where—where is—*It*?" I asked in a husky whisper, from a throat gone dry.

"Upstairs," answered Conrad in a low voice, showing that the silence and mystery of the house had laid a spell on him also. "Upstairs, in the library where he died."

I glanced up involuntarily. Somewhere above our head, the lone master of this grim house was stretched out in his last sleep—silent, his white face set in a grinning mask of death. Panic swept over me and I fought for control. After all, it was merely the corpse of a wicked old man, who was past harming anyone—this argument rang hollowly in my brain like the words of a frightened child who is trying to reassure himself.

I turned to Conrad. He had taken a time-yellowed envelope from an inside pocket.

"This," he said, removing from the envelope several pages of closely written, time-yellowed parchment, "is, in effect, the last word of John Grimlan, though God alone knows how many years ago it was written. He gave it to me ten years ago, immediately after his return from Mongolia. It was shortly after this that he had his first seizure.

"This envelope he gave me, sealed, and he made me swear that I would hide it carefully, and that I would not open it until he was dead, when I was to read the contents and follow their directions exactly. More, he made me swear that no matter what he said or did after giving me the envelope, I would go ahead as first directed. 'For,' he said with a fearful smile, 'the flesh is weak but I am a man of my word, and though I might, in a moment of weakness, wish to retract, it is far, far too late now. You may never understand the matter, but you are to do as I have said.' "

"Well?"

"Well," again Conrad wiped his brow, "tonight as he lay writhing in his death-agonies, his wordless howls were mingled with frantic admonitions to me to bring him the envelope and destroy it before his eyes! As he yammered this, he forced himself up on his elbows and with eyes staring and hair standing straight up on his head, he screamed at me in a manner to chill the blood. And he was shrieking for me to destroy the envelope, not to open it; and once he howled in his delirium for me to hew his body into pieces and scatter the bits to the four winds of heaven!"

An uncontrollable exclamation of horror escaped my dry lips.

"At last," went on Conrad, "I gave in. Remembering his commands ten years ago, I at first stood firm, but at last, as his screeches grew unbearably desperate, I turned to go for the envelope, even though that meant leaving him alone. But as I turned, with one last fearful convulsion in which blood-flecked foam flew from his writhing lips, the life went from his twisted body in a single great wrench."

He fumbled at the parchment.

"I am going to carry out my promise. The directions herein seem fantastic and may be the whims of a disordered mind, but I gave my word. They are, briefly, that I place his corpse on the great black ebony table in his library, with seven black candles burning about him. The doors and windows are to be firmly closed and fastened. Then, in the darkness which precedes dawn, I am to read the formula charm or spell which is contained in a smaller, sealed envelope inside the first, and which I have not yet opened."

"But is that all?" I cried. "No provisions as to the disposition of his fortune, his estate—or his corpse?"

"Nothing. In his will, which I have seen elsewhere, he leaves estate and fortune to a certain Oriental gentleman named in the document as—Malik Tous!"

"What!" I cried, shaken to my soul. "Conrad, this is madness heaped on madness! Malik Tous—good God! No mortal man was ever so named! That is the title of the foul god worshipped by the mysterious Yezidees—they of Mount Alamout the Accursed—whose Eight Brazen Towers rise in the mysterious wastes of deep Asia. His idolatrous symbol is the brazen peacock. And the Muhammadans, who hate his demon-worshipping devotees, say he is the essence of the evil of all the universe—the Prince of Darkness—Ahriman—the old Serpent—the veritable Satan! And you say Grimlan names this mythical demon in his will?"

"It is the truth," Conrad's throat was dry. "And look—he has scribbled a strange line at the corner of his parchment: 'Dig me no grave; I shall not need one.'"

Again a chill wandered down my spine.

"In God's name," I cried in a kind of frenzy, "let us get this incredible business over with!"

"I think a drink might help," answered Conrad, moistening his lips. "It seems to me I've seen Grimlan go into this cabinet for wine—" He bent to the door of an ornately carved mahogany cabinet, and after some difficulty opened it.

"No wine here," he said disappointedly, "and if ever I felt the need of stimulants—what's this?"

He drew out a roll of parchment, dusty, yellowed and half covered with spiderwebs. Everything in that grim house seemed, to my nervously excited senses, fraught with mysterious meaning and import, and I leaned over his shoulder as he unrolled it.

"It's a record of peerage," he said, "such a chronicle of births, deaths and so forth, as the old families used to keep, in the Sixteenth Century and earlier."

"What's the name?" I asked.

He scowled over the dim scrawls, striving to master the faded, archaic script.

"G-r-y-m—I've got it—Grymlann, of course. It's the records of old John's family—the Grymlanns of Toad's-health Manor, Suffolk—what an outlandish name for an estate! Look at the last entry."

Together we read, "John Grymlann, borne, March 10, 1630." And then we both cried out. Under this entry was freshly written, in a strange scrawling hand, "Died, March 10, 1930." Below this there was a seal of black wax, stamped with a strange design, something like a peacock with a spreading tail.

Conrad stared at me speechless, all the color ebbed from his face. I shook myself with the rage engendered by fear.

"It's the hoax of a madman!" I shouted. "The stage has been set with such great care that the actors have overstepped themselves. Whoever they are, they have heaped up so many incredible effects as to nullify them. It's all a very stupid, very dull drama of illusion."

And even as I spoke, icy sweat stood out on my body and I shook as with an ague. With a wordless motion Conrad turned toward the stairs, taking up a large candle from a mahogany table.

"It was understood, I suppose," he whispered, "that I should go through with this ghastly matter alone; but I had not the moral courage, and now I'm glad I had not."

A still horror brooded over the silent house as we went up the stairs. A faint breeze stole in from somewhere and set the heavy velvet hangings rustling and I visualized stealthy taloned fingers drawing aside the tapestries, to fix red gloating eyes upon us. Once I thought I heard the indistinct clumping of monstrous feet somewhere above us, but it must have been the heavy pounding of my own heart.

The stairs debouched into a wide dark corridor, in which our feeble candle cast a faint gleam which but illuminated our pale faces and made the shadows seem darker by comparison. We stopped at a heavy door, and I heard Conrad's breath draw in sharply as a man's will when he braces himself physically or mentally. I involuntarily clenched my fists until the nails bit into the palms; then Conrad thrust the door open.

A sharp cry escaped his lips. The candle dropped from his nerveless fingers and went out. The library of John Grimlan was ablaze with light, though the whole house had been in darkness when we entered it.

This light came from seven black candles placed at regular intervals about the great ebony table. On this table, between the candles—I had braced myself against the sight. Now in the face of the mysterious illumination and the sight of the thing on the table, my resolution nearly gave way. John Grimlan had been unlovely in life; in death he was hideous. Yes, he was hideous even though his face was mercifully covered with the same curious silken robe, which, worked in fantastic bird-like designs, covered his whole body except the crooked claw-like hands and the bare withered feet.

A strangling sound came from Conrad. "My God!" he whispered; "what is this? I laid his body out on the table and placed the candles about it, but I did not light them, nor did I place that robe over the body! And there were bedroom slippers on his feet when I left—"

He halted suddenly. We were not alone in the deathroom.

At first we had not seen him, as he sat in the great

armchair in a farther nook of a corner, so still that he
seemed a part of the shadows cast by the heavy
tapestries. As my eyes fell upon him, a violent shuddering shook me and a feeling akin to nausea racked
the pit of my stomach. My first impression was of
vivid, oblique yellow eyes which gazed unwinkingly
at us. Then the man rose and made a deep salaam,
and we saw that he was an Oriental. Now when I
strive to etch him clearly in my mind, I can resurrect
no plain image of him. I only remember those piercing eyes and the yellow, fantastic robe he wore.

We returned his salute mechanically and he spoke
in a low, refined voice, "Gentlemen, I crave your
pardon! I have made so free as to light the candles—
shall we not proceed with the business pertaining to
our mutual friend."

He made a slight gesture toward the silent bulk on
the table. Conrad nodded, evidently unable to speak.
The thought flashed through our minds at the same
time, that this man had also been given a sealed
envelope—but how had he come to the Grimlan
house so quickly? John Grimlan had been dead
scarcely two hours and to the best of our knowledge
no one knew of his demise but ourselves. And how
had he got into the locked and bolted house?

The whole affair was grotesque and unreal in the
extreme. We did not even introduce ourselves or ask
the stranger his name. He took charge in a matter-of-
fact way, and so under the spell of horror and illusion
were we that we moved dazedly, involuntarily obeying his suggestions, given us in a low, respectful
tone.

I found myself standing on the left side of the table
looking across its grisly burden at Conrad. The Oriental stood with arms folded and head bowed at the
head of the table, nor did it then strike me as being
strange that he should stand there, instead of Conrad
who was to read what Grimlan had written. I found

my gaze drawn to the figure worked on the breast of the stranger's robe, in black silk—a curious figure somewhat resembling a peacock and somewhat resembling a bat, or a flying dragon. I noted with a start that the same design was worked on the robe covering the corpse.

The doors had been locked, the windows fastened down.

Conrad, with a shaky hand, opened the inner envelope and fluttered open the parchment sheets contained therein. These sheets seemed much older than those containing the instructions to Conrad, in the larger envelope. Conrad began to read in a monotonous drone which had the effect of hypnosis on the hearer; so at times the candles grew dim in my gaze and the room and its occupants swam strange and monstrous, veiled and distorted like an hallucination. Most of what he read was gibberish; it meant nothing; yet the sound of it and the archaic style of it filled me with an intolerable horror.

"To ye contract elsewhere recorded, I, John Grymlann, herebye sweare by ye Name of ye Nameless One to keep goode faithe. Wherefore do I now write in blood these wordes spoken to me in thys grim & silent chamber in ye dedde citie of Koth, whereto no mortal manne hath attained but mee. These same wordes now writ down by mee to be rede over my bodie at ye appointed tyme to fulfill my part of ye bargain which I entered intoe of mine own free will & knowledge beinge of rite mynd & fiftie years of age this yeare of 1680, A. D. Here begynneth ye incantation:

"Before manner was, ye Elder ones were, & even yet their lord dwelleth amonge ye shadows to which if a manne sette his foote he maye not turn vpon his track."

The words merged into a barbaric gibberish as Conrad stumbled through an unfamiliar language—a language faintly suggesting the Phoenician, but shuddery with the touch of a hideous antiquity beyond any remembered earthly tongue. One of the candles flickered and went out. I made a move to relight it, but a motion from the silent Oriental stayed me. His eyes burned into mine, then shifted back to the still form on the table.

The manuscript had shifted back into its archaic English.

"—And ye mortal which gaineth to ye black citadels of Koth & speaks with ye Darke Lord whose face is hidden, for a price may he gain hys heartes desire, ryches & knowledge beyond countinge & lyffe beyond mortal span even two hundred and fiftie yeares."

Again Conrad's voice trailed off into unfamiliar gutturals. Another candle went out.

"—Let not ye mortals flynche as ye tyme draweth nigh for payement & ye fires of Hel laye hold vpon ye vytals as the sign of reckoninge. For ye Prince of Darkness taketh hys due in ye endde & he is not to bee cozened. What ye have promised, that shall ye deliver. *Augantha ne shuba*—"

At the first sound of those barbaric accents, a cold hand of terror locked about my throat. My frantic eyes shot to the candles and I was not surprised to see another flicker out. Yet there was no hint of any draft to stir the heavy black hangings. Conrad's voice wavered; he drew his hand across his throat, gagging momentarily. The eyes of the Oriental never altered.

"—Amonge ye sonnes of men glide strange shadows for ever. Men see ye tracks of ye talones but not ye feete that make them. Over ye souls of men spread great black wingges. There is but one Black Master though men called hym Sathanas & Beelzebub & Apolleon & Ahriman & Malik Tous—"

Mists of horror engulfed me. I was dimly aware of Conrad's voice droning on and on, both in English and in that other fearsome tongue whose horrific import I scarcely dared try to guess. And with stark fear clutching at my heart, I saw the candles go out, one by one. And with each flicker, as the gathering gloom darkened about us, my horror mounted. I could not speak, I could not move; my distended eyes were fixed with agonized intensity on the remaining candle. The silent Oriental at the head of that ghastly table was included in my fear. He had not moved nor spoken, but under his drooping lids, his eyes burned with devilish triumph; I knew that beneath his inscrutable exterior he was gloating fiendishly—but why—*why?*

But I *knew* that the moment the extinguishing of the last candle plunged the room into utter darkness, some nameless, abominable thing would take place. Conrad was approaching the end. His voice rose to the climax in gathering crescendo.

"Approacheth now ye moment of payment. Ye ravens are flying. Ye bats winge against ye skye. There are skulls in ye starres. Ye soul & ye bodie are promised and shall bee delivered uppe. Not to ye dust agayne nor ye elements from which springe lyfe—"

The candle flickered slightly. I tried to scream, but my mouth gaped to a soundless yammering. I tried to flee, but I stood frozen, unable even to close my eyes.

"—Ye abysse yawns & ye debt is to paye. Ye light fayles, ye shadows gather. There is no god but evil; no lite but darkness; no hope but doom—"

A hollow groan resounded through the room. *It seemed to come from the robe-covered thing on the table!* That robe twitched fitfully.

"Oh winges in ye black darke!"

I started violently; a faint swish sounded in the gathering shadows. The stir of the dark hangings? It sounded like the rustle of gigantic wings.

"Oh redde eyes in ye shadows! What is promised, what is writ in bloode is fulfilled! Ye lite is gulfed in blackness! Ya—Koth!"

The last candle went out suddenly and a ghastly unhuman cry that came not from my lips or from Conrad's burst unbearably forth. Horror swept over me like a black icy wave; in the blind dark I heard myself screaming terribly. Then with a swirl and a great rush of wind something swept the room, flinging the hangings aloft and dashing chairs and tables crashing to the floor. For an instant an intolerable odor burned our nostrils, a low hideous tittering mocked us in the blackness; then silence fell like a shroud.

Somehow, Conrad found a candle and lighted it. The faint glow showed us the room in fearful disarray—showed us each other's ghastly faces—and showed us the black ebony table—empty! The doors and windows were locked as they had been, but the Oriental was gone—and so was the corpse of John Grimlan.

Shrieking like damned men we broke down the door and fled frenziedly down the well-like staircase where the darkness seemed to clutch at us with clammy black fingers. As we tumbled down into the lower hallway, a lurid glow cut the darkness and the scent of burning wood filled our nostrils.

The outer doorway held momentarily against our frantic assault, then gave way and we hurtled into the outer starlight. Beyond us the flames leaped up with a crackling roar as we fled down the hill. Conrad glancing over his shoulder, halted suddenly, wheeled and flung up his arms like a madman, and screamed, "Soul and body he sold to Malik Tous, who is Satan, two hundred and fifty years ago! This was the night of payment—and my God—look! *Look!* The Fiend has claimed his own!

I looked, frozen with horror. Flames had enveloped the whole house with appalling swiftness, and now the great mass was etched against the shadowed sky, a crimson inferno. And above the holocaust hovered a gigantic black shadow like a monstrous bat, and from its dark clutch dangled a small white thing, like the body of a man, dangling limply. Then, even as we cried out in horror, it was gone and our dazed gaze met only the shuddering walls and blazing roof which crumpled into the flames with an earth-shaking roar.

Robert E. Howard

Silence falls on Mecca's walls,
Else god from god, Red-masked she
Sits, virgin in a dream a days
Votive once at each sublime in dews
A woman bares her pulsing loins

SILENCE FALLS ON MECCA'S WALLS

Silence falls on Mecca's walls
And true believers turn to stone;
A granite wind from out the East
Bears the rattle of bone on bone,
And to the harlot of the priest
Comes one no man has ever known.

The black stars fall on Mecca's wall,
The red stars gem the pallid night;
The yellow stars are hinged in grey
But Ammon-Hoteph's stars are white.
Who weaves a web to hold at bay
The castled king of Mekmet's light?

Darkness falls on Mecca's walls.
The cressets glimmer in the gloom;
Along the cornices and groins
The scorpion weaves his trail of doom.
A woman bares her pulsing loins
To One within a shadowy room.

The star-dust falls on Mecca's walls,
The bats' wings flash in Mekmet's face;
The lonely fanes rise black and stark.
What brought what Shape from what strange place,
Across the gulf of utter dark,
To span the void of cosmic space?

Silence falls on Mecca's walls
Like mist from some fiend-haunted fen.
Stars, shuttles in a demon's looms,
Weave over Mecca, dooms of men.
A woman laughs—and laughs again.

THE VALLEY OF THE WORM

I WILL tell you of Niord and the Worm. You have heard the tale before in many guises wherein the hero was named Tyr, or Perseus, or Siegfried, or Beowulf, or Saint George. But it was Niord who met the loathly demoniac thing that crawled hideously up from hell, and from which meeting sprang the cycle of hero-tales that revolves down the ages until the very substance of the truth is lost and passes into the limbo of all forgotten legends. I know whereof I speak, for I was Niord.

As I lie here awaiting death, which creeps slowly upon me like a blind slug, my dreams are filled with glittering visions and the pageantry of glory. It is not of the drab, disease-racked life of James Allison I dream, but all the gleaming figures of the mighty pageantry that have passed before, and shall come after; for I have faintly glimpsed, not merely the shapes that trail out behind, but shapes that come after, as a man in a long parade glimpses, far ahead, the line of figures that precede him winding over a distant hill, etched shadow-like against the sky. I am one and all the pageantry of shapes and guises and masks which have been, are, and shall be the visible manifestations of that illusive, intangible, but vitally existent spirit now promenading under the brief and temporary name of James Allison.

Each man on earth, each woman, is part and all of a similar caravan of shapes and beings. But they can not remember—their minds can not bridge the brief, awful gulfs of blackness which lie between those unstable shapes, and which the spirit, soul or ego, in spanning, shakes off its fleshy masks. I remember. Why I can remember is the strangest tale of all; but as I lie here with death's black wings slowly unfolding over me, all the dim folds of my previous lives are shaken out before my eyes, and I see myself in many forms and guises—braggart, swaggering, fearful, loving, foolish, all that men have been or will be.

I have been Man in many lands and many conditions; yet—and here is another strange thing—my line of reincarnation runs straight down one unerring channel. I have never been any but a man of that restless race men once called Nordheimr and later Aryans, and today name by many names and designations. Their history is my history, from the first mewling wail of a hairless white ape cub in the wastes of the arctic, to the death-cry of the last degenerate product of ultimate civilization, in some dim and unguessed future age.

My name has been Hialmar, Tyr, Bragi, Bran, Horsa, Eric, and John. I strode red-handed through the deserted streets of Rome behind the yellow-maned Brennus; I wandered through the violated plantations with Alaric and his Goths when the flame of burning villas lit the land like day and an empire was gasping its last under our sandalled feet; I waded sword in hand through the foaming surf from Hengist's galley to lay the foundations of England in blood and pillage; when Leif the Lucky sighted the broad white beaches of an unguessed world, I stood beside him in the bows of the dragon-ship, my golden beard blowing in the wind; and when Godfrey of Bouillon led his Crusaders over the walls of Jersualem, I was among them in steel cap and brigandine.

But it is of none of these things I would speak. I would take you back with me into an age beside which that of Brennus and Rome is as yesterday. I would take you back through, not merely centuries and millenniums, but epochs and dim ages unguessed by the wildest philosopher. Oh far, far and far will you fare into the nighted Past before you win beyond the boundaries of my race, blue-eyed, yellow-haired, wanderers, slayers, lovers, mighty in rapine and wayfaring.

It is the adventure of Niord Worm's-bane of which I would speak—the root-stem of a whole cycle of hero-tales which has not yet reached its end, the grisly underlying reality that lurks behind time-distorted myths of dragons, fiends and monsters.

Yet it is not alone with the mouth of Niord that I will speak. I am James Allison no less than I was Niord, and as I unfold the tale, I will interpret some of his thoughts and dreams and deeds from the mouth of the modern I, so that the saga of Niord shall not be a meaningless chaos to you. His blood is your blood, who are sons of Aryan; but wide misty gulfs of eons lie horrifically between, and the deeds and dreams of Niord seem as alien to your deeds and dreams as the primordial and lion-haunted forest seems alien to the white-walled city street.

It was a strange world in which Niord lived and loved and fought, so long ago that even my eon-spanning memory can not recognize landmarks. Since then the surface of the earth has changed, not once but a score of times; continents have risen and sunk, seas have changed their beds and rivers their courses, glaciers have waxed and waned, and the very stars and constellations have altered and shifted.

It was so long ago that the cradle-land of my race was still in Nordheim. But the epic drifts of my people had already begun, and blue-eyed, yellow-maned tribes flowed eastward and southward and westward, on century-long treks that carried them around the world and left their bones and their traces in strange lands and wild waste places. On one of these drifts I grew from infancy to manhood. My knowledge of that northern homeland was dim memories, like half-remembered dreams, of blinding white snow plains and ice fields, of great fires roaring in the circle of hide tents, of yellow manes flying in great winds, and a sun setting in a lurid wallow of crimson clouds, blazing on trampled snow where still dark forms lay in pools that were redder than the sunset.

That last memory stands out clearer than the others. It was the field of Jotunheim, I was told in later years, whereon had just been fought that terrible battle which was the Armageddon of the Æsir-folk, the subject of a cycle of hero-songs for long ages, and which still lives today in dim dreams of Ragnarok and Goetterdaemmerung. I looked on that battle as a mewling infant; so I must have lived about—but I will not name the age, for I would be called a madman, and historians and geologists alike would rise to dispute me.

But my memories of Nordheim were few and dim, paled by memories of that long, long trek upon which I had spent my life. We had not kept to a straight course, but our trend had been forever southward. Sometimes we had bided for a while in fertile upland valleys or rich river-traversed plains, but always we took up the trail again, and not always because of drouth or famine. Often we left countries teeming with game and wild grain to push into wastelands. On our trail we moved endlessly, driven only by our restless whim, yet blindly following a cosmic law, the workings of which we never guessed, any more than the wild geese guess in their flights around the world. So at last we came into the Country of the Worm.

I will take up the tale at the time when we came into jungle-clad hills reeking with rot and teeming with spawning life, where the tom-toms of a savage people pulsed incessantly through the hot breathless night. These people came forth to dispute our way—short, strongly built men, black-haired, painted, ferocious, but indisputably white men. We knew their breed of old. They were Picts, and of all alien races the fiercest. We had met their kind before in thick forests, and in upland valleys beside mountain lakes. But many moons had passed since those meetings.

I believe this particular tribe represented the easternmost drift of the race. They were the most primitive and ferocious of any I ever met. Already they were exhibiting hints of characteristics I have noted among black savages in jungle countries, though they had dwelt in these environs only a few generations. The abysmal jungle was engulfing them, was obliterating their pristine characteristics and shaping them in its own horrific mold. They were drifting into head-hunting, and cannibalism was but a step which I believe they must have taken before they became extinct. These things are natural adjuncts to the jungle; the Picts did not learn them from the black people, for then there were no blacks among those hills. In later years they came up from the south, and the Picts first enslaved and then were absorbed by them. But with that my saga of Niord is not concerned.

We came into that brutish hill country, with its squalling abysms of savagery and black primitiveness. We were a whole tribe marching on foot, old men, wolfish with their long beards and gaunt limbs, giant warriors in their prime, naked children running along the line of march, women with tousled yellow locks carrying babies which never cried—unless it were to scream from pure rage. I do not remember our numbers, except that there were some five hundred fighting-men—and by fighting-men I mean all males, from the child just strong enough to lift a bow, to the oldest of the old men. In that madly ferocious age all were fighters. Our women fought, when brought to bay, like tigresses, and I have seen a babe, not yet old enough to stammer articulate words, twist its head and sink its teeth in the foot that stamped out its life.

Oh, we were fighters! Let me speak of Niord. I am proud of him, the more when I consider the paltry crippled body of James Allison, the unstable mask I now wear. Niord was tall, with great shoulders, lean hips and mighty limbs. His muscles were long and swelling, denoting endurance and speed as well as strength. He could run all day without tiring, and he possessed a co-ordination that made his movements a blur of blinding speed. If I told you his full strength, you would brand me a liar. But there is no man on earth today strong enough to bend the bow Niord handled with ease. The longest arrow-flight on record is that of a Turkish archer who sent a shaft 482 yards. There was not a stripling in my tribe who could not have bettered that flight.

As we entered the jungle country we heard the tom-toms booming across the mysterious valley that slumbered between the brutish hills, and in a broad, open plateau we met our enemies. I do not believe these Picts knew us, even by legends, or they had never rushed so openly to the onset, though they outnumbered us. But there was no attempt at ambush. They swarmed out of the trees, dancing and singing their war-songs, yelling their barbarous threats. Our heads should hang in their idol-hut and our yellow-haired women should bear their sons. Ho! ho! ho! By Ymir, it was Niord who laughed then, not James Allison. Just so we of the Æsir laughed to hear their threats—deep thunderous laughter from broad and mighty chests. Our trail was laid in blood and embers through many lands. We were the slayers and ravishers, striding sword in hand across the world, and that these folk threatened us woke our rugged humor.

We went to meet them, naked but for our wolfhides, swinging our bronze swords, and our singing was like rolling thunder in the hills. They sent their arrows among us, and we gave back their fire. They could not match us in archery. Our arrows hissed in blinding clouds among them, dropping them like autumn leaves, until they howled and frothed like mad dogs and charged to hand-grips. And we, mad with the fighting joy, dropped our bows and ran to meet them, as a lover runs to his love.

By Ymir, it was a battle to madden and make drunken with the slaughter and the fury. The Picts were as ferocious as we, but ours was the superior physique, the keener wit, the more highly developed fighting-brain. We won because we were a superior race, but it was no easy victory. Corpses littered the blood-soaked earth; but at last they broke, and we cut them down as they ran, to the very edge of the trees. I tell of that fight in a few bald words. I can not paint the madness, the reek of sweat and blood, the panting, muscle-straining effort, the splintering of bones under mighty blows, the rending and hewing of quivering sentient flesh; above all the merciless abysmal savagery of the whole affair, in which there was neither rule nor order, each man fighting as he would or could. If I might do so, you would recoil in horror; even the modern I, cognizant of my close kinship with those times, stand aghast as I review that butchery. Mercy was yet unborn, save as some individual's whim, and rules of warfare were as yet undreamed of. It was an age in which each tribe and each human fought tooth and fang from birth to death, and neither gave nor expected mercy.

So we cut down the fleeting Picts, and our women came out on the field to brain the wounded enemies with stones, or cut their throats with copper knives. We did not torture. We were no more cruel than life demanded. The rule of life was ruthlessness, but there is no more wanton cruelty today than ever we dreamed of. It was not wanton bloodthirstiness that made us butcher wounded and captive foes. It was because we knew our chances of survival increased with each enemy slain.

Yet there was occasionally a touch of individual mercy, and so it was in this fight. I had been occupied with a duel with an especially valiant enemy. His tousled thatch of black hair scarcely came above my chin, but he was a solid knot of steel-spring muscles, than which lightning scarcely moved faster. He had an iron sword and a hide-covered buckler. I had a knotty-headed bludgeon. That fight was one that glutted even my battle-lusting soul. I was bleeding from a score of flesh wounds before one of my terrible, lashing strokes smashed his shield like cardboard, and an instant later my bludgeon glanced from his unprotected head. Ymir! Even now I stop to laugh and marvel at the hardness of that Pict's skull. Men of that age were assuredly built on a rugged plan! That blow should have splattered his brains like water. It did lay his scalp open horribly, dashing him senseless to the earth, where I let him lie, supposing him to be dead, as I joined in the slaughter of the fleeing warriors.

When I returned reeking with sweat and blood, my club horridly clotted with blood and brains, I noticed that my antagonist was regaining consciousness, and that a naked tousle-headed girl was preparing to give him the finishing touch with a stone she could scarcely lift. A vagrant whim caused me to check the blow. I had enjoyed the fight, and I admired the adamantine quality of his skull.

We made camp a short distance away, burned our dead on a great pyre, and after looting the corpses of the enemy, we dragged them across the plateau and cast them down in a valley to make a feast for the hyenas, jackals and vultures which were already gathering. We kept close watch that night, but we were not attacked, though far away through the jungle we could make out the red gleam of fires, and could faintly hear, when the wind veered, the throb of tom-toms and demoniac screams and yells—keenings for the slain or mere animal squallings of fury.

Nor did they attack us in the days that followed. We bandaged our captive's wounds and quickly learned his primitive tongue, which, however, was so different from ours that I can not conceive of the two languages having ever had a common source.

His name was Grom, and he was a great hunter and fighter, he boasted. He talked freely and held no grudge, grinning broadly and showing tusk-like teeth, his beady eyes glittering from under the tangled black mane that fell over his low forehead. His limbs were almost ape-like in their thickness.

He was vastly interested in his captors, though he could never understand why he had been spared; to the end it remained an inexplicable mystery to him. The Picts obeyed the law of survival even more rigidly than did the Æsir. They were the more practical, as shown by their more settled habits. They never roamed as far or as blindly as we. Yet in every line we were the superior race.

Grom, impressed by our intelligence and fighting qualities, volunteered to go into the hills and make peace for us with his people. It was immaterial to us, but we let him go. Slavery had not yet been dreamed of.

So Grom went back to his people, and we forgot about him, except that I went a trifle more cautiously about my hunting, expecting him to be lying in wait to put an arrow through my back. Then one day we heard a rattle of tom-toms, and Grom appeared at the edge of the jungle, his face split in his gorilla-grin, with the painted, skin-clad, feather-bedecked chiefs of the clans. Our ferocity had awed them, and our sparing of Grom further impressed them. They could not understand leniency; evidently we valued them too cheaply to bother about killing one when he was in our power.

So peace was made with much pow-wow, and sworn to with many strange oaths and rituals—we swore only by Ymir, and an Æsir never broke that vow. But they swore by the elements, by the idol which sat in the fetish-hut where fires burned forever and a withered crone slapped a leather-covered drum all night long, and by another being too terrible to be named.

Then we all sat around the fires and gnawed meat-bones, and drank a fiery concoction they brewed from wild grain, and the wonder is that the feast did not end in a general massacre; for that liquor had devils in it and made maggots writhe in our brain. But no harm came of our vast drunkenness, and thereafter we dwelt at peace with our barbarous neighbors. They taught us many things, and learned many more from us. But they taught us iron-workings, into which they had been forced by the lack of copper in those hills, and we quickly excelled them.

We went freely among their villages—mud-walled clusters of huts in hilltop clearings, overshadowed by giant trees—and we allowed them to come at will among our camps—straggling lines of hide tents on the plateau where the battle had been fought. Our young men cared not for their squat beady-eyed women, and our rangy clean-limbed girls with their tousled yellow heads were not drawn to the hairy-breasted savages. Familiarity over a period of years would have reduced the repulsion on either side, until the two races would have flowed together to form one hybrid people, but long before that time

the Æsir rose and departed, vanishing into the
mysterious hazes of the haunted south. But before
that exodus there came to pass the horror of the
Worm.

I hunted with Grom and he led me into brooding,
uninhabited valleys and up into silence-haunted hills
where no men had set foot before us. But there was
one valley, off in the mazes of the southwest, into
which he would not go. Stumps of shattered columns, relics of a forgotten civilization, stood among
the trees on the valley floor. Grom showed them to
me, as we stood among the trees on the valley floor.
Grom showed them to me, as we stood on the cliffs
that flanked the mysterious vale, but he would not
go down into it, and he disuaded me when I would
have gone alone. He would not speak plainly of the
danger that lurked there, but it was greater than that
of serpent or tiger, or the trumpeting elephants which
occasionally wandered up in devastating droves from
the south.

Of all beasts, Grom told me in the gutturals of his
tongue, the Picts feared only Satha, the great snake,
and they shunned the jungle where he lived. But
there was another thing they feared, and it was connected in some manner with the Valley of Broken
Stones, as the Picts called the crumbling pillars.
Long ago, when his ancestors had first come into the
country, they had dared that grim vale, and a whole
clan of them had perished, suddenly, horribly, and
unexplainably. At least Grom did not explain. The
horror had come up out of the earth, somehow, and
it was not good to talk of it, since it was believed that
It might be summoned by speaking of It—whatever
It was.

But Grom was ready to hunt with me anywhere
else; for he was the greatest hunter among the Picts,
and many and fearful were our adventures. Once I
killed, with the iron sword I had forged with my own

hands, that most terrible of all beasts—old saber-tooth, which men today call a tiger because he was more like a tiger than anything else. In reality he was almost as much like a bear in build, save for his unmistakably feline head. Saber-tooth was massive-limbed, with a low-hung, great, heavy body, and he vanished from the earth because he was too terrible a fighter, even for that grim age. As his muscles and ferocity grew, his brain dwindled until at last even the instinct of self-preservation vanished. Nature, who maintains her balance in such things, destroyed him because, had his super-fighting powers been allied with an intelligent brain, he would have de-stroyed all other forms of life on earth. He was a freak on the road of evolution—organic development gone mad and run to fangs and talons, to slaughter and destruction.

I killed saber-tooth in a battle that would make a saga in itself, and for months afterward I lay semi-delirious with ghastly wounds that made the toughest warriors shake their heads. The Picts said that never before had a man killed a saber-tooth single-handed. Yet I recovered, to the wonder of all.

While I lay at the doors of death there was a secession from the tribe. It was a peaceful secession, such as continually occurred and contributed greatly to the peopling of the world by yellow-haired tribes. Forty-five of the young men took themselves mates simultaneously and wandered off to found a clan of their own. There was no revolt; it was a racial custom which bore fruit in all the later ages, when tribes sprung from the same roots met, after centuries of separation, and cut one another's throats with joyous abandon. The tendency of the Aryan and the pre-Aryan was always toward disunity, clans splitting off the main stem, and scattering.

So these young men, led by one Bragi, my brother-in-arms, took their girls and venturing to the southwest, took up their abode in the Valley of Broken Stones. The Picts expostulated, hinting vaguely of a monstrous doom that haunted the vale, but the Æsir laughed. We had left our own demons and weirds in the icy wastes of the far blue north, and the devils of other races did not much impress us.

When my full strength was returned, and the grisly wounds were only scars, I girt on my weapons and strode over the plateau to visit Bragi's clan. Grom did not accompany me. He had not been in the Æsir camp for several days. But I knew the way. I remembered well the valley, from the cliffs of which I had looked down and seen the lake at the upper end, the trees thickening into forest at the lower extremity. The sides of the valley were high sheer cliffs, and a steep broad ridge at either end cut it off from the surrounding country. It was toward the lower or southwestern end that the valley-floor was dotted thickly with ruined columns, some towering high among the trees, some fallen into heaps of lichen-clad stones. What race reared them none knew. But Grom had hinted fearsomely of a hairy, apish monostrosity dancing loathsomely under the moon to a demoniac piping that induced horror and madness.

I crossed the plateau whereon our camp was pitched, descended the slope, traversed a shallow vegetation-choked valley, climbed another slope, and plunged into the hills. A half-day's leisurely travel brought me to the ridge on the other side of which lay the valley of the pillars. For many miles I had seen no sign of human life. The settlements of the Picts all lay many miles to the east. I topped the ridge and looked down into the dreaming valley with its still blue lake, its brooding cliffs and its broken columns jutting among the trees. I looked for smoke. I saw none, but I saw vultures wheeling in the sky over a cluster of tents on the lake shore.

I came down the ridge, warily and approached the

silent camp. In it I halted, frozen with horror. I was not easily moved. I had seen death in many forms, and had fled from or taken part in red massacres that spilled blood like water and heaped the earth with corpses. But here I was confronted with an organic devastation that staggered and appalled me. Of Bragi's embryonic clan, not one remained alive, and not one corpse was whole. Some of the hide tents still stood erect. Others were mashed down and flattened out, as if crushed by some monstrous weight, so that at first I wondered if a drove of elephants had stampeded across the camp. But no elephants ever wrought such destruction as I saw strewn on the bloody ground. The camp was a shambles, littered with bits of flesh and fragments of bodies—hands, feet, heads, pieces of human debris. Weapons lay about, some of them stained with a greenish slime like that which spurts from a crushed caterpillar.

No human foe could have committed this ghastly atrocity. I looked at the lake, wondering if nameless amphibian monsters had crawled from the calm waters whose deep blue told of unfathomed depths. Then I saw a print left by the destroyer. It was a track such as a titanic worm might leave, yards broad, winding back down the valley. The grass lay flat where it ran, and bushes and small trees had been crushed down into the earth, all horribly smeared with blood and greenish slime.

With berserk fury in my soul I drew my sword and started to follow it, when a call attracted me. I wheeled, to see a stocky form approaching me from the ridge. It was Grom the Pict, and when I think of the courage it must have taken for him to have overcome all the instincts planted in him by traditional teachings and personal experience, I realize the full depths of his friendship for me.

Squatting on the lake shore, spear in his hands, his black eyes ever roving fearfully down the brooding tree-waving reaches of the valley, Grom told me of the horror that had come upon Bragi's clan under the moon. But first he told me of it, as his sires had told the tale to him.

Long ago the Picts had drifted down from the northwest on a long, long trek, finally reaching these jungled-covered hills, where, because they were weary, and because the game and fruit were plentiful and there were no hostile tribes, they halted and built their mud-walled villages.

Some of them, a whole clan of that numerous tribe, took up their abode in the Valley of the Broken Stones. They found the columns and a great ruined temple back in the trees, and in that temple there was no shrine or altar, but the mouth of a shaft that vanished deep into the black earth, and in which there were no steps such as a human being would make and use. They built their village in the valley, and in the night, under the moon, horror came upon them and left only broken walls and bits of slime-smeared flesh.

In those days the Picts feared nothing. The warriors of the other clans gathered and sang their war-songs and danced their war dances, and followed a broad track of blood and slime to the shaft-mouth in the temple. They howled defiance and hurled down boulders which were never heard to strike bottom. Then began a thin demoniac piping, and up from the well pranced a hideous anthropomorphic figure dancing to the weird strains of a pipe it held in its monstrous hands. The horror of its aspect froze the fierce Picts with amazement, and close behind it a vast white bulk heaved up from the subterranean darkness. Out of the shaft came a slavering mad nightmare which arrows pierced but could not check, which swords carved but could not slay. It fell slobbering upon the warriors, crushing them to crimson pulp, tearing them to bits as an octopus might tear small fishes, sucking their blood from their mangled limbs and devouring them even as they screamed and struggled. The survivors fled, pursued to the very ridge, up which, apparently, the monster could not propel its quaking mountainous bulk.

After that they did not dare the silent valley. But the dead came to their shamans and old men in dreams and told them strange and terrible secrets. They spoke of an ancient race of semi-human beings which once inhabited that valley and reared those columns for their own weird inexplicable purpose. The white monster in the pits was their god, summoned up from the nighted abysses of mid-earth uncounted fathoms below the black mold, by sorcery unknown to the sons of men. The hairy anthropomorphic being was its servant, created to serve the god, a formless elemental spirit drawn up from below and cased in flesh, organic but beyond the understanding of humanity. The Old Ones had long vanished into the limbo from whence they crawled in the black dawn of the universe, but their bestial god and his inhuman slave lived on. Yet both were organic after a fashion, and could be wounded, though no human weapon had been found potent enough to slay them.

Bragi and his clan had dwelt for weeks in the valley before the horror struck. Only the night before, Grom, hunting above the cliffs, and by that token daring greatly, had been paralyzed by a high-pitched demon piping, and then by a mad clamor of human screaming. Stretched face down in the dirt, hiding his head in a tangle of grass, he had not dared to move, even when the shrieks died away in the slobbering, repulsive sounds of a hideous feast. When dawn broke he had crept shuddering to the cliffs to look down into the valley, and the sight of the devas-

tation, even when seen from afar, had driven him in
yammering flight far into the hills. But it had occurred to him, finally, that he should warn the rest of
the tribe, and returning, on his way to the camp on
the plateau, he had seen me entering the valley.

So spoke Grom, while I sat and brooded darkly,
my chin on my mighty fist. I can not frame in modern words the clan-feeling that in those days was a
living vital part of every man and woman. In a world
where talon and fang were lifted on every hand, and
the hands of all men raised against an individual,
except those of his own clan, tribal instinct was more
than the phrase it is today. It was as much a part of a
man as was his heart or his right hand. This was
necessary, for only thus banded together in unbreak-
able groups could mankind have survived in the
terrible environments of the primitive world. So now
the personal grief I felt for Bragi and the clean-
limbed young men and laughing white-skinned girls
was drowned in a deeper sea of grief and fury that
was cosmic in its depth and intensity. I sat grimly,
while the Pict squatted anxiously beside me, his gaze
roving from me to the menacing deeps of the valley
where the accursed columns loomed like broken teeth
of cackling hags among the waving leafy reaches.

I, Niord, was not one to use my brain over-much.
I lived in a physical world, and there were the old
men of the tribe to do my thinking. But I was one of
a race destined to become dominant mentally as well
as physically, and I was no mere muscular animal. So
as I sat there there came dimly and then clearly a
thought to me that brought a short fierce laugh from
my lips.

Rising, I bade Grom aid me, and we built a pyre
on the lake shore of dried wood, the ridge-poles of
the tents, and the broken shafts of spears. Then we
collected the grisly fragments that had been parts of

Bragi's band, and we laid them on the pile, and struck flint and steel to it.

The thick sad smoke crawled serpent-like into the sky, and turning to Grom, I made him guide me to the jungle where lurked that scaly horror, Satha, the great serpent. Grom gaped at me; not the greatest hunters among the Picts sought out the mighty crawling one. But my will was like a wind that swept him along my course, and at last he led the way. We left the valley by the upper end, crossing the ridge, skirting the tall cliffs, and plunged into the fastnesses of the south, which was peopled only by the grim denizens of the jungle. Deep into the jungle we went, until we came to a low-lying expanse, dark and dark beneath the great creeper-festooned trees, where our feet sank deep into the spongy silt, carpeted by rotting vegetation, and slimy moisture oozed up beneath their pressure. This, Grom told me, was the realm haunted by Satha, the great serpent.

Let me speak of Satha. There is nothing like him on earth today, nor has there been for countless ages. Like the meat-eating dinosaur, like old sabertooth, he was too terrible to exist. Even then he was a survival of a grimmer age when life and its forms were cruder and more hideous. There were not many of his kind then, though they may have existed in great numbers in the reeking ooze of the vast jungled-tangled swamps still farther south. He was larger than any phython of modern ages, and his fangs dripped with poison a thousand times more deadly than that of a king cobra.

He was never worshipped by the pure-blood Picts, though the blacks that came later deified him, and that adoration persisted in the hybrid race that sprang from the Negroes and their white conquerors. But to other peoples he was the nadir of evil horror, and tales of him became twisted into demonology; so in later ages Satha became the veritable devil of the

white races, and the Stygians first worshipped, and
then, when they became Egyptians, abhorred him
under the name of Set, the Old Serpent, while to the
Semites he became Leviathan and Satan. He was
terrible enough to be a god, for he was a crawling
death. I had seen a bull elephant fall dead in his
tracks from Satha's bite. I had seen him, had glimpsed
him writhing his horrific way through the dense jungle, had seen him take his prey, but had never
hunted him. He was too grim, even for the slayer of
old saber-tooth.

But now I hunted him, plunging farther and farther into the hot, breathless reek of his jungle, even
when friendship for me could not drive Grom farther. He urged me to paint my body and sing my
death-song before I advanced farther, but I pushed
on unheeding.

In a natural runway that wound between the shoul-
dering trees, I set a trap. I found a large tree, soft
and spongy of fiber, but thick-boled and heavy, and I
hacked through its base close to the ground with my
great sword, directing its fall so that when it toppled,
its top crashed into the branches of a smaller tree,
leaving it leaning across the runway, one end resting
on the earth, the other caught in the small tree.
Then I cut away the branches on the under side, and
cutting a slim tough sapling I trimmed it and stuck it
upright like a prop-pole under the leaning tree. Then,
cutting away the tree which supported it, I left the
great trunk poised precariously on the prop-pole, to
which I fastened a long vine, as thick as my wrist.

Then I went along through that primordial twilight
jungle until an over-powering fetid odor assailed my
nostrils, and from the rank vegetation in front of me,
Satha reared up his hideous head, swaying lethally
from side to side, while his forked tongue jetted in
and out, and his great yellow terrible eyes burned
icily on me with all the evil wisdom of the black

elder world that was when man was not. I backed
away, feeling no fear, only an icy sensation along my
spine, and Satha came sinuously after me, his shining eighty-foot barrel rippling over the rotting vegetation in mesmeric silence. His wedge-shaped head
was bigger than the head of the hugest stallion, his
trunk was thicker than a man's body, and his scales
shimmered with a thousand changing scintillations. I
was to Satha as a mouse is to a king cobra, but I was
fanged as no mouse ever was. Quick as I was, I knew
I could not avoid the lightning stroke of that great
triangular head; so I dared not let him come too
close. Subtly I fled down the runway, and behind me
the rush of the great supple body was like the sweep
of wind through the grass.

He was not far behind me when I raced beneath
the dead fall, and as the great shining length glided
under the trap, I gripped the vine with both hands
and jerked desperately. With a crash the great trunk
fell across Satha's scaly back, some six feet back of his
wedge-shaped head.

I had hoped to break his spine but I do not think
it did, for the great body coiled and knotted, the
mighty tail lashed and thrashed, mowing down the
bushes as if with a giant flail. At the instant of the
fall, the huge head had whipped about and struck the
tree with a terrific impact, the mighty fangs shearing
through the bark and woof like simitars. Now, as if
aware he fought an inanimate foe, Satha turned on me,
standing out of his reach. The scaly neck writhed and
arched, the mighty jaws gaped, disclosing fangs a foot
in length, from which dripped venom that might have
burned through solid stone.

I believe, what of his stupendous strength, that
Satha would have writhed from under the trunk, but
for a broken branch that had been driven deep into
his side, holding him like a barb. The sound of his
hissing filled the jungle and his eyes glared at me

with such concentrated evil that I shook despite myself. Oh, he knew it was I who had trapped him! Now as I came as close as I dared, and with a sudden powerful cast of my spear, transfixed his neck just below the gaping jaws, nailing him to the tree-trunk. Then I dared greatly, for he was far from dead, and I knew he would in an instant tear the spear from the wood and be free to strike. But in that instant I ran in, and swinging my sword with all my great power, I hewed off his terrible head.

The heavings and contortions of Satha's prisoned form in life were naught to the convulsions of his headless length in death. I retreated, dragging the gigantic head after me with a crooked pole, and a safe distance from the lashing, flying tail, I set to work. I worked with naked death then, and no man ever toiled more gingerly than did I. For I cut out the poison sacs at the base of the great fangs, and in the terrible venom I soaked the heads of eleven arrows, being careful that only the bronze points were in the liquid, which else had corroded away the wood of the tough shafts. While I was doing this, Grom, driven by comradeship and curiosity, came stealing nervously through the jungle, and his mouth gaped as he looked on the head of Satha.

For hours I seeped the arrowheads in the poison, until they were caked with a horrible green scum, and showed tiny flecks of corrosion where the venom had eaten into the solid bronze. I wrapped them carefully in broad, thick, rubber-like leaves, and then, though night had fallen and the hunting beasts were roaring on every hand, I went back through the jungled hills, Grom with me, until at dawn we came again to the high cliffs that loomed above the Valley of Broken Stones.

At the mouth of the valley I broke my spear, and I took all the unpoisoned shafts from my quiver, and snapped them. I painted my face and limbs as the

Æsir painted themselves only when they went forth to certain doom, and I sang my death-song to the sun as it rose over the cliffs, my yellow mane blowing in the morning wind.

Then I went down into the valley, bow in hand.

Grom could not drive himself to follow me. He lay on his belly in the dust and howled like a dying dog.

I passed the lake and the silent camp where the pyre-ashes still smoldered, and came under the thickening trees beyond. About me the columns loomed, mere shapeless heaps from the ravages of staggering eons. The trees grew more dense, and under their vast leafy branches the very light was dusky and evil. As in twilight shadow I saw the ruined temple, cyclopean walls staggering up from masses of decaying masonry and fallen blocks of stone. About six hundred yards in front of it a great column reared up in an open glade, eighty or ninety feet in height. It was so worn and pitted by weather and time that any child of my tribe could have climbed it, and I marked it and changed my plan.

I came to the ruins and saw huge crumbling walls upholding a domed roof from which many stones had fallen, so that it seemed like the lichen-grown ribs of some mythical monster's skeleton arching above me. Titanic columns flanked the open doorway through which ten elephants could have stalked abreast. Once there might have been inscriptions and hieroglyphics on the pillars and walls, but they were long worn away. Around the great room, on the inner side, ran columns in better state of preservation. On each of these columns was a flat pedestal, and some dim instinctive memory vaguely resurrected a shadowy scene wherein black drums roared madly, and on these pedestals monstrous beings squatted loathsomely in inexplicable rituals rooted in the black dawn of the universe.

There was no altar—only the mouth of a great

well-like shaft in the stone stone floor, with strange
obscene carvings all about the rim. I tore great pieces
of stone from the rotting floor and cast them down
the shaft which slanted down into utter darkness. I
heard them bound along the side, but I did not hear
them strike bottom. I cast down stone after stone,
each with a searing curse, and at last I heard a sound
that was not the dwindling rumble of the falling
stones. Up from the well floated a weird demon-
piping that was a symphony of madness. Far down in
the darkness I glimpsed the faint fearful glimmering
of a vast white bulk.

I retreated slowly as the piping grew louder, falling back through the broad doorway. I heard a scratching, scrambling noise, and up from the shaft and out
of the doorway between the colossal columns came a
prancing incredible figure. It went erect like a man,
but it was covered with fur, that was shaggiest where
its face should have been. If it had ears, nose and a
mouth I did not discover them. Only a pair of staring
red eyes leered from the furry mask. Its misshapen
hands held a strange set of pipes, on which it blew
weirdly as it pranced toward me with many a grotesque caper and leap.

Behind it I heard a repulsive obscene noise as of a
quaking unstable mass heaving up out of a well.
Then I nocked an arrow, drew the cord and sent the
shaft singing through the furry breast of the dancing
monostrosity. It went down as though struck by a
thunderbolt, but to my horror the piping continued,
though the pipes had fallen from the malformed hands.
Then I turned and ran fleetly to the column, up
which I swarmed before I looked back. When I
reached the pinnacle I looked, and because of the
shock and surprise of what I saw, I almost fell from
my dizzy perch.

Out of the temple the monstrous dweller in the
darkness had come, and I, who had expected a hor-

ror yet cast in some terrestrial mold, looked on the spawn of nightmare. From what subterranean hell it crawled in the long ago I know not, nor what black age it represented. But it was not a beast, as humanity knows beasts. I call it a worm for lack of a better term. There is no earthly language which has a name for it. I can only say it looked somewhat more like a worm than it did an octopus, a serpent or a dinosaur.

It was white and pulpy, and drew its quaking bulk along the ground, worm-fashion. But it had wide flat tentacles, and fleshy feelers, and other adjuncts the use of which I am unable to explain. And it had a long proboscis which it curled and uncurled like an elephant's trunk. Its forty eyes, set in a horrific circle, were composed of thousands of facets of as many scintillant colors which changed and altered in never-ending transmutation. But through all interplay of hue and glint, they retained their evil intelligence—intelligence there was behind those flickering facets, not human not yet bestial, but a night-born demoniac intelligence such as men in dreams vaguely sense throbbing titanically in the black gulfs outside our material universe. In size the monster was mountainous; its bulk would have dwarfed a mastodon.

But even as I shook with the cosmic horror of the thing, I drew a feathered shaft to my ear and arched it singing on its way. Grass and bushes were crushed flat as the monster came toward me like a moving mountain and shaft after shaft I sent with terrific force and deadly precision. I could not miss so huge a target. The arrows sank to the feathers or clear out of sight in the unstable bulk, each bearing enough poison to have stricken dead a bull elephant. Yet on it came, swiftly, appallingly, apparently heedless of both the shafts and the venom in which they were steeped. And all the time the hideous music played a maddening accompaniment, whining thinly from the pipes that lay untouched on the ground.

My confidence faded; even the poison of Satha was futile against this uncanny being. I drove my last shaft almost straight downward into the quaking white mountain, so close was the monster under my perch. Then suddenly its color altered. A wave of ghastly blue surged over it, and the vast bulk heaved in earthquake-like convulsions. With a terrible plunge it struck the lower part of the column, which crashed to falling shards of stone. But even with the impact, I leaped far out and fell through the empty air full upon the monster's back.

The spongy skin yielded and gave beneath my feet, and I drove my sword hilt deep, dragging it through the pulpy flesh, ripping a horrible yard-long wound, from which oozed a green slime. Then a flip of a cable-like tentacle flicked me from the titan's back and spun me three hundred feet through the air to crash among a cluster of giant trees.

The impact must have splintered half the bones in my frame, for when I sought to grasp my sword again and crawl anew to the combat, I could not move hand or foot, could only writhe helplessly with my broken back. But I could see the monster and I knew that I had won, even in defeat. The mountainous bulk was heaving and billowing, the tentacles were lashing madly, the antennae writhing and knotting, and the nauseous whiteness had changed to a pale and grisly green. It turned ponderously and lurched back toward the temple, rolling like a crippled ship in a heavy swell. Trees crashed and splintered as it lumbered against them.

I wept with pure fury because I could not catch up my sword and rush in to die glutting my berserk madness in mighty strokes. But the worm-god was death-stricken and needed not my futile sword. The demon pipes on the ground kept their infernal tune, and it was like the fiend's death-dirge. Then as the monster veered and floundered, I saw it catch up the corpse of its hairy slave. For an instant the apish form dangled in midair, gripped round by the trunk-like proboscis, then was dashed against the temple wall with a force that reduced the hairy body to a mere shapeless pulp. At that the pipes screamed out horribly, and fell silent forever.

The titan staggered on the brink of the shaft; then another change came over it—a frightful transfiguration the nature of which I can not yet describe. Even now when I try to think of it clearly, I am only chaotically conscious of a blasphemous, unnatural transmutation of form and substance, shocking and indescribable. Then the strangely altered bulk tumbled into the shaft to roll down into the ultimate darkness from whence it came, and I knew that it was dead. And as it vanished into the well, with a rending, grinding groan the ruined walls quivered from dome to base. They bent inward and buckled with deafening reverberation, the column splintered, and with a cataclysmic crash the dome itself came thundering down. For an instant the air seemed veiled with flying debris and stone-dust, through which the tree-tops lashed madly as in a storm or an earthquake convulsion. Then all was clear again and I stared, shaking the blood from my eyes. Where the temple had stood there lay only a colossal pile of shattered masonry and broken stones, and every column in the valley had fallen, to lie in crumbling shards.

In the silence that followed I heard Grom wailing a dirge over me. I bade him lay my sword in my hand, and he did so, and bent close to hear what I had to say, for I was passing swiftly.

"Let my tribe remember," I said, speaking slowly. "Let the tale be told from village to village, from camp to camp, from tribe to tribe, so that men may know that not man nor beast nor devil may prey in safety on the golden-haired people of Asgard. Let them build me a cairn where I lie and lay me therein with my bow and sword at hand, to guard this valley forever; so if the ghost of the god I slew comes up from below, my ghost will ever be ready to give it battle."

And while Grom howled and beat his hairy breast, death came to me in the Valley of the Worm.

THE SHADOW OF THE BEAST

As long as evil stars arise
Or moonlight fires the East,
May God in Heaven preserve us from
The Shadow of the Beast!

THE MADNESS began with the crack of a pistol. A man dropped with a bullet in his chest, and the man who had fired the shot turned to flee, snarling a brief threat at the pale-faced girl who stood, horror-struck, close by; then he dashed away among the trees on the edge of the camp, looking like an ape with his broad back and stooping gait.

Within an hour, grim-faced men were combing the pine woods with guns in their hands, and throughout the night the grisly hunt went on, while the victim of the fugitive lay fighting for his life.

"He's quiet now; they say he'll live," Joan said as she came out of the room where her young brother lay. Then she sank down into a chair and gave way to a burst of tears.

I sat down beside her and soothed her much as one would a child. I loved her, and she had shown that she returned my affection. It was my love for her that had drawn me from my Texas ranch to the

119

lumber camps in the shadow of the pine woods, where her brother looked after the interests of his company. I had reached my destination scarcely an hour after the shooting.

"Give me the details of all this," I said. "I haven't been able to get a coherent account of it."

"There isn't much to tell," she answered listlessly. "This man's name is Joe Cagle, and he's bad—in every sense of the word. Twice I've seen him peering in my window, and this morning he sprang out from behind a pile of lumber and caught me by the arm. I screamed, and Harry rushed up and struck him with a club. Then Cagle shot my brother, and— and before he ran away, he promised to revenge himself on me also. He's like a wild beast!"

"What threats did he make against you?" I asked, my hands involuntarily clenching.

"He said he'd come back and get me some night when the woods were dark," she answered wearily; and, with a fatalism that surprised and dismayed me, she added: "He will, too. When a man like him sets his mind on a girl, nothing but death can stop him."

"Then death will stop him," I said harshly, rising. "I'm going to join the posse. Don't leave this house tonight. By morning, Joe Cagle will be past harming any girl."

As I went out of the house I met one of the men who had been searching for the fugitive. He had sprained his ankle on a hidden root in the darkness and had returned to the camp on a borrowed horse.

"Naw, we ain't found no trace yet," he replied to my question. "We've done combed the country right around the camp, and the boys are spreading out towards the swamp. Don't look reasonable that he coulda got so far away with the short start he had, and us right after him on horseback; but Joe Cagle's more of a varmint than he is a man—looks like one uh these gorillas. I imagine he's hidin' in the swamp,

and if he is, it may take weeks to rout him out. He
can't be noplace else—like I said, we've done searched
the woods close by—all except the Deserted House,
uh course."

"Why not there? And where is this house?"

"Down the old tote road what ain't used no more,
'bout four miles. Aw, they ain't a man in the country
that'd go near that place, even to save his life. That
feller that killed the foreman a few years ago—they
chased him down the old tote road, and when he
seen he was goin' to have to go right past the Deserted House, he turned back and gave hisself up to
the mob. No sir—Joe Cagle ain't nowhere near that
house, you can bet!"

"Why does it have such a bad name?" I asked.

"Ain't nobody lived in it for twenty years. Last
man what owned it come crashin' out of a upstairs
window one night and was killed by the fall. Later a
young travellin' man stayed there all night on a bet,
and they found him outside the house next mornin'
—all smashed up like he'd fell a long ways. A back-
woodsman passin' that way late at night swore he'd
heard a terrible scream, then seen the travellin' man
come flyin' out of a second story window. He didn't
wait to see no more! But what give the Deserted
House the bad name in the first place was . . ."

But I was in no mood to listen to a long, drawn-out
ghost story, or whatever the man was about to tell
me. Almost every locality in the South has its "ha'nted"
house, and the tales attached to each are numberless.

I interrupted him to ask where I might likely find
the part of the posse which had penetrated most
deeply into the pine woods; and, having gotten instructions, made the man promise that he would
keep watch over Joan until I had returned. Then I
mounted his horse and rode away.

"Don't get lost," he shouted after me. "Them piney
woods is risky business for a stranger. Watch for the

light of the posse's torches through the trees. Don't
take the old branch road!"

A brisk canter brought me to the verge of a road
which led into the woods in the direction I wished to
go, and there I halted. Another road, one which was
little more than a dimly defined path, led away at
right angles. This was the old tote road which went
past the Deserted House. I hesitated. I had none of
the confidence that the others had shown that Joe
Cagle would shun the place. The more I thought of
it, the more I felt it likely that the fugitive would
take refuge there. From all acounts, he was an unusual man, a complete savage, so bestial, so low in
the scale of intelligence that even the superstitions of
the local people left him untouched. Why, then,
should not his animal craft bid him hide in the last
place his pursuers would think of looking—that same
animal-like nature that caused him to scorn the fears
of his more imaginative fellow men?

My decision reached, I reined my steed about and
started down the old road.

There is no darkness in the world so utterly devoid
of light as the blackness of the pine woods. The silent
trees rose like basaltic walls about me, shutting out
the stars. Except for the occasional eery sigh of the
wind through the branches, or the faraway hunting
cry of an owl, the silence was as absolute as the
darkness. The stillness bore heavily upon me. I
seemed to sense in the blackness about me the spirit
of the unconquerable swamplands, the primitive foe
of man whose abysmal savagery still defies his vaunted
civilization. In such surroundings anything seems possible. I did not wonder then at the tales of black
magic and voodoo rites said to take place in those
dark forests. Perhaps even the throb of a tom-tom,
summoning naked figures to leap and dance at some
firelit feast in the darkness, might not have surprised
me . . .

I shrugged my shoulders to rid myself of such thoughts. If voodoo worshippers did indeed worship secretly in these woods, there would be none tonight with the vengeful posse combing the country.

As my mount, bred in the pine country and sure-footed as a cat in the darkness, picked his way without my aid, I strained my senses to catch any sound such as a man might make. But not one stealthy footfall reached me, not a single rustle of the scanty underbrush. I knew Joe Cagle was armed and desperate. He might be waiting in ambush—might spring on me at any moment—but I felt no especial fear. In that veiling darkness he could see no better than I, and I would have as good a chance as he in a blind exchange of shots. And if it came to a hand-to-hand conflict—well, I weighed in at two hundred and five pounds, mostly bone and sinew, and life on the Texas range had hardened me to every sort of fighting, even to the death. To tell the truth, Cagle's threat to Joan had so enraged me that I had discarded all caution—it never occurred to me that I might be less than a match for the desperate, ape-like fugitive. If I could get my hands on him, I could crush him to pulp!

Surely I must be close to the Deserted House by now. I had no idea of the exact time, but far away in the east a faint glow began to spear through the masking blackness of the pines. The moon was rising. And on that instant, from somewhere in front of me, rattled a sudden volley of shots—then silence fell again, like a heavy fog. I had halted short, and now I hesitated. To me it had sounded as if all the reports had come from the same gun, and there had been no answering shots. What had happened out there in the grim darkness? Did those shots spell Joe Cagle's doom—or did they mean he had struck again? Or were they connected with Cagle at all? There was but one way to find out. Nudging my mount's ribs, I started on again at a swifter gait.

Moments later I entered a large clearing and a gaunt, dark building bulked against the stars. The Deserted House at last!

The moon glimmered eerily through the trees, etching out black shadows and throwing an illusive witchlight over the country. I saw, in this vague light, that the house had once been a mansion of the old colonial type. Sitting motionless for a moment in my saddle, a vision of lost glory passed before my mind—a vision of broad plantations, aristocratic Southern colonels, balls, dances, gallantry . . .

All gone now—blotted out by the Civil War. The pine trees grew where the plantation fields had flourished, the gallants and their ladies were long dead and forgotten, the mansion was crumbled into decay and ruin . . .

And now, what threat waited in those dark and dusty rooms where the mice gnawed and the owls roosted?

I swung from my saddle—and, as I did, my horse snorted suddenly, reared back violently upon his haunches, tearing the reins from my hands. I snatched for them again, but he wheeled and galloped away, vanishing like a goblin's shadow in the gloom. I stood, struck speechless, listening to the receding thunder of my mount's hoofs—and felt a cold finger trace its way down my spine. It is not a good experience to have your retreat so suddenly cut off in such foreboding surroundings.

However, I had not come to run from danger. I strode boldly up to the broad veranda, a heavy pistol in one hand and a darkened flashlight in the other. The massive pillars towered above me; the door sagged open upon broken hinges. Switching my flashlight on, I swept the broad hallway with a gleam of light— but only dust and decay met my eyes.

Turning the light off again, I entered warily.

As I stood there in the hall, trying to accustom my eyes to the gloom, I realized that I was doing as reckless a thing as a man could do. If Joe Cagle were hiding somewhere in the house, all he had to do was wait until I turned on my light—and then shoot me full of lead.

But I also thought again of his threats against Joan, who was even now doubtless waiting weak and fearful of his return. My determination steeled. If Joe Cagle was in that house, he was going to die.

I strode to the stairs, instinctively feeling that, if the fugitive were in the house at all, he would be somewhere in the second story. I groped my way up and came out on a landing, lit by the moonlight which streamed in at a window. The dust lay thick on the floor as if undisturbed for two decades, and I heard the whisper of bats' wings and the scampering of mice. No footprints in the dust betrayed a man's presence, but I felt sure that there were other stairways. Cagle might have come into the house through a window.

I went down the hallway—a horrible maze of black, menacing shadows and squares of moonlight that flooded in at the windows. There was no sound save the cushioned tread of my own feet in the deep dust on the floor. Room after room I passed, but my flashlight showed only moldered walls, sagging ceilings and broken furniture. At last, close to the end of the corridor, I came to a room whose door was shut. I halted, an intangible feeling working upon me to steel my nerves. My heart was pounding. Somehow, I knew that on the other side of that door lay something mysterious—something menacing . . .

Cautiously I turned on my flashlight. The dust in front of the door was disturbed: an arc of the floor just in front of it was brushed bare. The door had been opened and closed only a short time before. I tried the knob warily, winced at the rattle it made and expected a blast of lead through the door. Silence reigned. I tore the door open and leaped quickly aside.

There was no shot, no sound.

Crouching, gun cocked, I peered about the jamb and strained my eyes into the room. A faint acrid scent met my nostrils—gunpowder. Was it in this room that the shots I had heard had been fired?

Moonlight streamed over a broken sill, lending a vague radiance. I saw a dark, bulky form that had the semblance of a man lying close to the center of the floor. I crossed the threshold, bent over the figure and turned my light into the upturned face.

Joan would never again need to fear Joe Cagle's threats, for the shape on the floor was Joe Cagle— and he was dead.

Close to his outstretched hand lay a revolver. I picked it up, and found that all the chambers were filled with empty shells. Yet there was no wound upon the man. At whom had he fired—and what had killed him?

A second glance at his distorted features told me. I had seen that look once before in the eyes of a man struck by a rattlesnake—a man who had died with fear before the reptile's venom could possibly have killed him. Cagle's mouth gaped; his dead eyes stared hideously. He had died of fright—but what grisly thing had caused that fright . . . ?

At the thought, cold sweat started out on my brow and the short hairs prickled at the base of my skull. I was suddenly acutely aware of the silence and solitude of the place I was in at this midnight hour. . . .

Somewhere in the house a rat squeaked, and I started violently. I glanced up—then halted, frozen. Moonlight was on the opposite wall—and a shadow had suddenly and silently fallen across it.

I bounded to my feet, whirling toward the outer

door. That doorway stood empty. I sprang across the room and through another door, slamming it behind me . . .

Then I halted, shaken. Not a sound broke the stillness. What was it that had stood for an instant in the doorway opening into the hall, throwing its shadow into the room where I had stood? I was still trembling with an unaccountable fear. The thought of some desperate man was bad enough, but the glance I had had of that shadow had left upon my soul an impression of something strange and unholy—something *inhuman!*

The room in which I stood now also opened into the hallway. I started to cross to the hall door—then hesitated at the thought of confronting whatever lurked out there in the darkness. The door then sagged open . . .

I saw nothing, but my soul froze as a *hideous shadow fell across the floor and moved toward me!*

Etched blackly in the moonlight on the floor, it was as if some frightful shape stood in the doorway, throwing its lengthened and distorted shade across the boards to my feet. Yet the doorway was utterly empty!

I rushed across the room and through the door that opened into the next chamber. Still I was adjacent to the hallway—all these upstairs rooms seemed to open into the hall. I paused, shivering, my revolver gripped so tightly in my sweating hand that the barrel shook like a leaf. The pounding of my heart seemed thunderously loud in the silence. What in God's name was this horror which was hunting me through these dark rooms? What was it that threw a shadow, when its own substance was unseen? Silence lay like a dark mist; the ghostly radiance of the moon patterned the floor. Two rooms away lay the corpse of a man who had seen a thing so unnamably terrible that it had shattered his brain and taken away his life. And here stood I, alone with the unknown monster. . .

What was that? The creak of ancient hinges! I shrank back against the wall, my blood freezing. The door through which I had just come was slowly opening! A sudden gust of wind shuddered through. The door swung wide . . .

But I, nerving myself to meet the sight of some horror framed in the opening, saw—nothing!

Moonlight, as in all of the rooms on this side of the hall, streamed through the hall door and lay on the opposite wall. If any invisible thing was coming from that adjoining room, the moonlight was not at its back. Yet a distorted shadow fell across the moonlit wall—a shadow that grew as if cast by some being that moved forward!

Though the angle at which it was thrown deformed it, I saw it clearly—broad, shambling figure, stooped, head thrust forward, long manlike arms dangling—curiously human, yet fearsomely unhuman. All this I read in the approaching shadow, yet saw no solid form that might have cast it.

Then panic seized me and I fired my pistol again and again through the seemingly empty doorway in front of me, filling the empty house with crashing reverberations and the acrid smell of powder. Then in desperation I sent the last bullet straight into the gliding shadow, just as Joe Cagle must have done in the last terrible moment which preceded his death. The hammer fell hollowly on an empty shell and I hurled my empty gun wildly at the invisible menace. Not for an instant had the unseen thing halted—now the shadow was close upon me.

As I staggered back my flailing hands encountered the door, and tore at the knob. The door held—it was locked! Now on the wall beside me the shadow loomed up, black and horrific. Two great, tree-like arms were raised. . . .

With a scream I hurled my full weight against the door. It gave way with a splintering crash, and I fell through into the room beyond.

The rest is nightmare. I scrambled up without a glance behind me and rushed into the hall. At the far end I saw, as through a fog, the stair landing, and dashed toward it. The hall was long—it seemed to stretch into Eternities of time as I fled down it. And a black shadow kept pace with me, flying along the moonlit wall, vanishing for an instant in black darkness, reappearing an instant later in a square of moonlight let in by some outer window.

All down the hall it kept by my side, falling upon the wall at my left, telling me that whatever thing threw it was close at my back. Long has it been said that a ghost will fling a shadow in the moonlight, even though it be invisible itself to human sight— but no man ever lived whose ghost could throw such a silhouette as that bestial, unhuman shadow from which I fled in the grip of stark, unreasoning fear!

Now I was almost at the stair—*but now the shadow fell in front of me!* The thing was at my very back— was groping with unseen arms to clutch me. One swift glance over my shoulder gave me an added pang of horror: *on the dust of the corridor, close upon my footprints, other footprints were forming*— huge misshapen footprints that left the marks of talons! With a frantic scream I swerved to the right and leaped for an open window—without conscious thought, as a drowning man seizes a rope . . .

My shoulder struck the window-frame; I felt empty air under my hurtling body—caught one whirling, chaotic glimpse of the moon, the stars and the dark pine trees as the earth rushed up to meet me—then black oblivion crashed about me.

My first sensation of returning consciousness was of soft hands lifting my head and caressing my face. I lay still, my eyes closed, trying to orient myself—I could not remember where I was or what had happened. Then with a rush it all came back to me. My eyes must have flared wildly as I struggled to rise.

"Steve—oh, Steve! You're hurt!"

Surely I was insane, for the voice was Joan's! Yet—no! My head was cradled in her lap; her large, dark eyes, bright with tears, gazed down into mine.

"Joan! In God's name, what are you doing here?"

I sat up, drawing her into my arms. My head throbbed nauseatingly; I was sore and bruised. Above us rose the stark, grim wall of the Deserted House, and I could see the window from which I had fallen, dark above the twisted thorn-bush beside which I lay. I must have lain there for a long time, for now the moon hung red as blood close to the western horizon.

"The horse you rode away came back riderless. I couldn't stand to sit and wait—so I slipped out of the house and came here. They told me you'd gone to find the posse, but the horse came back the old tote road. There wasn't anyone to send, so I slipped away and came myself."

"Joan!" The sight of her kneeling there, so slender and forlorn in the dark, so frail and yet so full of love, took hold of my heart. Once more I drew her close and kissed her without speaking.

"Steve—" Her voice came low and frightened. "What happened to you? When I rode up, you were lying here in the thornbush, unconscious . . ."

"I see—only pure chance saved me from being killed just like those other two men who fell from those windows! Joan, tell me—what happened in that house twenty years ago to throw such a curse upon it?"

Joan shivered. "I don't know. The people who owned it before the war had to sell it afterwards; the tenants let it fall into disrepair, of course. But a

strange thing happened there just before the death
of the last tenant: a huge ape escaped from a circus
which was passing through the country and took
refuge in the house. The poor beast was suffering
terribly from maltreatment, and when his owners
tried to recapture him he fought them so fiercely
that they had to kill him. That was over twenty years
ago. Shortly after that, the owner fell from an upstairs window and was killed. Everyone supposed he
committed suicide or was walking in his sleep, but—"

"No!" A sudden inner chill made me shudder. "He
was hunted through the rooms of this very house by
a thing so terrible that death itself seemed a wel-
come escape. And that travelling man—I know what
killed him. And Joe Cagle—"

"Joe Cagle!" Joan started violently. "Where . . . ?"

"Don't worry—he's past harming you. Don't ask
me more. No, I didn't kill him; his death was more
horrible than any I could have dealt. There are worlds
and shadows of worlds beyond our ken, it seems, and
bestial earthbound spirits lurk in the dark shadows of
our own world beyond their time. Come—let us go."

Joan had brought two horses with her, and had
tethered them a short distance from the house. I
bade her mount and then, despite her anxious protests, I returned to the mansion. I went only as far as
a first story window, and I stayed only a few moments. Then I also mounted, and together Joan and I
rode slowly down the old tote road. The stars were
paling and the east was beginning to whiten with the
coming morn.

"You have not told me what haunts that house,"
said Joan in a hushed voice, "but I can guess. What
are we to do?"

For answer I turned in my saddle and pointed.
We had rounded a bend in the old road and could
just glimpse the old house through the trees. As we
looked, a red lance of flame leaped up; smoke bil-

lowed to the morning sky and, a few minutes later, a deep roar came to us as the whole building began to fall into the ravening flames—the flames that had grown from the fire I had ignited before we left. The ancients have always maintained that fire is the final destroyer—and, as I watched, I knew that the ghost of the dead ape was lain, and the shadow of the beast forever lifted from the pine lands.

OLD GARFIELD'S HEART

I WAS sitting on the porch when my grandfather hobbled out and sank down on his favorite chair with the cushioned seat, and began to stuff tobacco in his corn-cob pipe.

"I thought you'd be goin' to the dance," he said.

"I'm waiting for Doc Blaine," I answered. "I'm going over to old man Garfield's with him."

My grandfather sucked at his pipe awhile before he spoke again.

"Old Jim purty bad off?"

"Doc says he hasn't a chance."

"Who's takin' care of him?"

"Joe Braxton—against Garfield's wishes. But somebody had to stay with him."

My grandfaher sucked his pipe noisily, and watched the heat lightning playing away off up in the hills; then he said: "You think old Jim's the biggest liar in this county, don't you?"

"He tells some pretty tall tales," I admitted. "Some of the things he claimed he took part in, must have happened before he was born."

"I came from Tennessee to Texas in 1870," my grandfather said abruptly. "I saw this town of Lost Knob grow up from nothin'. There wasn't even a

133

log-hut store here when I came. But old Jim Garfield was here, livin' in the same place he lives now, only then it was a log cabin. He don't look a day older now than he did the first time I saw him."

"You never mentioned that before," I said in some surprise.

"I knew you'd put it down to an old man's maunderin's," he answered. "Old Jim was the first white man to settle in this country. He built his cabin a good fifty miles west of the frontier. God knows how he done it, for these hills swarmed with Comanches then.

"I remember the first time I ever saw him. Even then everybody called him 'old Jim.'

"I remember him tellin' me the same tales he's told you—how he was at the battle of San Jacinto when he was a youngster, and how he'd rode with Ewen Cameron and Jack Hayes. Only I believe him, and you don't."

"That was so long ago——" I protested.

"The last Indian raid through this country was in 1874," said my grandfather, engrossed in his own reminiscences. "I was in on that fight, and so was old Jim. I saw him knock old Yellow Tail off his mustang at seven hundred yards with a buffalo rifle.

"But before that I was with him in a fight up near the head of Locust Creek. A band of Comanches came down Mesquital, lootin' and burnin', rode through the hills and started back up Locust Creek, and a scout of us were hot on their heels. We ran on to them just at sundown in a mesquite flat. We killed seven of them, and the rest skinned out through the brush on foot. But three of our boys were killed, and Jim Garfield got a thrust in the breast with a lance.

"It was an awful wound. He lay like a dead man, and it seemed sure nobody could live after a wound like that. But an old Indian came out of the brush, and when we aimed our guns at him, he made the peace

sign and spoke to us in Spanish. I don't know why
the boys didn't shoot him in his tracks, because our
blood was heated with the fightin' and killin', but
somethin' about him made us hold our fire. He said
he wasn't a Comanche, but was an old friend of
Garfield's, and wanted to help him. He asked us to
carry Jim into a clump of mesquite, and leave him
alone with him, and to this day I don't know why we
did, but we did. It was an awful time—the wounded
moanin' and callin' for water, the starin' corpses strewn
about the camp, night comin' on, and no way of
knowin' that the Indians wouldn't return when dark
fell.

"We made camp right there, because the horses
were fagged out, and we watched all night, but the
Comanches didn't come back. I don't know what
went on out in the mesquite where Jim Garfield's
body lay, because I never saw that strange Indian
again, but durin' the night, I kept hearin' a weird
moanin' that wasn't made by the dyin' men, and an
owl hooted from midnight till dawn.

"And at sunrise Jim Garfield came walkin' out of
the mesquite, pale and haggard, but alive, and already the wound in his breast had closed and begun
to heal. And since then he's never mentioned that
wound, nor that fight, nor the strange Indian who
came and went so mysteriously. And he hasn't aged a
bit; he looks now just like he did then—a man of
about fifty."

In the silence that followed, a car began to purr
down the road, and twin shafts of light cut through
the dusk.

"That's Doc Blaine," I said. "When I come back
I'll tell you how Garfield is."

Doc Blaine was prompt with his prediction as we
drove the three miles of post-oak covered hills that
lay between Lost Knob and the Garfield farm.

"I'll be surprised to find him alive," he said,

"smashed up like he is. A man his age ought to have more sense than to try to break a young horse."

"He doesn't look so old," I remarked.

"I'll be fifty, my next birthday," answered Doc Blaine. "I've known him all my life, and he must have been at least fifty the first time I ever saw him. His looks are deceiving."

Old Garfield's dwelling-place was reminiscent of the past. The boards of the low squat house had never known paint. Orchard fence and corrals were built of rails.

Old Jim lay on his rude bed, tended crudely but efficiently by the man Doc Blaine had hired over the old man's protests. As I looked at him, I was impressed anew by his evident vitality. His frame was stooped but unwithered, his limbs rounded out with springy muscles. In his corded neck and in his face, drawn though it was with suffering, was apparent an innate virility. His eyes, though partly glazed with pain, burned with the same unquenchable element.

"He's been ravin'," said Joe Braxton stolidly.

"First white man in this country," muttered old Jim, becoming intelligible. "Hills no white man ever set foot in before. Gettin' too old. Have to settle down. Can't move on like I used to. Settle down here. Good country before it filled up with crowmen and squatters. Wish Ewen Cameron could see this country. The Mexicans shot him. Damn 'em!"

Doc Blaine shook his head. "He's all smashed up inside. He won't live till daylight."

Garfield unexpectedly lifted his head and looked at us with clear eyes.

"Wrong, Doc," he wheezed, his breath whistling with pain. "I'll live. What's broken bones and twisted guts? Nothin'! It's the heart that counts. Long as the heart keeps pumpin', a man can't die. My heart's sound. Listen to it! Feel it!"

He groped painfully for Doc Blaine's wrist, dragged

his hand to his bosom and held it there, staring up into the doctor's face with avid intensity.

"Regular dynamo, ain't it?" he gasped. "Stronger'n a gasoline engine!"

Blaine beckoned me. "Lay your hand here," he said, placing my hand on the old man's bare breast. "He does have a remarkable heart action."

I noted, in the light of the coal-oil lamp, a great livid scar as might be made by a flint-headed spear. I laid my hand directly on this scar, and an exclamation escaped my lips.

Under my hand old Jim Garfield's heart pulsed, but its throb was like no other heart action I have ever observed. Its power was astounding; his ribs vibrated to its steady throb. It felt more like the vibrating of a dynamo than the action of a human organ. I could feel its amazing vitality radiating from his breast, stealing up into my hand and up my arm, until my own heart seemed to speed up in response.

"I can't die," old Jim gasped. "Not so long as my heart's in my breast. Only a bullet through the brain can kill me. And even then I wouldn't be rightly dead, as long as my heart beats in my breast. Yet it ain't rightly mine, either. It belongs to Ghost Man, the Lipan chief. It was the heart of a god the Lipans worshipped before the Comanches drove 'em out of their native hills.

"I knew Ghost Man down on the Rio Grande, when I was with Ewen Cameron. I saved his life from the Mexicans once. He tied the string of ghost wampum between him and me—the wampum no man but me and him can see or feel. He came when he knowed I needed him, in that fight up on the headwaters of Locust Creek, when I got this scar.

"I was dead as a man can be. My heart was sliced in two, like the heart of a butchered beef steer.

"All night Ghost Man did magic, callin' my ghost back from spirit-land. I remember that flight, a little.

It was dark, and gray-like, and I drifted through gray mists and heard the dead wailin' past me in the mist. But Ghost Man brought me back.

"He took out what was left of my mortal heart, and put the heart of the god in my bosom. But it's his, and when I'm through with it, he'll come for it. It's kept me alive and strong for the lifetime of a man. Age can't touch me. What do I care if these fools here call me an old liar? What I know, I know. But hark'ee!"

His fingers became claws, clamping fiercely on Doc Blaine's wrist. His old eyes, old yet strangely young, burned fierce as those of an eagle under his bushy brows.

"If by some mischance I *should* die, now or later, promise me this! Cut into my bosom and take out the heart Ghost Man lent me so long ago! It's his. And as long as it beats in my body, my spirit'll be tied to that body, though my head be crushed like an egg underfoot! A livin' thing in a rottin' body! Promise!"

"All right, I promise," replied Doc Blaine, to humor him, and old Jim Garfield sank back with a whistling sigh of relief.

He did not die that night, nor the next, nor the next. I well remember the next day, because it was that day that I had the fight with Jack Kirby.

People will take a good deal from a bully, rather than to spill blood. Because nobody had gone to the trouble of killing him, Kirby thought the whole countryside was afraid of him.

He had bought steer from my father, and when my father went to collect for it, Kirby told him that he had paid the money to me—which was a lie. I went looking for Kirby, and came upon him in a bootleg joint, boasting of his toughness, and telling the crowd that he was going to beat me up and make me say that he had paid me the money, and that I had stuck it into my own pocket. When I heard him say that, I saw red, and ran in on him with a stockman's rifle, and cut him across the face, and in the neck, side, breast and belly, and the only thing that saved his life was the fact that the crowd pulled me off.

There was a preliminary hearing, and I was indicted on a charge of assault, and my trial was set for the following term of court. Kirby was as tough-fibered as a post-oak country bully ought to be, and he recovered, swearing vengeance, for he was vain of his looks, though God knows why, and I had permanently impaired them.

And while Jack Kirby was recovering, old man Garfield recovered too, to the amazement of everybody, especially Doc Blaine.

I well remember the night Doc Blaine took me again out to old Jim Garfield's farm. I was in Shifty Corlan's joint, trying to drink enough of the slop he called beer to get a kick out of it, when Doc Blaine came in and persuaded me to go with him.

As we drove along the winding old road in Doc's car, I asked: "Why are you insistent that I go with you this particular night? This isn't a professional call, is it?"

"No," he said. "You couldn't kill old Jim with a post-oak maul. He's completely recovered from injuries that ought to have killed an ox. To tell you the truth, Jack Kirby is in Lost Knob, swearing he'll shoot you on sight."

"Well, for God's sake!" I exclaimed angrily. "Now everybody'll think I left town because I was afraid of him. Turn around and take me back, damn it!"

"Be reasonable," said Doc. "Everybody knows you're not afraid of Kirby. Nobody's afraid of him now. His bluff's broken, and that's why he's so wild against you. But you can't afford to have any more trouble with him now, and your trial's only a short time off."

I laughed and said: "Well, if he's looking for me hard enough, he can find me as easily at old Garfield's as in town, because Shifty Corlan heard you say where we were going. And Shifty's hated me ever since I skinned him in that horseswap last fall. He'll tell Kirby where I went."

"I never thought of that," said Doc Blaine, worried.

"Hell, forget it," I advised. "Kirby hasn't got guts enough to do anything but blow."

But I was mistaken. Puncture a bully's vanity and you touch his one vital spot.

Old Jim had not gone to bed when we got there. He was sitting in the room opening on to his sagging porch, the room which was at once living-room and bedroom, smoking his old cob pipe and trying to read a newspaper by the light of his coal-oil lamp. All the windows and doors were wide open for the coolness, and the insects which swarmed in and fluttered around the lamp didn't seem to bother him.

We sat down and discussed the weather—which isn't so inane as one might suppose, in a country where men's livelihood depends on sun and rain, and is at the mercy of wind and drouth. The talk drifted into the other kindred channels, and after some time, Doc Blaine bluntly spoke of something that hung in his mind.

"Jim," he said, "that night I thought you were dying, you babbled a lot of stuff about your heart, and an Indian who lent you his. How much of that was delirium?"

"None, Doc," said Garfield, pulling at his pipe. "It was gospel truth. Ghost Man, the Lipan priest of the Gods of Night, replaced my dead, torn heart with one from somethin' he worshipped. I ain't sure myself just what that somethin' is—somethin' from away back and a long way off, he said. But bein' a god, it can do without its heart for awhile. But when I die—if I ever get my head smashed so my consciousness is destroyed—the heart must be given back to Ghost Man."

"You mean you were in earnest about cutting out your heart?" demanded Doc Blaine.

"It has to be," answered old Garfield. "A livin' thing in a dead thing is opposed to nat'er. That's what Ghost Man said."

"Who the devil *was* Ghost Man?"

"I told you. A witch-doctor of the Lipans, who dwelt in this country before the Comanches came down from the Staked Plains and drove 'em south across the Rio Grande. I was a friend to 'em. I reckon Ghost Man is the only one left alive."

"Alive? Now?"

"I dunno," confessed old Jim. "I dunno whether he's alive or dead. I dunno whether he was alive when he came to me after the fight on Locust Creek, or even if he was alive when I knowed him in the southern country. Alive as we understand life, I mean."

"What balderdash is this?" demanded Doc Blaine uneasily, and I felt a slight stirring in my hair. Outside was stillness, and the stars, and the black shadows of the post-oak woods. The lamp cast old Garfield's shadow grotesquely on the wall, so that it did not at all resemble that of a human, and his words were strange as words heard in a nightmare.

"I knowed you wouldn't understand," said old Jim. "I don't understand myself, and I ain't got the words to explain them things I feel and know without understandin'. The Lipans were kin to the Apaches, and the Apaches learnt curious things from the Pueblos. Ghost Man *was*—that's all I can say—alive or dead, I don't know, but he *was*. What's more, he *is*."

"Is it you or me that's crazy?" asked Doc Blaine.

"Well," said old Jim, "I'll tell you this much—Ghost Man knew Coronado."

"Crazy as a loon!" murmured Doc Blaine. Then he lifted his head. "What's that?"

"Horse turning in from the road," I said. "Sounds like it stopped."

I stepped to the door, like a fool, and stood etched in the light behind me. I got a glimpse of a shadowy bulk I knew to be a man on a horse; then Doc Blaine yelled: "Look out!" and threw himself against me, knocking us both sprawling. At the same instant I heard the smashing report of a rifle, and old Garfield grunted and fell heavily.

"Jack Kirby!" screamed Doc Blaine. "He's killed Jim!"

I scrambled up, hearing the clatter of retreating hoofs, snatched old Jim's shotgun from the wall, rushed recklessly out on to the sagging porch and let go both barrels at the fleeing shape, dim in the starlight. The charge was too light to kill at that range, but the bird-shot stung the horse and maddened him. He swerved, crashed headlong through a rail fence and charged across the orchard, and a peach tree limb knocked his rider out of the saddle. He never moved after he hit the ground. I ran out there and looked down at him. It was Jack Kirby, right enough, and his neck was broken like a rotten branch.

I let him lie, and ran back to the house. Doc Blaine had stretched old Garfield out on a bench he'd dragged in from the porch, and Doc's face was whiter than I'd ever seen it. Old Jim was a ghastly sight; he had been shot with an old-fashioned .45–70, and at that range the heavy ball had literally torn off the top of his head. His features were masked with blood and brains. He had been directly behind me, poor old devil, and he had stopped the slug meant for me.

Doc Blaine was trembling, though he was anything but a stranger to such sights.

"Would your pronounce him dead?" he asked.

"That's for you to say," I answered. "But even a fool could tell that he's dead."

"He *is* dead," said Doc Blaine in a strained unnatural voice. "Rigor mortis is already setting in. But feel his heart!"

I did, and cried out. The flesh was already cold and clammy; but beneath it that mysterious heart still hammered steadily away, like a dynamo in a deserted house. No blood coursed through those veins; yet the heart pounded, pounded, pounded, like the pulse of Eternity.

"A living thing in a dead thing," whispered Doc Blaine, cold sweat on his face. "This is opposed to nature. I am going to keep the promise I made him. I'll assume full responsibility. This is too monstrous to ignore."

Our implements were a butcher-knife and a hacksaw. Outside only the still stars looked down on the black post-oak shadows and the dead man that lay in the orchard. Inside, the old lamp flickered, making strange shadows move and shiver and cringe in the corners, and glistened on the blood on the floor, and the red-dabbled figure on the bench. The only sound inside was the crunch of the saw-edge in bone; outside an owl began to hoot weirdly.

Doc Blaine thrust a red-stained hand into the aperture he had made, and drew out a red, pulsing object that caught the lamplight. With a choked cry he recoiled, and the thing slipped from his fingers and fell on the table. And I too cried out involuntarily. For it did not fall with a soft meaty thud, as a piece of flesh should fall. It *thumped* hard on the table.

Impelled by an irresistible urge, I bent and gingerly picked up old Garfield's heart. The feel of it was brittle, unyielding, like steel or stone, but smoother than either. In size and shape it was the duplicate of a human heart, but it was slick and smooth, and its crimson surface reflected the lamplight like a jewel more lambent than any ruby; and in my hand it still throbbed mightily, sending vibratory radiations of energy up my arm until my own heart seemed swelling and bursting in response. It was cosmic *power*, beyond my comprehension, concentrated into the likeness of a human heart.

The thought came to me that here was a dynamo of life, the nearest approach to immortality that is possible for the destructible human body, the materialization of a cosmic secret more wonderful than the fabulous fountain sought for by Ponce de Leon. My soul was drawn into that unterrestrial gleam, and I suddenly wished passionately that it hammered and thundered in my own bosom in place of my paltry heart of tissue and muscle.

Doc Blaine ejaculated incoherently. I wheeled.

The noise of his coming had been no greater than the whispering of a night wind through the corn. There in the doorway he stood, tall, dark, inscrutable—an Indian warrior, in the paint, war bonnet, breech-clout and moccasins of an elder age. His dark eyes burned like fires gleaming deep under fathomless black lakes. Silently he extended his hand, and I dropped Jim Garfield's heart into it. Then without a word he turned and stalked into the night. But when Doc Blaine and I rushed out into the yard an instant later, there was no sign of any human being. He had vanished like a phantom of the night, and only something that looked like an owl was flying, dwindling from sight, into the rising moon.

PEOPLE OF THE DARK

I CAME to Dagon's Cave to kill Richard Brent. I went down the dusky avenues made by the towering trees, and my mood well-matched the primitive grimness of the scene. The approach to Dagon's Cave is always dark, for the mighty branches and thick leaves shut out the sun, and now the somberness of my own soul made the shadows seem more ominous and gloomy than was natural.

Not far away I heard the slow wash of the waves against the tall cliffs, but the sea itself was out of sight, masked by the dense oak forest. The darkness and the stark gloom of my surroundings gripped my shadowed soul as I passed beneath the ancient branches—as I came out into a narrow glade and saw the mouth of the ancient cavern before me. I paused, scanning the cavern's exterior and the dim reaches of the silent oaks.

The man I hated had not come before me! I was in time to carry out my grim intent. For a moment my resolution faltered, then like a wave there surged over me the fragrance of Eleanor Bland, a vision of wavy golden hair and deep gray eyes, changing and mystic as the sea. I clenched my hands until the knuckles showed white, and instinctively touched, the wicked snub-nosed revolver whose weight sagged my coat pocket.

But for Richard Brent, I felt certain I had already won this woman, desire for whom made my waking hours a torment and my sleep a torture. Whom did she love? She would not say; I did not believe she knew. Let one of us go away, I thought, and she would turn to the other. And I was going to simplify matters for her—and for myself. By chance I had overheard my blond English rival remark that he intended coming to lonely Dagon's Cave on an idle exploring outing—alone.

I am not by nature criminal. I was born and raised in a hard country, and have lived most of my life on the raw edges of the world, where a man took what he wanted, if he could, and mercy was a virtue little known. But it was a torment that racked me day and night that sent me out to take the life of Richard Brent. I have lived hard, and violently perhaps. When love overtook me, it also was fierce and violent. Perhaps I was not wholly sane, what with my love for Eleanor Bland and my hatred for Richard Brent. Under any other circumstances, I would have been glad to call him friend—a fine, rangy, upstanding young fellow, clear-eyed and strong. But he stood in the way of my desrie and he must die.

I stepped into the dimness of the cavern and halted. I had never before visited Dagon's Cave, yet a vague sense of misplaced familiarity troubled me as I gazed on the high arching roof, the even stone walls and the dusty floor. I shrugged my shoulders, unable to place the elusive feeling; doubtless it was evoked by a similarity to caverns in the mountain country of the American Southwest where I was born and spent my childhood.

And yet I knew that I had never seen a cave like this one, whose regular aspect gave rise to myths that it was not a natural cavern, but had been hewn

from the solid rock ages ago by the tiny hands of the
mysterious Little People, the prehistoric beings of
British legend. The whole countryside thereabouts
was a haunt for ancient folk lore.

The country folk were predominantly Celtic; here
the Saxon invaders had never prevailed, and the
legends reached back, in that long settled countryside, further than anywhere else in England—back
beyond the coming of the Saxons, aye, and incredibly beyond that distant age, beyond the coming of
the Romans, to those unbelievably ancient days when
the native Britons warred with black-haired Irish
pirates.

The Little People, of course, had their part in the
lore. Legend said that this cavern was one of their
last strongholds against the conquering Celts, and
hinted at lost tunnels, long fallen in or blocked up,
connecting the cave with a network of subterranean
corridors which honeycombed the hills. With these
chance meditations vying idly in my mind with grimmer speculations, I passed through the outer chamber of the cavern and entered a narrow tunnel, which,
I knew by former descriptions, connected with a
larger room.

It was dark in the tunnel, but not too dark for me
to make out the vague, half-defaced outlines of mysterious etchings on the stone walls. I ventured to
switch on my electric torch and examine them more
closely. Even in their dimness I was repelled by
their abnormal and revolting character. Surely no
men cast in human mold as we know it, scratched
those grotesque obscenities.

The Little People—I wondered if those anthropol-
ogists were correct in their theory of a squat Mongoloid aboriginal race, so low in the scale of evolution as
to be scarcely human, yet possessing a distinct, though
repulsive culture of their own. They had vanished
before the invading races, theory said, forming the

base of all Aryan legends of trolls, elves, dwarfs and witches. Living in caves from the start, these aborigines had retreated farther and farther into the caverns of the hills, before the conquerors, vanishing at last entirely, though folk-lore fancy pictures their descendants still dwelling in the lost chasms far beneath the hills, loathsome survivals of an outworn age.

I snapped off the torch and passed through the tunnel, to come out into a sort of doorway which seemed entirley too symmetrical to have been the work of nature. I was looking into a vast dim cavern, at a somewhat lower level than the outer chamber, and again I shuddered with a strange alien sense of familiarity. A short flight of steps led down from the tunnel to the floor of the cavern—tiny steps, too small for normal human feet, carved into the solid stone. Their edges were greatly worn away, as if by ages of use. I started the descent—my foot slipped suddenly. I instinctively knew what was coming—it was all in part with that strange feeling of familiarity—but I could not catch myself. I fell headlong down the steps and struck the stone floor with a crash that blotted out my senses. . . .

Slowly consciousness returned to me, with a throbbing of my head and a sensation of bewilderment. I lifted a hand to my head and found it caked with blood. I had received a blow, or had taken a fall, but so completely had my wits been knocked out of me that my mind was an absolute blank. Where I was, who I was, I did not know. I looked about, blinking in the dim light, and saw that I was in a wide, dusty cavern. I stood at the foot of a short flight of steps which led upward into some kind of tunnel. I ran my hand dazedly through my square-cut black mane, and my eyes wandered over my massive naked limbs and powerful torso. I was clad, I noticed absently, in a sort of loincloth, from the girdle of which swung an empty scabbard, and leathern sandals were on my feet.

Then I saw an object lying at my feet, and stooped and took it up. It was a heavy iron sword, whose broad blade was darkly stained. My fingers fitted instinctivley about its hilt with the familiarity of long usage. Then suddenly I remembered and laughed to think that a fall on his head should render me, Conan of the reavers, so completely daft. Aye, it all came back to me now. It had been a raid on the Britons, on whose coasts we continually swooped with torch and sword, from the island called Eire-ann. That day we of the black-haired Gael had swept suddenly down on a coastal village in our long, low ships and in the hurricane of battle which followed, the Britons had at last given up the stubborn contest and retreated, warriors, women and bairns, into the deep shadows of the oak forests, whither we seldom dared follow.

But I had followed, for there was a girl of my foes whom I desired with a burning passion, a lithe, slim young creature with wavy golden hair and deep gray eyes, changing and mystic as the sea. Her name was Tamera—well I knew it, for there was trade between the races as well as war, and I had been in the villages of the Britons as a peaceful visitor, in times of rare truce.

I saw her white half-clad body flickering among the trees as she ran with the swiftness of a doe, and I followed, panting with fierce eagerness. Under the dark shadows of the gnarled oaks she fled, with me in close pursuit, while far away behind us died out the shouts of slaughter and the clashing of swords. Then we ran in silence, save for her quick labored panting, and I was so close behind her as we emerged into a narrow glade before a somber-mouthed cavern, that I caught her flying golden tresses with one mighty hand. She sank down with a despairing wail, and even so, a shout echoed her cry and I wheeled quickly to face a rangy young Briton who sprang from among the trees, the light of desperation in his eyes.

"Vertorix!" the girl wailed, her voice breaking in a sob, and fiercer rage welled up in me, for I knew the lad was her lover.

"Run for the forest, Tamera!" he shouted, and leaped at me as a panther leaps, his bronze ax whirling like a flashing wheel about his head. And then sounded the clangor of strife and the hard-drawn panting of combat.

The Briton was as tall as I, but he was lithe where I was massive. The advantage of sheer muscular power was mine, and soon he was on the defensive, striving desperately to parry my heavy strokes with his ax. Hammering on his guard like a smith on an anvil, I pressed him relentlessly, driving him irresistibly before me. His chest heaved, his breath came in labored gasps, his blood dripped from scalp, chest and thigh where my whistling blade had cut the skin, and all but gone home. As I redoubled my strokes and he bent and swayed beneath them like a sapling in a storm, I heard the girl cry: "Vertorix! Vertorix! The cave. Into the cave!"

I saw his face pale with a fear greater than that induced by my hacking sword.

"Not there!" he gasped. "Better a clean death! In Il-marenin's name, girl, run in the forest and save yourself!"

"I will not leave you!" she cried. "The cave; it is our one chance!"

I saw her flash past us like a flying wisp of white and vanish in the cavern, and with a despairing cry, the youth launched a wild desperate stroke that nigh cleft my skull. As I staggered beneath the blow I had barely parried, he sprang away, leaped into the cavern after the girl and vanished in the gloom.

With a maddened yell that invoked all my grim Gaelic gods, I sprang recklessly after them, not reckoning if the Briton lurked beside the entrance to brain me as I rushed in. But a quick glance showed the chamber empty and a wisp of white disappearing through a dark doorway in the back wall.

I raced across the cavern and came to a sudden halt as an ax licked out of the gloom of the entrance and whistled perilously close to my black-maned head. I gave back suddenly. Now the advantage was with Vertorix, who stood in the narrow mouth of the corridor where I could hardly come at him without exposing myself to the devastating stroke of his ax.

I was near frothing with fury and the sight of a slim white form among the deep shadows behind the warrior drove me into a frenzy. I attacked savagely but warily, thrusting venomously at my foe, and drawing back from his strokes. I wished to draw him out into a wide lunge, avoid it and run him through before he could recover his balance. In the open I could have beat him down by sheer power and heavy blows, but here I could only use the point and that at a disadvantage; I always preferred the edge. But I was stubborn; if I could not come at him with a finishing stroke, neither could he or the girl escape me while I kept him hemmed in the tunnel.

It must have been the realization of this fact that prompted the girl's action, for she said something to Vertorix about looking for a way leading out, and though he cried out fiercely forbidding her to venture away into the darkness, she turned and ran swiftly down the tunnel to vanish in the dimness. My wrath rose appallingly and I nearly got my head split in my eagerness to bring down my foe before she found a means for their escape.

Then the cavern echoed with a terrible scream and Vertorix cried out like a man death-stricken, his face ashy in the gloom. He whirled, as if he had forgotten me and my sword, and raced down the tunnel like a madman, shrieking Tamera's name. From far away, as if from the bowels of the earth, I seemed to hear her answering cry, mingled with a strange sibilant clamor that electrified me with nameless but instinctive horror. Then silence fell, broken only by Vertorix's frenzied cries, receding farther and farther into the earth.

Recovering myself I sprang into the tunnel and raced after the Briton as recklessly as he had run after the girl. And to give me my due, red-handed reaver though I was, cutting down my rival from behind was less in my mind than discovering what dread thing had Tamera in its clutches.

As I ran along I noted absently that the sides of the tunnel were scrawled with monstrous pictures, and realized suddenly and creepily that this must be the dread Cavern of the Children of the Night, tales of which had crossed the narrow sea to resound horrifically in the ears of the Gaels. Terror of me must have ridden Tamera hard to have driven her into the cavern shunned by her people, where it was said, lurked the survivals of that grisly race which inhabited the land before the coming of the Picts and Britons, and which had fled before them into the unknown caverns of the hills.

Ahead of me the tunnel opened into a wide chamber, and I saw the white form of Vertorix glimmer momentarily in the semi-darkness and vanish in what appeared to be the entrance of a corridor opposite the mouth of the tunnel I had just traversed. Instantly there sounded a short, fierce shout and the crash of a hard-driven blow, mixed with the hysterical screams of a girl and a medley of serpentlike hissing that made my hair bristle. And at that instant I shot out of the tunnel, running at full speed, and realized too late the floor of the cavern lay several feet below the level of the tunnel. My flying feet missed the tiny steps and I crashed terrifically on the solid stone floor.

Now as I stood in the semidarkness, rubbing my aching head, all this came back to me, and I stared fearsomely across the vast chamber at that black cryptic corridor into which Tamera and her lover had disappeared, and over which silence lay like a pall. Gripping my sword, I warily crossed the great still cavern and peered into the corridor. Only a denser darkness met my eyes. I entered, striving to pierce the gloom, and as my foot slipped on a wide wet smear on the stone floor, the raw acrid scent of fresh-spilled blood met my nostrils. Someone or something had died there, either the young Briton or his unknown attacker.

I stood there uncertainly, all the supernatural fears that are the heritage of the Gael rising in my primitive soul. I could turn and stride out of these accursed mazes, into the clear sunlight and down to the clean blue sea where my comrades, no doubt, impatiently awaited me after the routing of the Britons. Why should I risk my life among these grisly rat dens? I was eaten with curiosity to know what manner of beings haunted the cavern, and who were called the Children of the Night by the Britons, but in it was my love for the yellow-haired girl which drove me down that dark tunnel—and love her I did, in my way, and would have been kind to her, and carried her away to my island haunt.

I walked softly along the corridor, blade ready. What sort of creatures the Children of the Night were, I had no idea, but the tales of the Britons had lent them a distinctly inhuman nature.

The darkness closed around me as I advanced, until I was moving in utter blackness. My groping left hand encountered a strangely carven doorway, and at that instant something hissed like a viper beside me and slashed fiercely at my thigh. I struck

back savagely and felt my blind stroke crunch home,
and something fell at my feet and died. What thing I
had slain in the dark I could not know, but it must
have been at least partly human because the shallow
gash in my thigh had been made with a blade of
some sort, and not by fangs or talons. And I sweated
with horror, for the gods know, the hissing voice of
the Thing had resembled no human tongue I had
ever heard.

And now in the darkness ahead of me I heard the
sound repeated, mingled with horrible slitherings, as
if numbers of reptilian creatures were approaching. I
stepped quickly into the entrance my groping hand
had discovered and came near repeating my headlong fall, for instead of letting into another level
corridor, the entrance gave onto a flight of dwarfish
steps on which I floundered wildly.

Recovering my balance I went on cautiously, groping along the sides of the shaft for support. I seemed
to be descending into the very bowels of the earth,
but I dared not turn back. Suddenly, far below me, I
glimpsed a faint eerie light. I went on, perforce, and
came to a spot where the shaft opened into another
great vaulted chamber; and I shrank back, aghast.

In the center of the chamber stood a grim, black
altar; it had been rubbed all over with a sort of
phosphorous, so that it glowed dully, lending a semi-
illumination to the shadowy cavern. Towering behind it on a pedestal of human skulls, lay a cryptic
black object, carven with mysterious hieroglyphics.
The Black Stone! The ancient, ancient Stone before
which, the Britons said, the Children of the Night
bowed in gruesome worship, and whose origin was
lost in the black mists of a hideously distant past.
Once, legend said, it had stood in that grim circle of
monoliths called Stonehenge, before its votaries had
been driven like chaff before the bows of the Picts.

But I gave it but a passing, shuddering glance.

Two figures lay, bound with rawhide thongs, on the glowing black altar. One was Tamera; the other was Vertorix, blood-stained and disheveled. His bronze ax, crusted with clotted blood, lay near the altar. And before the glowing stone squatted Horror.

Though I had never seen one of those ghoulish aborigines, I knew this thing for what it was, and shuddered. It was a man of a sort, but so low in the stage of life that its distorted humanness was more horrible than its bestiality.

Erect, it could not have been five feet in height. Its body was scrawny and deformed, its head disproportionately large. Lank snaky hair fell over a square inhuman face with flabby writhing lips that bared yellow fangs, flat spreading nostrils and great yellow slant eyes. I knew the creature must be able to see in the dark as well as a cat. Centuries of skulking in dim caverns had lent the race terrible and inhuman attributes. But the most repellent feature was its skin: scaly, yellow and mottled, like the hide of a serpent. A loincloth made of a real snake's skin girt its lean loins, and its taloned hands gripped a short stone-tipped spear and a sinister-looking mallet of polished flint.

So intently was it gloating over its captives, it evidently had not heard my stealthy descent. As I hesitated in the shadows of the shaft, far above me I heard a soft sinister rustling that chilled the blood in my veins. The Children were creeping down the shaft behind me, and I was trapped. I saw other entrances opening on the chamber, and I acted, realizing that an alliance with Vertorix was our only hope. Enemies though we were, we were men, cast in the same mold, trapped in the lair of these indescribable monstrosities.

As I stepped from the shaft, the horror beside the altar jerked up his head and glared full at me. And as he sprang up, I leaped and he crumpled, blood spurting, as my heavy sword split his reptilian heart. But even as he died, he gave tongue in an abhorrent shriek which was echoed far up the shaft. In desperate haste I cut Vertorix's bonds and dragged him to his feet. And I turned to Tamera, who in that dire extremity did not shrink from me, but looked up at me with pleading, terror-dilated eyes. Vertorix wasted no time in words, realizing chance had made allies of us. He snatched up his ax as I freed the girl.

"We can't go up the shaft," he explained swiftly; "we'll have the whole pack upon us quickly. They caught Tamera as she sought for an exit, and overpowered me by sheer numbers when I followed. They dragged us hither and all but that carrion scattered—bearing word of the sacrifice through all their burrows, I doubt not. Il-marenin alone knows how many of my people, stolen in the night, have died on that altar. We must take our chance in one of these tunnels—all lead to hell! Follow me!"

Seizing Tamera's hand he ran fleetly into the nearest tunnel and I followed. A glance back into the chamber before a turn in the corridor blotted it from view showed a revolting horde streaming out of the shaft. The tunnel slanted steeply upward, and suddenly ahead of us we saw a bar of gray light. But the next instant our cries of hope changed to curses of bitter disappointment. There was daylight, aye, drifting in through a cleft in the vaulted roof, but far, far above our reach. Behind us the pack gave tongue exultingly. And I halted.

"Save yourselves if you can," I growled. "Here I make my stand. They can see in the dark and I cannot. Here at least I can see them. Go!"

But Vertorix halted also. "Little use to be hunted like rats to our doom. There is no escape. Let us meet our fate like men."

Tamera cried out, wringing her hands, but she clung to her lover.

"Stand behind me with the girl," I grunted. "When I fall, dash out her brains with your ax lest they take her alive again. Then sell your own life as high as you may, for there is none to avenge us."

His keen eyes met mine squarely.

"We worship different gods, reaver," he said, "but all gods love brave men. Mayhap we shall meet again, beyond the Dark."

"Hail and farewell, Briton!" I growled, and our right hands gripped like steel.

"Hail and farewell, Gael!"

And I wheeled as a hideous horde swept up the tunnel and burst into the dim light, a flying nightmare of streaming snaky hair, foam-flecked lips and glaring eyes. Thundering my war-cry I sprang to meet them and my heavy sword sang and a head spun grinning from its shoulder on an arching fountain of blood. They came upon me like a wave and the fighting madness of my race was upon me. I fought as a maddened beast fights and at every stroke I clove through flesh and bone, and blood spattered in a crimson rain.

Then as they surged in and I went down beneath the sheer weight of their numbers, a fierce yell cut the din and Vertorix's ax sang above me, splattering blood and brains like water. The press slackened and I staggered up, trampling the writhing bodies beneath my feet.

"A stair behind us!" the Briton was screaming. "Half hidden in an angle of the wall! It must lead to daylight! Up it, in the name of Il-marenin!"

So we fell back, fighting our way inch by inch. The vermin fought like blood-hungry devils, clambering over the bodies of the slain to screech and hack. Both of us were streaming blood at every step when we reached the mouth of the shaft, into which Tamera had preceded us.

Screaming like very fiends the Children surged in

to drag us down. The shaft was not as light as had been the corridor, and it grew darker as we climbed, but our foes could only come at us from in front. By the gods, we slaughtered them till the stair was littered with mangled corpses and the Children frothed like mad wolves! Then suddenly they abandoned the fray and raced back down the steps.

"What portends this?" gasped Vertorix, shaking the bloody sweat from his eyes.

"Up the shaft, quick!" I panted. "They mean to mount some other stair and come at us from above!"

So we raced up those accursed steps, slipping and stumbling, and as we fled past a black tunnel that opened into the shaft, far down it we heard a frightful howling. An instant later we emerged from the shaft into a winding corridor, dimly illumined by a vague gray light filtering in from above, and somewhere in the bowels of the earth I seemed to hear the thunder of rushing water. We started down the corridor and as we did so, a heavy weight smashed on my shoulders, knocking me headlong, and a mallet crashed again and again on my head, sending dull red flashes of agony across my brain. With a volcanic wrench I dragged my attacker off and under me, and tore out his throat with my naked fingers. And his fangs met in my arm in his death-bite.

Reeling up, I saw that Tamera and Vertorix had passed out of sight. I had been somewhat behind them, and they had run on, knowing nothing of the fiend which had leaped on my shoulders. Doubtless they thought I was still close on their heels. A dozen steps I took, then halted. The corridor branched and I knew not which way my companions had taken. At blind venture I turned into the left-hand branch, and staggered on in the semidarkness. I was weak from fatigue and loss of blood, dizzy and sick from the blows I had received. Only the thought of Tamera kept me doggedly on my feet. Now distinctly I heard the sound of an unseen torrent.

That I was not far underground was evident by the dim light which filtered in from somewhere above, and I momentarily expected to come upon another stair. But when I did, I halted in black despair; instead of up, it led down. Somewhere far behind me I heard faintly the howls of the pack, and I went down, plunging into utter darkness. At last I struck a level and went along blindly. I had given up all hope of escape, and only hoped to find Tamera—if she and her lover had not found a way of escape—and die with her. The thunder of rushing water was above my head now, and the tunnel was slimy and dank. Drops of moisture fell on my head and I knew I was passing under the river.

Then I blundered again upon steps cut in the stone, and these led upward. I scrambled up as fast as my stiffening wounds would allow—and I had taken punishment enough to have killed an ordinary man. Up I went and up, and suddenly daylight burst on me through a cleft in the solid rock. I stepped into the blaze of the sun. I was standing on a ledge high above the rushing waters of a river which raced at awesome speed between towering cliffs. The ledge on which I stood was close to the top of the cliff; safety was within arm's length. But I hesitated and such was my love for the golden-haired girl that I was ready to retrace my steps through those black tunnels on the mad hope of finding her. Then I started.

Across the river I saw another cleft in the cliff-wall which fronted me, with a ledge similar to that on which I stood, but longer. In olden times, I doubt not, some sort of primitive bridge connected the two ledges—possibly before the tunnel was dug beneath the riverbed. Now as I watched, two figures emerged upon that other ledge—one gashed, dust-stained, limping, gripping a bloodstained ax; the other slim, white and girlish.

Vertorix and Tamera! They had taken the other branch of the corridor at the fork and had evidently followed the windows of the tunnel to emerge as I had done, except that I had taken the left turn and passed clear under the river. And now I saw that they were in a trap. On that side the cliffs rose half a hundred feet higher than on my side of the river, and so sheer a spider could scarce have scaled them. There were only two ways of escape from the ledge: back through the fiend-haunted tunnels, or straight down to the river which raved far beneath.

I saw Vertorix look up the sheer cliffs and then down, and shake his head in despair. Tamera put her arms about his neck, and though I could not hear their voices for the rush of the river, I saw them smile, and then they went together to the edge of the ledge. And out of the cleft swarmed a loathsome mob, as foul reptiles writhe up out of the darkness, and they stood blinking in the sunlight like the night-things they were. I gripped my sword-hilt in the agony of my helplessness until the blood trickled from under my fingernails. Why had not the pack followed me instead of my companions?

The Children hesitated an instant as the two Britons faced them, then with a laugh Vertorix hurled his ax far out into the rushing river, and turning, caught Tamera in a last embrace. Together they sprang far out and still locked in each other's arms, hurtled downward, struck the madly foaming water that seemed to leap up to meet them, and vanished. And the wild river swept on like a blind, insensate monster, thundering along the echoing cliffs.

A moment I stood frozen, then like a man in a dream I turned, caught the edge of the cliff above me and wearily drew myself up and over, and stood on my feet above the cliffs, hearing like a dim dream the roar of the river far beneath.

I reeled up, dazedly clutching my throbbing head, on which dried blood was clotted. I glared wildly about me. I had clambered the cliffs—no, by the thunder of Crom, I was still in the cavern! I reached for my sword—

The mists faded and I stared about dizzily, orienting myself with space and time. I stood at the foot of the steps down which I had fallen. I who had been Conan the reaver, was John O'Brien. Was all that grotesque interlude a dream? Could a mere dream appear so vivid? Even in dreams, we often know we are dreaming, but Conan the reaver had no cognizance of any other existence. More, he remembered his own past life as a living man remembers, though in the waking mind of John O'Brien, that memory faded into dust and mist. But the adventures of Conan in the Cavern of the Children stood clearetched in the mind of John O'Brien.

I glanced across the dim chamber toward the entrance of the tunnel into which Vertorix had followed the girl. But I looked in vain, seeing only the bare blank wall of the cavern. I crossed the chamber, switched on my electric torch—miraculously unbroken in my fall—and felt along the wall.

Ha! I started, as from an electric shock! Exactly where the entrance should have been, my fingers detected a difference in material, a section which was rougher than the rest of the wall. I was convinced that it was of comparatively modern workmanship; the tunnel had been walled up.

I thrust against it, exerting all my strength, and it seemed to me that the section was about to give. I drew back, and taking a deep breath, launched my full weight against it, backed by all the power of my giant muscles. The brittle, decaying wall gave way with a shattering crash and I catapulted through in a shower of stones and falling masonry.

I scrambled up, a sharp cry escaping me. I stood in a tunnel, and I could not mistake the feeling of similarity this time. Here Vertorix had first fallen foul of the Children, as they dragged Tamera away, and here where I now stood the floor had been awash with blood.

I walked down the corridor like a man in a trance. Soon I should come to the doorway on the left—aye, there it was, the strangely carven portal, at the mouth of which I had slain the unseen being which reared up in the dark beside me. I shivered momentarily. Could it be possible that remnants of that foul race still lurked hideously in these remote caverns?

I turned into the doorway and my light shone down a long, slanting shaft, with tiny steps cut into the solid stone. Down these had Conan the reaver gone groping and down them went I, John O'Brien, with memories of that other life filling my brain with vague phantasms. No light glimmered ahead of me but I came into the great dim chamber I had known of yore, and I shuddered as I saw the grim black altar etched in the gleam of my torch. Now no bound figures writhed there, no crouching horror gloated before it. Nor did the pyramid of skulls support the Black Stone before which unknown races had bowed before Egypt was born out of time's dawn. Only a littered heap of dust lay strewn where the skulls had upheld the hellish thing. No, that had been no dream: I was John O'Brien, but I had been Conan of the reavers in that other life, and that grim interlude a brief episode of reality which I had relived.

I entered the tunnel down which we had fled, shining a beam of light ahead, and saw the bar of gray light drifting down from above—just as in that other, lost age. Here the Briton and I, Conan, had turned at bay. I turned my eyes from the ancient cleft high up in the vaulted roof, and looked for the stair. There it was, half concealed by an angle in the wall.

I mounted, remembering how hardly Vertorix and I had gone up so many ages before, with the horde hissing and frothing at our heels. I found myself tense with dread as I approached the dark, gaping entrance through which the pack had sought to cut us off. I had snapped off the light when I came into the dim-lit corridor below, and now I glanced into the well of blackness which opened on the stair. And with a cry I started back, nearly losing my footing on the worn steps. Sweating in the semidarkness I switched on the light and directed its beam into the cryptic opening, revolver in hand.

I saw only the bare rounded sides of a small shaftlike tunnel and I laughed nervously. My imagination was running riot; I could have sworn that hideous yellow eyes glared terribly at me from the darkness, and that a crawling something had scuttered away down the tunnel. I was foolish to let these imaginings upset me. The Children had long vanished from these caverns; a nameless and abhorrent race closer to the serpent than the man, they had centuries ago faded back into the oblivion from which they had crawled in the black dawn ages of the earth.

I came out of the shaft into the winding corridor, which, as I remembered of old, was lighter. Here from the shadows a lurking thing had leaped on my back while my companions ran on, unknowing. What a brute of a man Conon had been, to keep going after receiving such savage wounds! Aye, in that age all men were iron.

I came to the place where the tunnel forked and as before I took the left-hand branch and came to the shaft that led down. Down this I went, listening for the roar of the river, but not hearing it. Again the darkness shut in about the shaft, so I was forced to have recourse to my electric torch again, lest I lose my footing and plunge to my death. Oh, I, John O'Brien, am not nearly so sure-footed as was I, Conan the reaver; no, nor as tigerishly powerful and quick, either.

I soon struck the dank lower level and felt again the dampness that denoted my position under the river-bed, but still I could not hear the rush of the water. And indeed I knew that whatever mighty river had rushed roaring to the sea in those ancient times, there was no such body of water among the hills today. I halted, flashing my light about. I was in a vast tunnel, not very high of roof, but broad. Other smaller tunnels branched off from it and I wondered at the network which apparently honeycombed the hills.

I cannot describe the grim, gloomy effect of those dark, low-roofed corridors far below the earth. Over all hung an overpowering sense of unspeakable antiquity. Why had the little people carved out these mysterious crypts, and in which black age? Were these caverns their last refuge from the onrushing tides of humanity, or their castles since time immemorial? I shook my head in bewilderment; the bestiality of the Children I had seen, yet somehow they had been able to carve these tunnels and chambers that might balk modern engineers. Even supposing they had but completed a task begun by nature, still it was stupendous work for a race of dwarfish aborigines.

Then I realized with a start that I was spending more time in these gloomy tunnels than I cared for, and began to hunt for the steps by which Conan had ascended. I found them and, following them up, breathed again deeply in relief as the sudden glow of daylight filled the shaft. I came out upon the ledge, now worn away until it was little more than a bump on the face of the cliff. And I saw the great river, which had roared like a prisoned monster between the sheer walls of its narrow canyon, had dwindled away with the passing eons until it was no more than a tiny stream, far beneath me, trickling soundlessly among the stones on its way to the sea.

Aye, the surface of the earth changes; the rivers swell or shrink, the mountains heave and topple, the lakes dry up, the continents alter; but under the earth the work of lost, mysterious hands slumbers untouched by the sweep of Time. Their work, aye, but what of the hands that reared that work? Did they, too, lurk beneath the bosoms of the hills?

How long I stood there, lost in dim speculations, I do not know, but suddenly, glancing across at the other ledge, crumbling and weathered, I shrank back into the entrance behind me. Two figures came out upon the ledge and I gasped to see that they were Richard Brent and Eleanor Bland. Now I remembered why I had come to the cavern and my hand instinctively sought the revolver in my pocket. They did not see me. But I could see them, and hear them plainly, too, since no roaring river now thundered between the ledges.

"By gad, Eleanor," Brent was saying, "I'm glad you decided to come with me. Who would have guessed there was anything to those old tales about hidden tunnels leading from the cavern? I wonder how that section of wall came to collapse? I thought I heard a crash just as we entered the outer cave. Do you suppose some beggar was in the cavern ahead of us, and broke it in?"

"I don't know," she answered. "I remember—oh, I don't know. It almost seems as if I'd been here before, or dreamed I had. I seem to faintly remember, like a far-off nightmare, running, running, running endlessly through these dark corridors with hideous creatures on my heels. . . ."

"Was I there?" jokingly asked Brent.

"Yes, and John, too," she answered. "But you were

not Richard Brent, and John was not John O'Brien. No, and I was not Eleanor Bland, either. Oh, it's so dim and far-off I can't describe it at all. It's hazy and misty and terrible."

"I understand, a little," he said unexpectedly. "Ever since we came to the place where the wall had fallen and revealed the old tunnel, I've had a sense of familiarity with the place. There was horror and danger and battle—and love, too."

He stepped nearer the edge to look in the gorge, and Eleanor cried out sharply and suddenly, seizing him in a convulsive grasp.

"Don't Richard, don't! Hold me, oh, hold me tight!"

He caught her in his arms. "Why, Eleanor, dear, what's the matter?"

"Nothing," she faltered, but she clung closer to him and I saw she was trembling. "Just a strange feeling—rushing dizziness and fright, just as if I were falling from a great height. Don't go near the edge, Dick; it scares me."

"I won't dear," he answered, drawing her closer to him, and continuing hesitantly: "Eleanor, there's something I've wanted to ask you for a long time—well, I haven't the knack of putting things in an elegant way. I love you, Eleanor; always have. You know that. But if you don't love me, I'll take myself off and won't annoy you any more. Only please tell me one way or another, for I can't stand it any longer. Is it I or the American?"

"You, Dick," she answered, hiding her face on his shoulder. "It's always been you, though I didn't know it. I think a great deal of John O'Brien. I didn't know which of you I really loved. But today as we came through those terrible tunnels and climbed those fearful stairs, and just now, when I thought for some strange reason we were falling from the ledge, I realized it was you I loved—that I always loved you, through more lives than this one. Always!"

Their lips met and I saw her golden head cradled on his shoulder. My lips were dry, my heart cold, yet my soul was at peace. They belonged to each other. Eons ago they lived and loved, and because of that love they suffered and died. And I, Conan, had driven them to that doom.

I saw them turn toward the cleft, their arms about each other, then I heard Tamera—I mean Eleanor—shriek, I saw them both recoil. And out of the cleft a horror came writhing, a loathsome, brain-shattering thing that blinked in the clean sunlight. Aye, I knew it of old—vestige of a forgotten age, it came writhing its horrid shape up out of the darkness of the Earth and the lost pact to claim its own.

What three thousand years of retrogression can do to a race hideous in the beginning, I saw, and shuddered. And instinctivley I knew that in all the world it was the only one of its kind, a monster that had lived on. God alone knows how many centuries, wallowing in the slime of its dank subterranean lairs. Before the Children had vanished, the race must have lost all human semblance, living as they did, the life of the reptile. This thing was more like a giant serpent than anything else, but it had aborted legs and snaky arms with hooked talons. It crawled on its belly, writhing back mottled lips to bare needle-like fangs, which I felt must drip with venom. It hissed as it reared up its ghastly head on a horribly long neck, while its yellow slanted eyes glittered with all the horror that is spawned in the black lairs under the earth.

I knew those eyes had blazed at me from the dark tunnel opening on the stair. For some reason the creature had fled from me, possibly because it feared my light, and it stood to reason that it was the only one remaining in the caverns, else I had been set upon in the darkness. But for it, the tunnels could be traversed in safety.

Now the reptilian thing writhed toward the humans trapped on the ledge. Brent had thrust Eleanor behind him and stood, face ashy, to guard her as best he could. And I gave thanks silently that I, John O'Brien, could pay the debt I, Conan the reaver, owed these lovers since long ago.

The monster reared up and Brent, with cold courage, sprang to meet it with his naked hands. Taking quick aim, I fired once. The shot echoed like the crack of doom between the towering cliffs, and the Horror, with a hideously human scream, staggered wildly, swayed and pitched headlong, knotting and writhing like a wounded python, to tumble from the sloping ledge and fall plumme-like to the rocks far below.

WORMS OF THE EARTH

"STRIKE IN the nails, soldiers, and let our guest see
the reality of our good Roman justice!"

The speaker wrapped his purple cloak closer about
his powerful frame and settled back into his official
chair, much as he might have settled back in his seat
at the Circus Maximus to enjoy the clash of gladiatorial swords. Realization of power colored his every
move. Whetted pride was necessary to Roman satisfaction, and Titus Sulla was justly proud; for he was
military governor of Eboracum and answerable only
to the Emperor of Rome. He was a strongly built
man of medium height, with the hawklike features of
the pure-bred Roman. Now a mocking smile curved
his full lips, increasing the arrogance of his haughty
aspect. Distinctly military in apperance, he wore the
golden-scaled corselet and chased breastplate of his
rank, with the short stabbing-sword at his belt, and
he held on his knee the silvered helmet with its
plumed crest. Behind him stood a clump of impassive
soldiers with shield and spear—blond titans from the
Rhineland.

Before him was taking place the scene which apparently gave him so much real gratification—a scene
common enough wherever stretched the far-flung

boundaries of Rome. A rude cross lay flat upon the barren earth and on it was bound a man—half-naked, wild of aspect with his corded limbs, glaring eyes and shock of tangled hair. His executioners were Roman soldiers, and with heavy hammers they prepared to pin the victim's hands and feet to the wood with iron spikes.

Only a small group of men watched this ghastly scene, in the dread place of execution beyond the city walls: the governor and his watchful guards; a few young Roman officers; the man to whom Sulla had referred as "guest" and who stood like a bronze image, unspeaking. Beside the gleaming splendor of the Roman, the quiet garb of this man seemed drab, almost somber.

He was dark, but he did not resemble the Latins around him. There was about him none of the warm, almost Oriental sensuality of the Mediterranean which colored their features. The blond barbarians behind Sulla's chair were less unlike the man in facial outline than were the Romans. Not his were the full curving lips, nor the rich waving locks suggestive of the Greek. Nor was his dark complexion the rich olive of the south; rather it was the bleak darkness of the north. The whole aspect of the man vaguely suggested the shadowed mists, the gloom, the cold and icy wind of the naked northern lands. Even his black eyes were savagely cold, like black fires burning through fathoms of ice.

His height was only medium but there was something about him which transcended mere physical bulk—a certain fierce innate vitality, comparable only to that of a wolf or a panther. In every line of his supple, compact body, as well as in his coarse straight hair and thin lips, this was evident—in the hawklike set of the head on the corded neck, in the broad square shoulders, in the deep chest, the lean loins, the narrow feet. Built with the savage economy of a panther, he was an image of dynamic potentialities, pent in with iron self-control.

At his feet crouched one like him in complexion— but there the resemblance ended. This other was a stunted giant, with gnarly limbs, thick body, a low sloping brow and an expression of dull ferocity, now clearly mixed with fear. If the man on the cross resembled, in a tribal way, the man Titus Sulla called guest, he far more resembled the stunted crouching giant.

"Well, Partha Mac Othna," said the governor with studied effrontery, "when you return to your tribe, you will have a tale to tell of the justice of Rome, who rules the south."

"I will have a tale," answered the other in a voice which betrayed no emotion, just as his dark face, schooled to immobility, showed no evidence of the maelstrom in his soul.

"Justice to all under the rule of Rome," said Sulla. "*Pax Romana!* Reward for virtue, punishment for wrong!" He laughed inwardly at his own black hypocrisy, then continued: "You see, emissary of Pictland, how swiftly Rome punishes the transgressor."

"I see," answered the Pict in a voice which strongly curbed anger made deep with menace, "that the subject of a foreign king is dealt with as though he were a Roman slave."

"He has been tried and condemned in an unbiased court," retorted Sulla.

"Aye! and the accuser was a Roman, the witnesses Roman, the judge Roman! He committed murder? In a moment of fury he struck down a Roman merchant who cheated, tricked and robbed him, and to injury added insult—aye, and a blow! Is his king but a dog, that Rome crucifies his subjects at will, condemned by Roman courts? Is his king too weak or foolish to do justice, were he informed and formal charges brought against the offender?"

"Well," said Sulla cynically, "you may inform Bran Mak Morn yourself. Rome, my friend, makes no account of her actions to barbarian kings. When savages come around us, let them act with discretion or suffer the consequences."

The Pict shut his iron jaws with a snap that told Sulla further badgering would elicit no reply. The Roman made a gesture to the executioners. One of them seized a spike and placing it against the thick wrist of the victim smote heavily. The iron point sank deep through the flesh, crunching against the bones. The lips of the man on the cross writhed, though no moan escaped him. As a trapped wolf fights against his cage, the bound victim instinctively wrenched and struggled. The veins swelled in his temples, sweat beaded his low forehead, the muscles in arms and legs writhed and knotted. The hammers fell in inexorable strokes, driving the cruel points deeper and deeper, through wrists and ankles; blood flowed in a black river over the hands that held the spikes, staining the wood of the cross, and the splintering of bones was distinctly heard. Yet the sufferer made no outcry, though his blackened lips writhed back until the gums were visible, and his shaggy head jerked involuntarily from side to side.

The man called Partha Mac Othna stood like an iron image, eyes burning from an inscrutable face, his whole body as hard as iron from the tension of his control. At his feet crouched his misshapen servant, hiding his face from the grim sight, his arms locked about his master's knees. Those arms gripped like steel and under his breath the fellow mumbled ceaselessly as if in invocation.

The last stroke fell; the cords were cut from arm and leg, so that the man would hang supported by the nails alone. He had ceased his struggling that only twisted the spikes in his agonizing wounds. His bright black eyes, unglazed, had not left the face of the man called Partha Mac Othna; in them lingered a desperate shadow of hope. Now the soldiers lifted the cross and set the end of it in the hole prepared, stamped the dirt about it to hold it erect.

The Pict hung in mid-air, suspended by the nails in his flesh, but still no sound escaped his lips. His eyes still hung on the somber face of the emissary, but the shadow of hope was fading.

"He'll live for days!" said Sulla cheerfully. "These Picts are harder than cats to kill! I'll keep a guard of ten soldiers watching day and night to see that no one takes him down before he dies. Ho, there, Valerius, in honor of our esteemed neighbor, King Bran Mak Morn, give him a cup of wine!"

With a laugh the young officer came forward, holding a brimming wine-cup, and rising on his toes, lifted it to the parched lips of the sufferer. In the black eyes flared a red wave of unquenchable hatred; writhing his head aside to avoid even touching the cup, he spat full into the young Roman's eyes. With a curse Valerius dashed the cup to the ground, and before any could halt him, wrenched out his sword and sheathed it in the man's body.

Sulla rose with an imperious exclamation of anger; the man called Partha Mac Othna had started violently, but he bit his lip and said nothing. Valerius seemed somewhat surprised at himself as he sullenly cleaned his sword. The act had been instinctive, following the insult to Roman pride, the one thing unbearable.

"Give up your sword, young sir!" exclaimed Sulla. "Centurion Publius, place him under arrest. A few days in a cell with stale bread and water will teach you to curb your patrician pride, in matters dealing with the will of the empire. What, you young fool, do you not realize that you could not have made the dog a more kindly gift? Who would not rather desire a quick death on the sword than the slow agony on the cross? Take him away. And you, centurion, see that guards remain at the cross so that the body is not cut down until the ravens pick bare the bones. Partha Mac Othna, I go to a banquet at the house of Demetrius—will you not accompany me?"

The emissary shook his head, his eyes fixed on the limp form which sagged on the black-stained cross. He made no reply. Sulla smiled sardonically, then rose and strode away, followed by his secretary who bore the gilded chair ceremoniously, and by the stolid soldiers, with whom walked Valerius, head sunken.

The man called Partha Mac Othna flung a wide fold of his cloak about his shoulder, halted a moment to gaze at the grim cross with its burden, darkly etched against the crimson sky, where the clouds of night were gathering. Then he stalked away, followed by his silent servant.

2

In an inner chamber of Eboracum, the man called Partha Mac Othna paced tigerishly to and fro. His sandaled feet made no sound on the marble tiles.

"Grom!" he turned to the gnarled servant, "well I know why you held my knees so tightly—why you muttered aid of the Moon-Woman—you feared I would lose my self-control and make a mad attempt to succor the poor wretch. By the gods, I believe that was what the dog Roman wished—his iron-cased watchdogs watched me narrowly, I know, and his baiting was harder to bear than ordinarily.

"Gods black and white, dark and light!" he shook his clenched fists above his head in the black gust of his passion. "That I should stand by and see a man of mine butchered on a Roman cross—without justice and with no more trial than that farce! Black gods of

R'lyeh, even you would I invoke to the ruin and
destruction of those butchers! I swear by the Nameless Ones, men shall die howling for that deed, and
Rome shall cry out as a woman in the dark who
treads upon an adder!"

"He knew you, master," said Grom.

The other dropped his head and covered his eyes
with a gesture of savage pain.

"His eyes will haunt me when I lie dying. Aye, he
knew me, and almost until the last, I read in his eyes
the hope that I might aid him. Gods and devils, is
Rome to butcher my people beneath my very eyes?
Then I am not king but dog!"

"Not so loud, in the name of all the gods!" exclaimed Grom in affright. "Did these Romans suspect you were Bran Mak Morn, they would nail you
on a cross beside that other."

"They will know it ere long," grimly answered the
king. "Too long I have lingered here in the guise of
an emissary, spying upon my enemies. They have
thought to play with me, these Romans, masking
their contempt and scorn only under polished satire.
Rome is courteous to barbarian ambassadors, they
give us fine houses to live in, offer us slaves, pander
to our lusts with women and gold and wine and
games, but all the while they laugh at us; their very
courtesy is an insult, and sometimes—as today—
their contempt discards all veneer. Bah! I've seen
through their baitings—have remained imperturb-
ably serene and swallowed their studied insults. But
this—by the fiends of Hell, this is beyond human
endurance! My people look at me; if I fail them—if I
fail even one—even the lowest of my people, who
will aid them? To whom shall they turn? By the
gods, I'll answer the gibes of these Roman dogs with
black shaft and trenchant steel!"

"And the chief with the plumes?" Grom meant the

governor, and his gutturals thrummed with the blood-lust. "He dies?" He flicked out a length of steel.

Bran scowled. "Easier said than done. He dies—but how may I reach him? By day his German guards keep at his back; by night they stand at door and window. He has many enemies, Romans as well as barbarians. Many a Briton would gladly slit his throat."

Grom seized Bran's garment, stammering as fierce eagerness broke the bonds of his inarticulate nature.

"Let me go, master! My life is worth nothing. I will cut him down in the midst of his warriors!"

Bran smiled fiercely and clapped his hand on the stunted giant's shoulder with a force that would have felled a lesser man.

"Nay, old war-dog, I have too much need of thee! You shall not throw your life away uselessly. Sulla would read the intent in your eyes, besides, and the javelins of his Teutons would be through you ere you could reach him. Not by the dagger in the dark will we strike this Roman, not by the venom in the cup nor the shaft from the ambush."

The king turned and paced the floor a moment, his head bent in thought. Slowly his eyes grew murky with a thought so fearful he did not speak it aloud to the waiting warrior.

"I have become somewhat familiar with the maze of Roman politics during my stay in this accursed waste of mud and marble," said he. "During a war on the Wall, Titus Sulla, as governor of this province, is supposed to hasten thither with his centuries. But this Sulla does not do; he is no coward, but the bravest avoid certain things—to each man, however bold, his own particular fear. So he sends in his place Caius Camillus, who in times of peace patrols the fens of the west, lest the Britons break over the border. And Sulla takes his place in the Tower of Trajan. Ha!"

He whirled and gripped Grom with steely fingers.

"Grom, take the red stallion and ride north! Let no grass grow under the stallion's hoofs! Ride to Cormac na Connacht and tell him to sweep the frontier with sword and torch! Let his wild Gaels feast their fill of slaughter. After a time I will be with him. But for a time I have affairs in the west."

Grom's black eyes gleamed and he made a passionate gesture with his crooked hand—an instinctive move of savagery.

Bran drew a heavy bronze seal from beneath his tunic.

"This is my safe-conduct as an emissary to Roman courts," he said grimly. "It will open all gates between this house and Baal-dor. If any official questions you too closely—here!"

Lifting the lid of an iron-bound chest, Bran took out a small, heavy leather bag which he gave into the hands of the warrior.

"When all keys fail at a gate," he said, "try a golden key. Go now!"

There was no ceremonious farewell between the barbarian king and his barbarian vassal. Grom flung up his arm in a gesture of salute; then turning, he hurried out.

Bran stepped to a barred window and gazed out into the moonlit streets.

"Wait until the moon sets," he muttered grimly. "Then I'll take the road to—Hell! But before I go I have a debt to pay."

The stealthy clink of a hoof on the flags reached him.

"With the safe-conduct and gold, not even Rome can hold a Pictish reaver," muttered the king. "Now I'll sleep until the moon sets."

With a snarl at the marble friezework and fluted columns, as symbols of Rome, he flung himself down on a couch, from which he had long since impatiently torn the cushions and silk stuffs, as too soft for his hard body. Hate and black passion for vengeance seethed in him, yet he went instantly to sleep. The first lesson he had learned in his bitter hard life was to snatch sleep any time he could, like a wolf that snatches sleep on the hunting trail. Generally his slumber was as light and dreamless as a panther's, but tonight it was otherwise.

He sank into fleecy gray fathoms of slumber and in a timeless, misty realm of shadows he met the tall, lean, white-bearded figure of old Gonar, the priest of the Moon, high counsellor to the king. And Bran stood aghast, for Gonar's face was white as driven snow and he shook with ague. Well might Bran stand appalled, for in all the years of his life he had never before seen Gonar the Wise show any sign of fear.

"What now, old one?" asked the king. "Goes all well in Baal-dor?"

"All is well in Baal-dor where my body lies sleeping," answered old Gonar. "Across the void I have come to battle with you for your soul. King, are you mad, this thought you have in your brain?"

"Gonar," answered Bran somberly, "this day I stood still and watched a man of mine die on the cross of Rome. What his name or his rank, I do not know. I do not care. He might have been a faithful unknown warrior of mine, he might have been an outlaw. I only know that he was mine; the first scents he knew were the scents of the heather; the first light he saw was the sunrise on the Pictish hills. He belonged to me, not to Rome. If punishment was just, then none but me should have dealt it. If it were to be tried, none but me should have been his judge. The same blood flowed in our veins; the same fire maddened our brains; in infancy we listened to the same old tales, and in youth we sang the same old songs. He was bound to my heartstrings, as every man and every woman and every child of Pictland is bound. It was mine to protect him! Now it is mine to avenge him."

"But in the name of the gods, Bran," expostulated the wizard, "take your vengeance in another way! Return to the heather—mass your warriors—join with Cormac and his Gaels, and spread a sea of blood and flame the length of the great Wall!"

"All that I will do," grimly answered Bran. "But now—*now*—I will have a vengeance such as no Roman ever dreamed of! Ha, what do they know of the mysteries of this ancient isle, which sheltered strange life long before Rome rose from the marshes of the Tiber?"

"Bran, there are weapons too foul to use, even against Rome!"

Bran barked short and sharp as a jackal.

"Ha! There are no weapons I would not use against Rome! My back is at the wall. By the blood of the fiends, has Rome fought me fair? Bah! I am a barbarian king with a wolfskin mantle and an iron crown, fighting with my handful of bows and broken pikes against the queen of the world. What have I? The heather hills, the wattle huts, the spears of my shock-headed tribesmen! And I fight Rome—with her armored legions, her broad fertile plains and rich seas—her mountains and her rivers and her gleaming cities—her wealth, her steel, her gold, her mastery and her wrath. By steel and fire I will fight her—and by subtlety and treachery—by the thorn in the foot, the adder in the path, the venom in the cup, the dagger in the dark; aye," his voice sank somberly, "and by the worms of the earth!"

"But it is madness!" cried Gonar. "You will perish in the attempt you plan—you will go down to Hell and you will not return! What of your people then?"

"If I cannot serve them I had better die," growled the king.

"But you cannot reach the beings you seek," cried

Gonar. "For untold centuries they have dwelt apart. There is no door by which you can come to them. Long ago they severed the bonds that bound them to the world we know."

"Long ago," answered Bran somberly, "you told me that nothing in the universe was separated from the stream of Life—a saying the truth of which I have often seen evident. No race, no form of life but is close-knit somehow, by some manner, to the rest of Life and the world. Somewhere there is a thin link connecting *those* I seek to the world I know. Somewhere there is a Door. And somewhere among the bleak fens of the west I will find it."

Stark horror flooded Gonar's eyes and he gave back crying, "Wo! Wo! Wo! to Pictdom! Wo to the unborn kingdom! Wo, black wo to the sons of men!"

Bran awoke to a shadowed room and the starlight on the window-bars. The moon had sunk from sight, though its glow was still faint above the housetops. Memory of his dream shook him and he swore beneath his breath.

Rising, he flung off cloak and mantle, donning a light shirt of black mesh-mail, and girding a sword and dirk. Going again to the iron-bound chest he lifted several compact bags and emptied the clinking contents into the leathern pouch at his girdle. Then wrapping his wide cloak about him, he silently left the house. No servants there were to spy on him—he had impatiently refused the offer of slaves which it was Rome's policy to furnish her barbarian emissaries. Gnarled Grom had attended to all Bran's simple needs.

The stables fronted on the courtyard. A moment's groping in the dark and he placed his hand over the great stallion's nose, checking the nicker of recognition. Working without a light he swiftly bridled and saddled the great brute, and went through the court-

yard into a shadowy side-street, leading him. The
moon was setting, the border of floating shadows
widening along the western wall. Silence lay on the
marble palaces and mud hovels of Eboracum under
the cold stars.

Bran touched the pouch at his girdle, which was
heavy with minted gold that bore the stamp of Rome.
He had come to Eboracum posing as an emissary of
Pictdom, to act the spy. But being a barbarian, he
had not been able to play his part in aloof formality
and sedate dignity. He retained a crowded memory
of wild feasts where wine flowed in fountains; of
white-bosomed Roman women, who, sated with civi-
lized lovers, looked with something more than favor
on a virile barbarian; of gladiatorial games; and of
other games where dice clicked and spun and tall
stacks of gold changed hands. He had drunk deeply
and gambled recklessly, after the manner of barbarians, and he had had a remarkable run of luck, due
possibly to the indifference with which he won or
lost. Gold to the Pict was so much dust, flowing
through his fingers. In his land there was no need of
it. But he had learned its power in the boundaries of
civilization.

Almost under the shadow of the northwestern wall
he saw ahead of him loom the great watch tower
which was connected with and reared above the
outer wall. One corner of the castle-like fortress,
farthest from the wall, served as a dungeon. Bran left
his horse standing in a dark alley, with the reins
hanging on the ground, and stole like a prowling wolf
into the shadows of the fortress.

The young officer Valerius was awakened from a
light, unquiet sleep by a stealthy sound at the barred
window. He sat up, cursing softly under his breath
as the faint starlight which etched the window-bars
fell across the bare stone floor and reminded him of
his disgrace. Well, in a few days, he ruminated, he'd

be well out of it; Sulla would not be too harsh on a man with such high connections; then let any man or woman gibe at him! Damn that insolent Pict! But wait, he thought suddenly, remembering; what of the sound which had roused him?

"Hssst!" it was a voice from the window.

Why so much secrecy? It could hardly be a foe—yet, why should it be a friend? Valerius rose and crossed his cell, coming close to the window. Outside all was dim in the starlight and he made out but a shadowy form close to the window.

"Who are you?" he leaned close against the bars, straining his eyes into the gloom.

His answer was a snarl of wolfish laughter, a long flicker of steel in the starlight. Valerius reeled away from the window and crashed to the floor, clutching his throat, gurgling horribly as he tried to scream. Blood gushed through his fingers, forming about his twitching body a pool that reflected the dim starlight dully and redly.

Outside Bran glided away like a shadow, without pausing to peer into the cell. In another minute the guards would round the corner on their regular routine. Even now he heard the measured tramp of their iron-clad feet. Before they came in sight he had vanished and they clumped stolidly by the cell windows with no intimation of the corpse that lay on the floor within.

Bran rode to the small gate in the western wall, unchallenged by the sleepy watch. What fear of foreign invasion in Eboracum?—and certain well-organized thieves and women-stealers made it profitable for the watchmen not to be too vigilant. But the single guardsman at the western gate—his fellows lay drunk in a nearby brothel—lifted his spear and bawled for Bran to halt and give an account of himself. Silently the Pict reined closer. Masked in the dark cloak, he seemed dim and indistinct to the Roman, who was only aware of the glitter of his cold eyes in the gloom. But Bran held up his hand against the starlight and the soldier caught the gleam of gold; in the other hand he saw a long sheen of steel. The soldier understood, and he did not hesitate between the choice of a golden bribe or a battle to the death with this unknown rider who was apparently a barbarian of some sort. With a grunt he lowered his spear and swung the gate open. Bran rode through, casting a handful of coins to the Roman. They fell about his feet in a golden shower, clinking against the flags. He bent in greedy haste to retrieve them and Bran Mak Morn rode westward like a flying ghost in the night.

3

Into the dim fens of the west came Bran Mak Morn. A cold wind breathed across the gloomy waste and against the gray sky a few herons flapped heavily. The long reeds and marsh grass waved in broken undulations and out across the desolation of the wastes a few still meres reflected the dull light. Here and there rose curiously regular hillocks above the general levels, and gaunt against the somber sky Bran saw a marching line of upright monoliths—menhirs, reared by what nameless hands?

A faint blue line to the west lay the foothills that beyond the horizon grew to the wild mountains of Wales where dwelt still wild Celtic tribes—fierce blue-eyed men that knew not the yoke of Rome. A row of well-garrisoned watch towers held them in check. Even now, far away across the moors, Bran glimpsed the unassailable keep men called the Tower of Trajan.

These barren wastes seemed the dreary accomplishment of desolation, yet human life was not utterly lacking. Bran met the silent men of the fen, reticent, dark of eye and hair, speaking a strange mixed tongue whose long-blended elements had forgotten their pristine separate sources. Bran recognized a certain kinship in these people to himself, but he looked on them with the scorn of a pure-blooded patrician for men of fixed strains.

Not that the common people of Caledonia were altogether pure-blooded; they got their stocky bodies and massive limbs from a primitive Teutonic race which had found its way into the northern tip of the isle even before the Celtic conquest of Britain was completed, and had been absorbed by the Picts. But the chiefs of Bran's folk had kept their blood from foreign taint since the beginnings of time, and he himself was a pure-bred Pict of the Old Race. But these fenmen, overrun repeatedly by British, Gaelic and Roman conquerors, had assimilated blood of each, and in the process almost forgotten their original language and lineage.

For Bran came of a race that was very old, which had spread over western Europe in one vast Dark Empire, before the coming of the Aryans, when the ancestors of the Celts, the Hellenes and the Germans were one primal people, before the days of tribal splitting-off and westward drift.

Only in Caledonia, Bran brooded, had his people resisted the flood of Aryan conquest. He had heard of a Pictish people called Basques, who in the crags of the Pyrenees called themselves an unconquered race; but he knew that they had paid tribute for centuries to the ancestors of the Gaels, before these Celtic conquerors abandoned their mountain realm and set sail for Ireland. Only the Picts of Caledonia had remained free, and they had been scattered into small feuding tribes—he was the first acknowledged king in five hundred years—the beginning of a new dynasty—no, a revival of an ancient dynasty under a

new name. In the very teeth of Rome he dreamed of
empire.

He wandered through the fens, seeking a Door.
Of his quest he said nothing to the dark-eyed fenmen.
They told him news that drifted from mouth to
mouth—a tale of war in the north, the skirl of war
pipes along the winding Wall, of gathering-fires in
the heather, of flame and smoke and rapine and the
glutting of Gaelic swords in the crimson sea of slaughter. The eagles of the legions were moving north-
ward and the ancient road resounded to the measured
tramp of the ironclad feet. And Bran, in the fens of
the west, laughed, well pleased.

In Eboracum, Titus Sulla gave secret word to seek
out the Pictish emissary with the Gaelic name who
had been under suspicion, and who had vanished the
night young Valerius was found dead in his cell with
his throat ripped out. Sulla felt that this sudden
bursting flame of war on the Wall was connected
closely with his execution of a condemned Pictish
criminal, and he set his spy system to work, though
he felt sure that Partha Mac Othna was by this time
far beyond his reach. He prepared to march from
Eboracum, but he did not accompany the consider-
able force of legionaries which he sent north. Sulla
was a brave man, but each man has his own dread,
and Sulla's was Cormac na Connacht, the black-haired
prince of the Gaels, who had sworn to cut out the
governor's heart and eat it raw. So Sulla rode with
his ever-present bodyguard, westward, where lay
the Tower of Trajan with its warlike commander,
Caius Camillus, who enjoyed nothing more than taking his superior's place when the red waves of war
washed at the foot of the Wall. Devious politics, but
the legate of Rome seldom visited this far isle, and
what with his wealth and intrigues, Titus Sulla was
the highest power in Britain.

And Bran, knowing all this, patiently waited his

coming, in the deserted hut in which he had taken up his abode.

One gray evening he strode on foot across the moors, a stark figure, blackly etched against the dim crimson fire of the sunset. He felt the incredible antiquity of the slumbering land, as he walked like the last man on the day after the end of the world! Yet at last he saw a token of human life—a drab hut of wattle and mud, set in the reedy breast of the fen.

A woman greeted him from the open door and Bran's somber eyes narrowed with a dark suspicion. The woman was not old, yet the evil wisdom of ages was in her eyes; her garments were ragged and scanty, her black locks tangled and unkempt, lending her an aspect of wildness well in keeping with her grim surroundings. Her red lips laughed but there was no mirth in her laughter, only a hint of mockery, and under the lips her teeth showed sharp and pointed like fangs.

"Enter, master," said she, "if you do not fear to share the roof of the witch-woman of Dagon-moor!"

Bran entered silently and sat down on a broken bench while the woman busied herself with the scanty meal cooking over an open fire on the squalid hearth. He studied her lithe, almost serpentine motions, the ears which were almost pointed, the yellow eyes which slanted curiously.

"What do you seek in the fens, my lord?" she asked, turning toward him with a supple twist of her whole body.

"I seek a Door," he answered, chin resting on his fist. "I have a song to sing to the worms of the earth!"

She started upright, a jar falling from her hands to shatter on the hearth.

"This is an ill saying, even spoken in chance," she stammered.

"I speak not by chance but by intent," he answered.

She shook her head. "I know not what you mean."

"Well you know," he returned. "Aye, you know well! My race is very old—they reigned in Britain before the nations of the Celts and the Hellenes were born out of the womb of peoples. But my people were not first in Britain. By the mottles on your skin, by the slanting of your eyes, by the taint in your veins, I speak with full knowledge and meaning."

Awhile she stood silent, her lips smiling but her face inscrutable.

"Man, are you mad?" she asked, "that in your madness you come seeking that from which strong men fled screaming in old times?"

"I seek a vengeance," he answered, "that can be accomplished only by Them I seek."

She shook her head.

"You have listened to a bird singing; you have dreamed empty dreams."

'I have heard a viper hiss," he growled, "and I do not dream. Enough of this weaving of words. I came seeking a link between two worlds; I have found it."

"I need lie to you no more, man of the North," answered the woman. "They you seek still dwell beneath the sleeping hills. They have drawn *apart*, farther and farther from the world you know."

"But they still steal forth in the night to grip women straying on the moors," said he, his gaze on her slanted eyes. She laughed wickedly.

"What would you of me?"

"That you bring me to Them."

She flung back her head with a scornful laugh. His left hand locked like iron in the breast of her scanty garment and his right closed on his hilt. She laughed in his face.

"Strike and be damned, my northern wolf! Do you think that such life as mine is so sweet that I would cling to it as a babe to the breast?"

His hand fell away.

"You are right. Threats are foolish. I will buy your aid."

"How?" the laughing voice hummed with mockery.

Bran opened his pouch and poured into his cupped palm a stream of gold.

"More wealth than the men of the fen ever dreamed of."

Again she laughed. "What is this rusty metal to me? Save it for some white-breasted Roman woman who will play the traitor for you!"

"Name me a price!" he urged. "The head of an enemy—"

"By the blood in my veins, with its heritage of ancient hate, who is mine enemy but thee?" she laughed, and springing, struck catlike. But her dagger splintered on the mail beneath his cloak, and he flung her off with a loathsome flit of his wrist which tossed her sprawling across her grass-strewn bunk. Lying there, she laughed up at him.

"I will name you a price, my wolf, and it may be in days to come you will curse the armor that broke Atla's dagger!" She rose and came close to him, her disquietingly long hands fastened fiercely into his cloak. "I will tell you, Black Bran, king of Caledon! Oh, I knew you when you came into my hut with your black hair and your cold eyes! I will lead you to the doors of Hell if you wish—and the price shall be the kisses of a king!

"What of my blasted and bitter life, I, whom mortal men loathe and fear? I have not known the love of men, the clasp of a strong arm, the sting of human kisses, I, Atla, the were-woman of the moors! What have I known but the lone winds of the fens, the dreary fire of cold sunsets, the whispering of the marsh grasses?—the faces that blink up at me in the waters of the meres, the foot-pad of night—things in the gloom, the glimmer of red eyes, the grisly murmur of nameless beings in the night!

"I am half human, at least! Have I not known sorrow and yearning and crying wistfulness, and the drear ache of loneliness? Give to me, king—give me your fierce kisses and your hurtful barbarian's embrace. Then in the long drear years to come I shall not utterly eat out my heart in vain envy of the white-bosomed women of men; for I shall have a memory few of them can boast—the kisses of a king! One night of love, O king, and I will guide you to the gates of Hell!"

Bran eyed her somberly; he reached forth and gripped her arm in his iron fingers. An involuntary shudder shook him at the feel of her sleek skin. He nodded slowly and, drawing her close to him, forced his head down to meet her lifted lips.

4

The cold gray mists of dawn wrapped King Bran like a clammy cloak. He turned to the woman whose slanted eyes gleamed in the gray gloom.

"Make good your part of the contract," he said roughly. "I sought a link between worlds, and in you I found it. I seek the one thing sacred to Them. It shall be the Key opening the Door that lies unseen between me and Them. Tell me how I can reach it."

"I will," the red lips smiled terribly. "Go to the mound men call Dagon's Barrow. Draw aside the stone that blocks the entrance and go under the dome of the mound. The floor of the chamber is made of seven great stones, six grouped about the seventh. Lift out the center stone—and you will see!"

"Will I find the Black Stone?" he asked.

"Dagon's Barrow is the Door to the Black Stone," she answered, "if you dare follow the Road."

"Will the symbol be well guarded?" He unconsciously loosened his blade in its sheath. The red lips curled mockingly.

"If you meet any on the Road, you will die as no mortal man has died for long centuries. The Stone is not guarded, as men guard their treasures. Why should They guard what man has never sought? Perhaps They will be near, perhaps not. It is a chance you must take, if you wish the Stone. Beware, king of Pictdom! Remember it was your folk who, so long ago, cut the thread that bound Them to human life. They were almost human then—they overspread the land and knew the sunlight. Now they have drawn *apart*. They know not the sunlight and they shun the light of the moon. Even the starlight they hate. Far, far apart have they drawn, who might have been men in time, but for the spears of your ancestors."

The sky was overcast with misty gray, through which the sun shone coldly yellow when Bran came to Dagon's Barrow, a round hillock overgrown with rank grass of a curious fungoid appearance. On the eastern side of the mound showed the entrance of a crudely built stone tunnel which evidently penetrated the barrow. One great stone blocked the entrance to the tomb. Bran laid hold of the sharp edges and exerted all his strength. It held fast. He drew his sword and worked the blade between the blocking stone and the sill. Using the sword as a lever, he worked carefully, and managed to loosen the great stone and wrench it out. A foul charnel-house scent flowed out of the aperture, and the dim sunlight seemed less to illuminate the cavern-like opening than to be fouled by the rank darkness which clung there.

Sword in hand, ready for he knew not what, Bran groped his way into the tunnel, which was long and narrow, built up of heavy joined stones, and was too low for him to stand erect. Either his eyes became somewhat accustomed to the gloom, or the darkness was, after all, somewhat lightened by the sunlight filtering in through the entrance. At any rate, he came into a round, low chamber and was able to make out its general dome-like outline. Here, no doubt, in old times, had reposed the bones of him for whom the stones of the tomb had been joined and the earth heaped high above them; but now of those bones no vestige remained on the stone floor. And bending close and straining his eyes, Bran made out the strange, startlingly regular pattern of that floor: six well-cut slabs clustered about a seventh, six-sided stone.

He drove his sword-point into a crack and pried carefully. The edge of the central stone tilted slightly upward. A little work and he lifted it out and leaned it against the curving wall. Straining his eyes downward he saw only the gaping blackness of a dark well, with small, worn steps that led downward and out of sight. He did not hesitate. Though the skin between his shoulders crawled curiously, he swung himself into the abyss and felt the clinging blackness swallow him.

Groping downward, he felt his feet slip and stumble on steps too small for human feet. With one hand pressed hard against the side of the well he steadied himself, fearing a fall into unknown and unlighted depths. The steps were cut into solid rock, yet they were greatly worn away. The farther he progressed, the less like steps they became, mere bumps of worn stone. Then the direction of the shaft changed sharply. It still led down, but at a shallow slant down which he could walk, elbows braced against the hollowed sides, head bent low beneath the curved roof. The steps had ceased altogether and the stone felt slimy to the touch, like a serpent's lair. What beings, Bran wondered, had slithered up and down this slanting shaft, for how many centuries?

The tunnel narrowed until Bran found it rather difficult to shove through. He lay on his back and pushed himself along with his hands, feet first. Still he knew he was sinking deeper and deeper into the very guts of the earth; how far below the surface he was, he dared not contemplate. Then ahead a faint witch-fire gleam tinged the abysmal blackness. He grinned savagely and without mirth. If They he sought came suddenly upon him, how could he fight in that narrow shaft? But he had put the thought of personal fear behind him when he began this hellish quest. He crawled on, thoughtless of all else but his goal.

And he came at last into a vast space where he could stand upright. He could not see the roof of the place, but he got an impression of dizzying vastness. The blackness pressed in on all sides, and behind him he could see the entrance to the shaft from which he had just emerged—a black well in the darkness. But in front of him a strange grisly radiance glowed about a grim altar built of human skulls. The source of that light he could not determine, but on the altar lay a sullen, night-black object—the Black Stone!

Bran wasted no time in giving thanks that the guardians of the grim relic were nowhere near. He caught up the Stone, and gripping it under his left arm, crawled into the shaft. When a man turns his back on peril, its clammy menace looms more grisly than when he advances upon it. So Bran, crawling back up the nighted shaft with his grisly prize, felt the darkness turn on him and slink behind him, grinning with dripping fangs. Clammy sweat beaded his flesh and he hastened to the best of his ability, ears strained for some stealthy sound to betray that fell shapes were at his heels. Strong shudders shook him, despite himself, and the short hair on his neck prickled as if a cold wind blew at his back.

When he reached the first of the tiny steps he felt

as if he had attained to the outer boundaries of the mortal world. Up them he went, stumbling and slipping, and with a deep gasp of relief, came out into the tomb, whose spectral grayness seemed like the blaze of noon in comparison to the stygian depths he had just traversed. He replaced the central stone and strode into light of the outer day, and never was the cold yellow light of the sun more grateful, as it dispelled the shadows of black-winged nightmares of fear and madness that seemed to have ridden him up out of the black deeps. He shoved the great blocking stone back into place, and picking up the cloak he had left at the mouth of the tomb, he wrapped it about the Black Stone and hurried away, a strong revulsion and loathing shaking his soul and lending wings to his strides.

A gray silence brooded over the land. It was desolate as the blind side of the moon; yet Bran felt the potentialities of life—under his feet, in the brown earth—sleeping, but how soon to waken, and in what horrific fashion?

He came through the tall, masking reeds to the still deep mere called Dagon's Mere. No slightest ripple ruffled the cold blue water to give evidence of the grisly monster legend said dwelt beneath. Bran closely scanned the breathless landscape. He saw no hint of life, human or unhuman. He sought the instincts of his savage soul to know if any unseen eyes fixed their lethal gaze upon him, and found no response. He was alone as if he were the last man on earth.

Swiftly he unwrapped the Black Stone, and as it lay in his hands like a solid, sullen block of darkness, he did not seek to learn the secret of its material nor scan the cryptic characters carved thereon. Weighing it in his hands and calculating the distance, he flung it far out, so that it fell almost exactly in the middle of the lake. A sullen splash and the waters closed over it. There was a moment of shimmering flashes on the bosom of the lake; then the blue surface stretched placid and unrippled again.

5

The were-woman turned swiftly as Bran approached her door. Her slant-eyes widened.

"You! And alive! And sane!"

"I have been into Hell and I have returned," he growled. "What is more, I have that which I sought."

"The Black Stone?" she cried. "You really dared steal it? Where is it?"

"No matter; but last night my stallion screamed in his stall and I heard something crunch beneath his thundering hoofs which was not the wall of the stable—and there was blood on his hoofs when I came to see, and blood on the floor of the stall. And I have heard stealthy sounds in the night, and noises beneath my dirt floor, as if worms burrowed deep in the earth. They know I have stolen their Stone. Have you betrayed me?"

She shook her head.

"I keep your secret; they do not need my word to know you. The farther they have retreated from the world of men, the greater have grown their powers in other uncanny ways. Some dawn your hut will stand empty, and if men dare investigate they will find nothing—except crumbling bits of earth on the dirt floor."

Bran smiled terribly.

"I have not planned and toiled thus far to fall prey to the talons of vermin. If They strike me down in the night, They will never know what became of their idol—or whatever it be to Them. I would speak with Them."

"Dare you come with me and meet Them in the night?" she asked.

"Thunder of all gods!" he snarled. "Who are you to ask me if I dare? Lead me to Them and let me bargain for a vengeance this night. The hour of retribution draws nigh. This day I saw silvered helmets and bright shields gleam across the fens—the new commander has arrived at the Tower of Trajan and Caius Camillus has marched to the Wall."

That night the king went across the dark desolation of the moors with the silent were-woman. The night was thick and still as if the land lay in ancient slumber. The stars blinked vaguely, mere points of red struggling through the unbreathing gloom. Their gleam was dimmer than the glitter in the eyes of the woman who glided beside the king. Strange thoughts shook Bran, vague, titanic, primeval. Tonight ancestral linkings with these slumbering fens stirred in his soul and troubled him with the fantasmal, eon-veiled shapes of monstrous dreams. The vast age of his race was borne upon him; where now he walked an outlaw and an alien, dark-eyed kings in whose mold he was cast had reigned in old times. The Celtic and Roman invaders were as strangers to this ancient isle beside his people. Yet his race likewise had been invaders, and there was an older race than his—a race whose beginnings lay lost and hidden back beyond the dark oblivion of antiquity.

Ahead of them loomed a low range of hills, which formed the easternmost extremity of those straying chains which far away climbed at last to the mountains of Wales. The woman led the way up what might have been a sheep-path, and halted before a wide, black, gaping cave.

"A door to those you seek, O king!" her laughter rang hateful in the gloom. "Dare ye enter?"

His fingers closed in her tangled locks and he shook her viciously.

"Ask me but once more if I dare," he grated, "and your head and shoulders part company! Lead on."

Her laughter was like sweet deadly venom. They passed into the cave and Bran struck flint and steel. The flicker of the tinder showed him a wide, dusty cavern, on the roof of which hung clusters of bats. Lighting a torch, he lifted it and scanned the shadowy recesses, seeing nothing but dust and emptiness.

"Where are They?" he growled.

She beckoned him to the back of the cave and leaned against the rough wall, as if casually. But the king's keen eyes caught the motion of her hand pressing hard against a projecting ledge. He recoiled as a round black well gaped suddenly at his feet. Again her laughter slashed him like a keen silver knife. He held the torch to the opening and again saw small worn steps leading down.

"They do not need those steps," said Atla. "Once they did, before your people drove them into the darkness. But you will need them."

She thrust the torch into a niche above the well; it shed a faint red light into the darkness below. She gestured into the well and Bran loosened his sword and stepped into the shaft. As he went down into the mystery of the darkness, the light was blotted out above him, and he thought for an instant Atla had covered the opening again. Then he realized that she was descending after him.

The descent was not a long one. Abruptly Bran felt his feet on a solid floor. Atla swung down beside him and stood in the dim circle of light. Bran could not see the limits of the place into which he had come.

"Many caves in these hills," said Atla, her voice sounding small and strangely brittle in the vastness, "are but doors to greater caves which lie beneath, even as a man's words and deeds are but small indications of the dark caverns of murky thought lying behind and beneath."

And now Bran was aware of movement in the gloom. The darkness was filled with stealthy noises not like those made by any human foot. Abruptly sparks began to flash and float in the blackness, like flickering fireflies. Closer they came until they girdled him in a wide half-moon. And beyond the ring gleamed other sparks, a solid sea of them, fading a way in the gloom until the farthest were mere tiny pinpoints of light. And Bran knew they were the slanted eyes of the beings who had come upon him in such numbers that his brain reeled at the contemplation—and at the vastness of the cavern.

Now that he faced his ancient foes, Bran knew no fear. He felt the waves of terrible menace emanating from them, the grisly hate, the inhuman threat to body, mind and soul. More than a member of a less ancient race, he realized the horror of his position, but he did not fear, though he confronted the ultimate Horror of the dreams and legends of his race. His blood raced fiercely, but it was with the hot excitement of the hazard, not the drive of terror.

"They know you have the Stone, O king," said Atla, and though he knew she feared, though he felt her physical efforts to control her trembling limbs, there was no quiver of fright in her voice. "You are in deadly peril; they know your breed of old—oh, they remember the days when their ancestors were men! I cannot save you; both of us will die as no human has died for ten centuries. Speak to them, if you will; they can understand your speech, though you may not understand theirs. But it will avail not—you are human—and a Pict."

Bran laughed, and the closing ring of fire shrank back at the savagery in his laughter. Drawing his sword with a soul-chilling rasp of steel, he set his back against what he hoped was a solid stone wall.

Facing the glittering eyes with his sword gripped in his right hand and his dirk in his left, he laughed as a blood-hungry wolf snarls.

"Aye," he growled, "I am a Pict, a son of those warriors who drove your brutish ancestors before them like chaff before the storm!—who flooded the land with your blood and heaped high your skulls for a sacrifice to the Moon-Woman! You who fled of old before my race, dare ye now snarl at your master? Roll on me like a flood, now, if ye dare! Before your viper fangs drink my life I will reap your multitudes like ripened barley—of your severed heads will I build a tower and of your mangled corpses will I rear up a wall! Dogs of the dark, vermin of Hell, worms of the earth, rush in and try my steel! When Death finds me in this dark cavern, your living will howl for the scores of your dead and your Black Stone will be lost to you forever—for only I know where it is hidden, and not all the tortures of all the Hells can wring the secret from my lips!"

Then followed a tense silence; Bran faced the firelit darkness, tensed like a wolf at bay, waiting the charge; at his side the woman cowered, her eyes ablaze. Then from the silent ring that hovered beyond the dim torchlight rose a vague abhorrent murmur. Bran, prepared as he was for anything, started. Gods, was *that* the speech of creatures which had once been called men?

Atla straightened, listening intently. From her lips came the same hideous soft sibilances, and Bran, though he had already known the grisly secret of her being, knew that never again could he touch her save with soul-shaken loathing.

She turned to him, a strange smile curving her red lips dimly in the ghostly light.

"They fear you, O king! By the black secrets of R'lyeh, who are you that Hell itself quails before you? Not your steel, but the stark ferocity of your soul has driven unused fear into their strange minds. They will buy back the Black Stone at any price."

"Good," Bran sheathed his weapons. "They shall promise not to molest you because of your aid of me. And," his voice hummed like the purr of a hunting tiger, "They shall deliver into my hands Titus Sulla, governor of Eboracum, now commanding the Tower of Trajan. This They can do—how, I know not. But I know that in the old days, when my people warred with these Children of the Night, babes disappeared from guarded huts and none saw the stealers come or go. Do They understand?"

Again rose the low frightful sounds, and Bran, who feared not their wrath, shuddered at their voices.

"They understand," said Atla. "Bring the Black Stone to Dagon's Ring tomorrow night when the earth is veiled with the blackness that foreruns the dawn. Lay the Stone on the altar. There They will bring Titus Sulla to you. Trust Them; They have not interfered in human affairs for many centuries, but They will keep their word."

Bran nodded and, turning, climbed up the stairs with Atla close behind him. At the top he turned and looked down once more. As far as he could see floated a glittering ocean of slanted yellow eyes upturned. But the owners of those eyes kept carefully beyond the dim circle of torchlight and of their bodies he could see nothing. Their low hissing speech floated up to him, and he shuddered as his imagination visualized, not a throng of biped creatures, but a swarming, swaying myriad of serpents, gazing up at him with their glittering, unwinking eyes.

He swung into the upper cave and Atla thrust the blocking stone back in place. It fitted into the entrance of the well with uncanny precision; Bran was unable to discern any crack in the apparently solid floor of the cavern. Atla made a motion to extinguish the torch but the king stayed her.

"Keep it so until we are out of the cave," he grunted. "We might tread on an adder in the dark."

Atla's sweetly hateful laughter rose maddeningly in the flickering gloom.

6

It was not long before sunset when Bran came again to the reed-grown marge of Dagon's Mere. Casting cloak and sword-belt on the ground, he stripped himself of his short leathern breeches. Then gripping his naked dirk in his teeth, he went into the water with the smooth ease of a diving seal. Swimming strongly, he gained the center of the small lake, and turning, drove himself downward.

The mere was deeper than he had thought. It seemed he would never reach the bottom, and when he did, his groping hands failed to find what he sought. A roaring in his ears warned him, and he swarm to the surface.

Gulping deep of the refreshing air, he dived again, and again his quest was fruitless. A third time he sought the depth, and this time his groping hands met a familiar object in the silt of the bottom. Grasping it, he swarm up to the surface.

The Stone was not particularly bulky, but it was heavy. He swarm leisurely, and suddenly was aware of a curious stir in the waters about him which was not caused by his own exertions. Thrusting his face below the surface, he tried to pierce the blue depths with his eyes and thought to see a dim, gigantic shadow hovering there.

He swarm faster, not frightened, but wary. His feet struck the shallows and he waded up on the shelving shore. Looking back he saw the waters swirl and subside. He shook his head, swearing. He had discounted the ancient legend which made Dagon's Mere the lair of a nameless water-monster, but now he had a feeling as if his escape had been narrow. The time-worn myths of the ancient land were taking form and coming to life before his eyes. What primeval shape lurked below the surface of that treacherous mere, Bran could not guess, but he felt that the fenmen had good reason for shunning the spot, after all.

Bran donned his garments, mounted the black stallion and rode across the fens in the desolate crimson of the sunset's afterglow, with the Black Stone wrapped in his cloak. He rode, not to his hut, but to the west, in the direction of the Tower of Trajan and the Ring of Dagon. As he covered the miles that lay between, the red stars winked out. Midnight passed him in the moonless night and still Bran rode on. His heart was hot for his meeting with Titus Sulla. Atla had gloated over the anticipation of watching the Roman writhe under torture, but no such thought was in the Pict's mind. The governor should have his chance with weapons—with Bran's own sword he should face the Pictish king's dirk, and live or die according to his prowess. And though Sulla was famed throughout the provinces as a swordsman, Bran felt no doubt as to the outcome.

Dagon's Ring lay some distance from the Tower—a sullen circle of tall, gaunt stones planted upright, with a rough-hewn stone altar in the center. The Romans looked on these menhirs with aversion; they thought the Druids had reared them; but the Celts supposed Bran's people, the Picts, had planted them— and Bran well knew what hands reared those grim monoliths in lost ages, though for what reasons, he but dimly guessed.

The king did not ride straight to the Ring. He was consumed with curiosity as to how his grim allies intended carrying out their promise. That They could snatch Titus Sulla from the very midst of his men, he felt sure, and he believed he knew how They would do it. He felt the gnawings of a strange misgiving, as if he had tampered with powers of unknown breadth and depth, and had loosed forces which he could not control. Each time he remembered that reptilian murmur, those slanted eyes of the night before, a cold breath passed over him. They had been abhorrent enough when his people drove Them into the caverns under the hills, ages ago; what had long centuries of retrogression made of Them? In their nighted, subterranean life, had They retained any of the attributes of humanity at all?

Some instinct prompted him to ride toward the Tower. He knew he was near; but for thick darkness he could have plainly seen its stark outline tusking the horizon. Even now he should be able to make it out dimly. An obscure, shuddery premonition shook him, and he spurred the stallion into swift canter.

And suddenly Bran staggered in his saddle as from a physical impact, so stunning was the surprise of what met his gaze. The impregnable Tower of Trajan was no more! Bran's astounded gaze rested on a gigantic pile of ruins—of shattered stone and crumbled granite, from which jutted the jagged and splintered ends of broken beams. At one corner of the tumbled heap one tower rose out of the waste of crumpled masonry, and it leaned drunkenly as if its foundations had been half cut away.

Bran dismounted and walked forward, dazed by bewilderment. The moat was filled in places by fallen stones and brown pieces of mortared wall. He crossed over and came among the ruins. Where, he knew, only a few hours before the flags had resounded to the martial tramp of iron-clad feet, and the walls had echoed to the clang of shields and the blast of loud-throated trumpets, a horrific silence reigned.

Almost under Bran's feet, a broken shape writhed and groaned. The king bent down to the legionary, who lay in a sticky red pool of his own blood. A single glance showed the Pict that the man, horribly crushed and shattered, was dying.

Lifting the bloody head, Bran placed his flask to the pulped lips, and the Roman instinctively drank deep, gulping through splintered teeth. In the dim starlight Bran saw his glazed eyes roll.

"The walls fell," muttered the dying man. "They crashed down like the skies falling on the day of doom. Ah Jove, the skies rained shards of granite and hailstones of marble!"

"I have felt no earthquake shock," Bran scowled, puzzled.

"It was no earthquake," muttered the Roman. "Before last dawn it began, the faint dim scratching and clawing far below the earth. We of the guard heard it—like rats burrowing, or like worms hollowing out the earth. Titus laughed at us, but all day long we heard it. Then at midnight the Tower quivered and seemed to settle—as if the foundations were being dug away—"

A shudder shook Bran Mak Morn. The worms of the earth! Thousands of vermin digging like moles far below the castle, burrowing away the foundations—gods, the land must be honeycombed with tunnels and caverns—these creatures were even less human than he had thought—what ghastly shapes of darkness had he invoked to his aid?

"What of Titus Sulla?" he asked, again holding the flask to the legionary's lips; in that moment the dying Roman seemed to him almost like a brother.

"Even as the Tower shuddered we heard a fearful scream from the governor's chamber," muttered the soldier. "We rushed there—as we broke down the door we heard his shrieks—they seemed to recede—*into the bowels of the earth!* We rushed in; the chamber was empty. His blood-stained sword lay on the floor; in the stone flags of the floor a black hole gaped. Then—the—towers—reeled—the—roof—broke;—through—a—storm—of—crashing—walls—I crawled."

A strong convulsion shook the broken figure.

"Lay me down," whispered the Roman. "I die."

He had ceased to breathe before Bran could comply. The Pict rose, mechanically cleansing his hands. He hastened from the spot, and as he galloped over the darkened fens, the weight of the accursed Black Stone under his cloak was as the weight of a foul nightmare on a mortal breast.

As he approached the Ring, he saw an eery glow within, so that the gaunt stones stood etched like the ribs of a skeleton in which a witch-fire burns. The stallions snorted and reared as Bran tied him to one of the menhirs. Carrying the Stone he strode into the grisly circle and saw Atla standing beside the altar, one hand on her hips, her sinuous body swaying in a serpentine manner. The altar glowed all over with ghastly light, and Bran knew someone, probably Atla, had rubbed it with phosphorus from some dank swamp or quagmire.

He strode forward and, whipping his cloak from about the Stone, flung the accursed thing onto the altar.

"I have fulfilled my part of the contract," he growled.

"And They theirs," she retorted. "Look!—They come!"

He wheeled, his hand instinctivley dropping to his sword. Outside the Ring the great stallion screamed savagely and reared against his tether. The night wind moaned through the waving grass and an abhorrent soft hissing mingled with it. Between the menhirs flowed a dark tide of shadows, unstable and chaotic. The Ring filled with glittering eyes which hovered beyond the dim, illusive circle of illumination cast by the phosphorescent altar. Somewhere in the darkness a human voice tittered and gibbered idiotically. Bran stiffened, the shadows of a horror clawing at his soul.

He strained his eyes, trying to make out the shapes of those who ringed him. But he glimpsed only billowing masses of shadow which heaved and writhed and squirmed with almost fluid consistency.

"Let them make good their bargain!" he exclaimed angrily.

"Then see, O king!" cried Atla in a voice of piercing mockery.

There was a stir, a seething in the writing shadows, and from the darkness crept, like a four-legged animal, a human shape that fell down and groveled at Bran's feet and writhed and mowed, and lifting a death's-head, howled like a dying dog. In the ghastly light, Bran, soul-shaken, saw the blank glassy eyes, the bloodless features, the loose, writhing, froth-covered lips of sheer lunacy—gods, was this Titus Sulla, the proud lord of life and death in Eboracum's proud city?

Bran bared his sword.

"I had thought to give this stroke in vengeance," he said somberly. "I give it in mercy—*Vale Caesar!*"

The steel flashed in the eery light and Sulla's head rolled to the foot of the glowing altar, where it lay staring up at the shadowed sky.

"They harmed him not!" Atla's hateful laugh slashed the sick silence. "It was what he saw and came to know that broke his brain! Like all his heavy-footed race, he knew nothing of the secrets of this ancient land. This night he has been dragged through the deepest pits of Hell, where even you might have blenched!"

"Well for the Romans that they know not the secrets of this accursed land!" Bran roared, maddened, "with its monster-haunted meres, its foul witch-women, and its lost caverns and subterranean realms where spawn in the darkness shapes of Hell!"

"Are they more foul than a mortal who seeks their aid?" cried Atla with a shriek of fearful mirth. "Give them their Black Stone!"

A cataclysmic loathing shook Bran's soul with red fury.

"Aye, take your cursed Stone!" he roared, snatching it from the altar and dashing it among the shadows with such savagery that bones snapped under its impact. A hurried babble of grisly tongues rose and the shadows heaved in turmoil. One segment of the mass detached itself for an instant, and Bran cried out in fierce revulsion, though he caught only a fleeting glimpse of the thing, had only a brief impression of a broad, strangely flattened head, pendulous writhing lips that bared curved, pointed fangs, and a hideously misshapen, dwarfish body that seemed—*mottled*—all set off by those unwinking reptilian eyes. Gods!—the myths had prepared him for horror in human aspect, horror induced by bestial visage and stunted deformity—but this was the horror of nightmare and the night.

"Go back to Hell and take your idol with you!" he yelled, brandishing his clenched fists to the skies, as the thick shadows receded, flowing back and away from him like the foul waters of some black flood. "Your ancestors were men, though strange and monstrous—but gods, ye have become in ghastly fact what my people called ye in scorn!

"Worms of the earth, back into your holes and burrows! Ye foul the air and leave on the clean earth the slime of the serpents ye have become! Gonar was right—there are shapes too foul to use even against Rome!"

He sprang from the Ring as a man flees the touch of a coiling snake, and tore the stallion free. At his elbow Atla was shrieking with fearful laughter, all human attributes dropped from her like a cloak in the night.

"King of Pictland!" she cried. "King of fools! Do you blench at so small a thing? Stay and let me show you real fruits of the pits! Ha! ha! ha! Run, fool, run! But you are stained with the taint—you have called them forth and they will remember! And in their own time they will come to you again!"

He yelled a wordless curse and struck her savagely in the mouth with his open hand. She staggered, blood starting from her lips, but her fiendish laughter only rose higher.

Bran leaped into the saddle, wild for the clean heather and the cold blue hills of the north where he could plunge his sword into clean slaughter and his sickened soul into the red maelstrom of battle, and forget the horror which lurked below the fens of the west. He gave the frantic stallion the rein, and rode through the night like a hunted ghost, until the hellish laughter of the howling were-woman died out in the darkness behind.

PIGEONS FROM HELL

1. The Whistler in the Dark

GRISWELL AWOKE suddenly, every nerve tingling with a premonition of imminent peril. He stared about wildly, unable at first to remember where he was, or what he was doing there. Moonlight filtered in through the dusty windows, and the great empty room with its lofty ceiling and gaping black fireplace was spectral and unfamiliar. Then as he emerged from the clinging cobwebs of his recent sleep, he remembered where he was and how he came to be there. He twisted his head and stared at his companion, sleeping on the floor near him. John Branner was but a vaguely bulking shape in the darkness that the moon scarcely grayed.

Griswell tried to remember what had awakened him. There was no sound in the house, no sound outside except the mournful hoot of an owl, far away in the piny woods. Now he had captured the elusive memory. It was a dream, a nightmare so filled with dim terror that it had frightened him awake. Recollection flooded back, vividly etching the abominable vision.

Or was it a dream? Certainly it must have been,

but it had blended so curiously with recent actual events that it was difficult to know where reality left off and fantasy began.

Dreaming, he had seemed to relive his past few waking hours, in accurate detail. The dream had begun, abruptly, as he and John Banner came in sight of the house where they now lay. They had come rattling and bouncing over the stumpy, uneven old road that led through the pinelands, he and John Branner, wandering far afield from their New England home, in search of vacation pleasure. They had sighted the old house with its balustraded galleries rising amidst a wilderness of weeds and bushes, just as the sun was setting behind it. It dominated their fancy, rearing black and stark and gaunt against the low lurid rampart of sunset, barred by the black pines.

They were tired, sick of bumping and pounding all day over woodland roads. The old deserted house stimulated their imagination with its suggestion of antebellum splendor and ultimate decay. They left the automobile beside the rutty road, and as they went up the winding walk of crumbling bricks, almost lost in the tangle of rank growth, pigeons rose from the balustrades in a fluttering, feathery crowd and swept away with a low thunder of beating wings.

The oaken door sagged on broken hinges. Dust lay thick on the floor of the wide, dim hallway, on the broad steps of the stair that mounted up from the hall. They turned into a door opposite the landing, and entered a large room, empty, dusty, with cobwebs shining thickly in the corners. Dust lay thick over the ashes in the great fireplace.

They discussed gathering wood and building a fire, but decided against it. As the sun sank, darkness came quickly, the thick, black, absolute darkness of the pinelands. They knew that rattlesnakes and copperheads haunted Southern forests, and they did not care to go groping for firewood in the dark. They ate frugally from tins, then rolled in their blankets fully clad before the empty fireplace, and went instantly to sleep.

This, in part, was what Griswell had dreamed. He saw again the gaunt house looming stark against the crimson sunset; saw the flight of the pigeons as he and Branner came up the shattered walk. He saw the dim room in which they presently lay, and he saw the two forms that were himself and his companion, lying wrapped in their blankets on the dusty floor. Then from that point his dream altered subtly, passed out of the realm of the commonplace and became tinged with fear. He was looking into a vague, shadowy chamber, lit by the gray light of the moon which streamed in from some obscure source. For there was no window in that room. But in the gray light he saw three silent shapes that hung suspended in a row, and their stillness and their outlines woke chill horror in his soul. There was no sound, no word, but he sensed a Presence of fear and lunacy crouching in a dark corner . . . Abruptly he was back in the dusty, high-ceilinged room, before the great fireplace.

He was lying in his blankets, staring tensely through the dim door and across the shadowy hall, to where a beam of moonlight fell across the balustraded stair, some seven steps up from the landing. And there was something on the stair, a bent, misshapen, shadowy thing that never moved fully into the beam of light. But a dim yellow blur that might have been a face was turned toward him, as if *something* crouched on the stair, regarding him and his companion. Fright crept chilly through his veins, and it was then that he awoke—if indeed he had been asleep.

He blinked his eyes. The beam of moonlight fell across the stair just as he had dreamed it did; but no figure lurked there. Yet his flesh still crawled from the fear the dream or vision had roused in him; his legs felt as if they had been plunged in ice-water. He made an involuntary movement to awaken his companion, when a sound paralyzed him.

It was the sound of whistling on the floor above. Eery and sweet it rose, not carrying any tune, but piping shrill and melodious. Such a sound in a supposedly deserted house was alarming enough; but it was more than the fear of a physical invader that held Griswell frozen. He could not himself have defined the horror that gripped him. But Branner's blankets rustled, and Griswell saw he was sitting upright. His figure bulked dimly in the soft darkness, the head turned toward the stair as if the man were listening intently. More sweetly and more subtly evil rose that weird whistling.

"John!" whispered Griswell from dry lips. He had meant to shout—to tell Branner that there was somebody upstairs, somebody who could mean them no good; that they must leave the house at once. But his voice died dryly in his throat.

Branner had risen. His boots clumped on the floor as he moved toward the door. He stalked leisurely into the hall and made for the lower landing, merging with the shadows that clustered black about the stair.

Griswell lay incapable of movement, his mind a whirl of bewilderment. Who was that whistling upstairs? Griswell saw him pass the spot where the moonlight rested, saw his head tilted back as if he were looking at something Griswell could not see, above and beyond the stair. But his face was like that of a sleep-walker. He moved across the bar of moonlight and vanished from Griswell's view, even as the latter tried to shout to him to come back. A ghastly whisper was the only result of his effort.

The whistling sank to a lower note, died out. Griswell heard the stairs creaking under Branner's measured tread. Now he had reached the hallway above, for Griswell heard the clump of his feet moving along it. Suddenly the footfalls halted, and the whole night seemed to hold its breath. Then an awful scream split the stillness, and Griswell started up, echoing the cry.

The strange paralysis that had held him was broken. He took a step toward the door, then checked himself. The footfalls were resumed. Branner was coming back. He was not running. The tread was even more deliberate and measured than before. Now the stairs began to creak again. A groping hand, moving along the balustrade, came into the bar of moonlight; then another, and a ghastly thrill went through Griswell as he saw that the other hand gripped a hatchet—a hatchet which dripped blackly. *Was* that Branner who was coming down that stair?

Yes! The figure had moved into the bar of moonlight now, and Griswell recognized it. Then he saw Branner's face, and a shriek burst from Griswell's lips. Branner's face was bloodless, corpse-like; gouts of blood dripped darkly down it; his eyes were glassy and set, and blood oozed from the great gash *which cleft the crown of his head!*

Griswell never remembered exactly how he got out of that accursed house. Afterward he retained a mad, confused impression of smashing his way through a dusty cobwebbed window, of stumbling blindly across the weed-choked lawn, gibbering his frantic horror. He saw the black wall of the pines, and the moon floating in a blood-red mist in which there was neither sanity nor reason.

Some shred of sanity returned to him as he saw the automobile beside the road. In a world gone suddenly mad, that was an object reflecting prosaic reality; but even as he reached for the door, a dry chilling whir sounded in his ears, and he recoiled from the swaying undulating shape that arched up from its scaly coils on the driver's seat and hissed sibilantly at him, darting a forked tongue in the moonlight.

Wtih a sob of horror he turned and fled down the road, as a man runs in a nightmare. He ran without purpose or reason. His numbed brain was incapable of conscious thought. He merely obeyed the blind primitive urge to run—run—until he fell exhausted.

The black walls of the pines flowed endlessly past him; so he was seized with the illusion that he was getting nowhere. But presently a sound penetrated the fog of his terror—the steady, inexorable patter of feet behind him. Turning his head, he saw *something* loping after him—wolf or dog, he could not tell which, but its eyes glowed like balls of green fire. With a gasp he increased his speed, reeled around a bend in the road, and heard a horse snort; saw it rear and heard its rider curse; saw the gleam of blue steel in the man's lifted hand.

He staggered and fell, catching at the rider's stirrup.

"For God's sake, help me!" he panted. "The thing! It killed Branner—it's coming after me! *Look!*"

Twin balls of fire gleamed in the fringe of bushes at the turn of the road. The rider swore again, and on the heels of his profanity came the smashing report of his six-shooter—again and yet again. The fire-sparks vanished, and the rider, jerking his stirrup free from Griswell's grasp spurred his horse at the bend. Griswell staggered up, shaking in every limb. The rider was out of sight only a moment; then he came galloping back.

"Took to the brush. Timber wolf, I reckon, though I never heard of one chasin' a man before. Do you know what it was?"

Griswell could only shake his head weakly.

The rider, etched in the moonlight, looked down at him, smoking pistol still lifted in his right hand. He was a compactly-built man of medium height, and his broad-brimmed planter's hat and his boots marked him as a native of the country as definitely as Griswell's garb stamped him as a stranger.

"What's all this about, anyway?"

"I don't know," Griswell answered helplessly. "My name's Griswell, John Branner—my friend who was travelling with me—we stopped at a deserted house back down the road to spend the night. Something——" at the memory he was choked by a rush of horror. "My God!" he screamed. 'I must be mad! *Something* came and looked over the balustrade of the stair—something with a yellow face! I thought I dreamed it, but it must have been real. Then somebody began whistling upstairs, and Branner rose and went up the stairs walking like a man in his sleep, or hypnotized. I heard him scream—or someone screamed; then he came down the stair again with a bloody hatchet in his hand—and my God, sir he was *dead!* His head had been split open. I saw his brains and clotted blood oozing down his face, and his face was that of a dead man. *But he came down the stair!* As God is my witness, John Branner was murdered in that dark upper hallway, and then his dead body came stalking down the stairs with a hatchet in its hand—to kill me!"

The rider made no reply; he sat his horse like a statue, outlined against the stars, and Griswell could not read his expression, his face shadowed by his hat-brim.

"You think I'm mad," he said hopelessly. "Perhaps I am."

"I don't know what to think," answered the rider. "If it was any house but the old Blassenville Manor— well, we'll see. My name's Buckner. I'm sheriff of this county. Took a nigger over to the county-seat in the next county and was ridin' back late."

He swung off his horse and stood beside Griswell, shorter than the lanky New Englander, but much harder knit. There was a natural manner of decision and certainty about him, and it was easy to believe that he would be a dangerous man in any sort of a fight.

"Are you afraid to go back to the house?" he asked, and Griswell shuddered, but shook his head, the dogged tenacity of Puritan ancestors asserting itself.

"The thought of facing that horror again turns me sick. But poor Branner—" he choked again. "We must find his body. My God!" he cried, unmanned by the abysmal horror of the thing; "*what* will we find? If a dead man walks, what——"

"We'll see." The sheriff caught the reins in the crook of his left elbow and began filling the empty chambers of his big blue pistol as they walked along.

As they made the turn Griswell's blood was ice at the thought of what they might see lumbering up the road with bloody, grinning death-mask, but they saw only the house looming spectrally among the pines, down the road. A strong shudder shook Griswell.

"God, how *evil* that house looks, against those black pines! It looked sinister from the very first— when he went up the broken walk and saw those pigeons fly up from the porch——"

"Pigeons?" Buckner cast him a quick glance. "You saw the pigeons?"

"Why, yes! Scores of them perching on the porch railing."

They strode on for a moment in silence, before Buckner said abruptly: "I've lived in this country all my life. I've passed the old Blassenville place a thousand times, I reckon, at all hours of the day and night. But I never saw a pigeon anywhere around it, or anywhere else in these woods."

"There were scores of them," repeated Griswell, bewildered.

"I've seen men who swore they'd seen a flock of pigeons perched along the balusters just at sundown," said Buckner slowly. "Niggers, all of them except one man. A tramp. He was buildin' a fire in the yard, aimin' to camp there that night. I passed along there about dark, and he told me about the pigeons. I came back by there the next mornin'. The ashes of his fire were there, and his tin cup, and skillet where he'd fried pork, and his blankets looked like they'd been slept in. Nobody ever saw him again. That was twelve years ago. The niggers say they can see the pigeons, but no nigger would pass along this road between sun-down and sun-up. They say the pigeons are the souls of the Blassenvilles, let out of hell at sunset. The niggers say the red glare in the west is the light from hell, because then the gates of hell are open, and the Blassenvilles fly out."

"Who were the Blassenvilles?" asked Griswell, shivering.

"They owned all this land here. French-English family. Came here from the West Indies before the Louisiana Purchase. The Civil War ruined them, like it did so many. Some were killed in the War; most of the others died out. Nobody's lived in the Manor since 1890 when Miss Elizabeth Blassenville, the last of the line, fled from the old house one night like it was a plague spot, and never came back to it—this your auto?"

They halted beside the car, and Griswell stared morbidly at the grim house. Its dusty panes were empty and blank; but they did not seem blind to him. It seemed to him that ghastly eyes were fixed hungrily on him through those darkened panes. Buckner repeated his question.

"Yes. Be careful. There's a snake on the seat—or there was."

"Not there now," grunted Buckner, tying his horse and pulling an electric torch out of the saddle-bag. "Well, let's have a look."

He strode up the broken brick-walk as matter-of-

factly as if he were paying a social call on friends.
Griswell followed close at his heels, his heart pounding suffocatingly. A scent of decay and moldering vegetation blew on the faint wind, and Griswell grew faint with nausea, that rose from a frantic abhorrence of these black woods, these ancient plantation houses that hid forgotten secrets of slavery and bloody pride and mysterious intrigues. He had thought of the South as a sunny, lazy land washed by soft breezes laden with spice and warm blossoms, where life ran tranquilly to the rhythm of black folk singing in sun-bathed cottonfields. But now he had discovered another, unsuspected side—a dark, brooding, fear-haunted side, and the discovery repelled him.

The oaken door sagged as it had before. The blackness of the interior was intensified by the beam of Buckner's light playing on the sill. That beam sliced through the darkness of the hallway and roved up the stair, and Griswell held his breath, clenching his fists. But no shape of lunacy leered down at them. Buckner went in, walking light as a cat, torch in one hand, gun in the other.

As he swung his light into the room across from the stairway, Griswell cried out—and cried out again, almost fainting with the intolerable sickness at what he saw. A trail of blood drops led across the floor, crossing the blankets Branner had occupied, which lay between the door and those in which Griswell had lain. And Griswell's blankets had a terrible occupant. John Branner lay there, face down, his cleft head revealed in merciless clarity in the steady light. His outstretched hand still gripped the haft of a hatchet, and the blade was imbedded deep in the blanket and the floor beneath, just where Griswell's head had lain when he slept there.

A momentary rush of blackness engulfed Griswell. He was not aware that he staggered, or that Buckner caught him. When he could see and hear again, he was violently sick and hung his head against the mantel, retching miserably.

Buckner turned the light full on him, making him blink. Buckner's voice came from behind the blinding radiance, the man himself unseen.

"Griswell, you've told me a yarn that's hard to believe. I saw something chasin' you, but it might have been a timber wolf, or a mad dog.

"If you're holdin' back anything, you better spill it. What you told me won't hold up in any court. You're bound to be accused of killin' your partner. I'll have to arrest you. If you'll give me the straight goods now, it'll make it easier. Now, didn't you kill this fellow, Branner?

"Wasn't it something like this: you quarreled, he grabbed a hatchet and swung at you, but you dodged and then let *him* have it?"

Griswell sank down and hid his face in his hands, his head swimming.

"Great God, man. I didn't murder John! Why, we've been friends ever since we were children in school together. I've told you the truth. I don't blame you for not believing me. But God help me, it is the truth!"

The light swung back to the gory head again, and Griswell closed his eyes.

He heard Buckner grunt.

"I believe this hatchet in his hand is the one he was killed with. Blood and brains plastered on the blade, and hairs stickin' to it—hairs exactly the same color as his. This makes it tough for you, Griswell."

"How so?" the New Englander asked dully.

"Knocks any plea of self-defense in the head. Branner couldn't have swung at you with this hatchet after you split his skull with it. You must have pulled the ax out of his head, stuck it into the floor and clamped his fingers on it to make it look like he'd attacked you. And it would have been damned clever—if you'd used another hatchet."

"But I didn't kill him," groaned Griswell. "I have no intention of pleading self-defense."

"That's what puzzles me," Buckner admitted frankly, straightening. "What murderer would rig up such a crazy story as you've told me, to prove his innocence? Average killer would have told a logical yarn, at least. Hmmm! Blood drops leadin' from the door. The body was dragged—no, couldn't have been dragged. The floor isn't smeared. You must have carried it here, after killin' him in some other place. But in that case, why isn't there any blood on your clothes? Of course you could have changed clothes and washed your hands. But the fellow hasn't been dead long."

"He walked downstairs and across the room," said Griswell hopelessly. "He came to kill me. I knew he was coming to kill me when I saw him lurching down the stair. He struck where I would have been, if I hadn't awakened. That window—I burst out at it. You see it's broken."

"I see. But if he walked then, why isn't he walkin' now?"

"I don't know! I'm too sick to think straight. I've been fearing that he'd rise up from the floor where he lies and come at me again. When I heard that wolf running up the road after me, I thought it was John chasing me—John, running through the night with his bloody ax and his bloody head, and his death-grin!"

His teeth chattered as he lived that horror over again.

Buckner let his light play across the floor.

"The blood drops lead into the hall. Come on. We'll follow them."

Griswell cringed. "They lead upstairs."

Buckner's eyes were fixed hard on him.

"Are you afraid to go upstairs, with me?"

Griswell's face was gray.

"Yes. But I'm going, with you or without you. The thing that killed poor John may still be hiding up there."

"Stay behind me," ordered Buckner. "If anything jumps us, I'll take care of it. But for your own sake, I warn you that I shoot quicker than a cat jumps, and I don't often miss. If you've got any ideas of layin' me out from behind, forget them."

"Don't be a fool!" Resentment got the better of his apprehension, and this outburst seemed to reassure Buckner more than any of his protestations of innocence.

"I want to be fair," he said quietly. "I haven't indicted and condemmned you in my mind already. If only half of what you're tellin' me is the truth, you've been through a hell of an experience and I don't want to be too hard on you. But you can see how hard it is for me to believe all you've told me."

Griswell wearily motioned for him to lead the way, unspeaking. They went out into the hall, paused at the landing. A thin string of crimson drops, distinct in the thick dust, led up the steps.

"Man's tracks in the dust," grunted Buckner. "Go slow. I've got to be sure of what I see, because we're obliteratin' them as we go up. Hmmm! One set goin' up, one comin' down. Same man. Not your tracks. Branner was a bigger man than you are. Blood drops all the way—blood on the bannisters like a man had laid his bloody hand there—a smear of stuff that looks—*brains*. Now what——"

"He walked down the stair, a dead man," shuddered Griswell. "Groping with one hand—the other gripping the hatchet that killed him."

"Or was carried," muttered the sheriff. "But if somebody carried him—*where are the tracks?*"

They came out into the upper hallway, a vast, empty space of dust and shadows where time-crusted windows repelled the moonlight and the ring of Buckner's torch seemed inadequate. Griswell trembled like a leaf. Here, in darkness and horror, John Branner had died.

"Somebody whistled up here," he muttered. "John came, as if he were being called."

Buckner's eyes were blazing strangely in the light.

"The footprints lead down the hall," he muttered. "Same as on the stair—one set going, one coming. Same prints—*Judas!*"

Behind him Griswell stifled a cry, for he had seen what prompted Buckner's exclamation. A few feet from the head of the stair Branner's footprints stopped abruptly, then returned, treading almost in the other tracks. And where the trail halted there was a great splash of blood on the dusty floor—and other tracks met it—tracks of bare feet, narrow but with splayed toes. They too receded in a second line from the spot.

Buckner bent over them, swearing.

"The tracks meet! And where they meet there's blood and brains on the floor! Branner must have been killed on that spot—with a blow from a hatchet. Bare feet coming out of the darkness to meet shod feet—then both turned away again; the shod feet went downstairs, the bare feet went back down the hall." He directed his light down the hall. The footprints faded into darkness, beyond the reach of the beam. On either hand the closed doors of chambers were cryptic portals of mystery.

"Suppose your crazy tale *was* true," Buckner muttered, half to himself. "These aren't your tracks. They look like a woman's. Suppose somebody did whistle, and Branner went upstairs to investigate. Suppose somebody met him here in the dark and split his head. The signs and tracks would have been, in that case, just as they really are. But if that's so, why isn't Branner lyin' here where he was killed? Could he have lived long enough to take the hatchet away from whoever killed him, and stagger downstairs with it?"

"No, no!" Recollection gagged Griswell. "I *saw* him on the stair. He was dead. No man could live a minute after receiving such a wound."

"I believe it," muttered Buckner. "But—it's madness! Or else it's *too* clever—yet, what sane man would think up and work out such an elaborate and utterly insane plan to escape punishment for murder, when a simple plea of self-defense would have been so much more effective? No court would recognize that story. Well, let's follow these other tracks. They lead down the hall—here, what's this?"

With an icy clutch at his soul, Griswell saw the light was beginning to grow dim.

"This battery is new," muttered Buckner, and for the first time Griswell caught an edge of fear in his voice. "Come on—out of here quick!"

The light had faded to a faint red glow. The darkness seemed straining into them, creeping with black cat-feet. Buckner retreated, pushing Griswell stumbling behind him as he walked backward, pistol cocked and lifted, down down the dark hall. In the growing darkness Griswell heard what sounded like the stealthy opening of a door. And suddenly the blackness about them was vibrant with menace. Griswell knew Buckner sensed it as well as he, for the sheriff's hard body was tense and taut as a stalking panther's.

But without haste he worked his way to the stair and backed down it, Griswell preceded him, and fighting the panic that urged him to scream and burst into mad flight. A ghastly thought brought icy sweat out of his flesh. *Suppose the dead man were creeping up the stair behind them in the dark, face frozen in the death-grin, blood-caked hatchet lifted to strike?*

This possibility so overpowered him that he was scarcely aware when his feet struck the level of the lower hallway, and he was only then aware that the light had grown brighter as they descended, until it now gleamed with its full power—but when Buckner turned it back up the stairway, it failed to illuminate the darkness that hung like a tangible fog at the head of the stair.

"The damn thing was conjured," muttered Buckner. "Nothin' else. It couldn't act like that naturally."

"Turn the light into the room," begged Griswell. "See if John—if John is——"

He could not put the ghastly thought into words, but Buckner understood.

He swung the beam around, and Griswell had never dreamed that the sight of the gory body of a murdered man could bring such relief.

"He's still there," grunted Buckner. "If he walked after he was killed, he hasn't walked since. But that thing——"

Again he turned the light up the stair, and stood chewing his lip and scowling. Three times he half lifted his gun. Griswell read his mind. The sheriff was tempted to plunge back up that stair, take his chance with the unknown. But common sense held him back.

"I wouldn't have a chance in the dark," he muttered. "And I've got a hunch the light would go out again."

He turned and faced Griswell squarely.

"There's no use dodgin' the question. There's something hellish in this house, and I believe I have an inklin' of what it is. I don't believe you killed Branner. Whatever killed him is up there—now. There's a lot about your yarn that don't sound sane; but there's nothin' sane about a flashlight goin' out like this one did. I don't believe that thing upstairs is human. I never met anything I was afraid to tackle in the dark before, but I'm not goin' up there until daylight. It's not long until dawn. We'll wait for it out there on that gallery."

The stars were already paling when they came out on the broad porch. Buckner seated himself on the balustrade, facing the door, his pistol dangling in his fingers. Griswell sat down near him and leaned back against a crumbling pillar. He shut his eyes, grateful for the faint breeze that seemed to cool his throbbing brain. He experienced a dull sense of unreality. He was a stranger in a strange land, a land that had become suddenly imbued with black horror. The shadow of the noose hovered above him, and in that dark house lay John Branner, with his butchered head—like the figments of a dream these facts spun and eddied in his brain until all merged in a gray twilight as sleep came uninvited to his weary soul.

He awoke to a cold white dawn and full memory of the horrors of the night. Mists curled about the stems of the pines, crawled in smoky wisps up the broken walk. Buckner was shaking him.

"Wake up! It's daylight."

Griswell rose, wincing at the stiffness of his limbs. His face was gray and old.

"I'm ready. Let's go upstairs."

"I've already been!" Buckner's eyes burned in the early dawn. "I didn't wake you up. I went as soon as it was light. I found nothin'."

"The tracks of the bare feet——"

"Gone!"

"*Gone?*"

"Yes, gone! The dust had been disturbed all over the hall, from the point where Branner's tracks ended; swept into corners. No chance of trackin' anything there now. Something obliterated those tracks while we sat here, and I didn't hear a sound. I've gone through the whole house. Not a sign of anything."

Griswell shuddered at the thought of himself sleeping alone on the porch while Buckner conducted his exploration.

"What shall we do?" he asked listlessly. "With those tracks gone, there goes my only chance of proving my story."

"We'll take Branner's body into the county-seat," answered Buckner. "Let me do the talkin'. If the authorities knew the facts as they appear, they'd insist on you being confined and indicted. I don't believe you killed Branner—but neither a district attorney, judge nor jury would believe what you told me, or what happened to us last night. I'm handlin' this thing my own way. I'm not goin' to arrest you until I've exhausted every other possibility.

"Say nothing' about what's happened here, when we get to town. I'll simply tell the district attorney that John Branner was killed by a party or parties unknown, and that I'm workin' on the case.

"Are you game to come back with me to this house and spend the night here, sleepin' in that room as you and Branner slept last night?"

Griswell went white, but answered as stoutly as his ancestors might have expressed their determination to hold their cabins in the teeth of the Pequots: "I'll do it."

"Let's go then; help me pack the body out to your auto."

Griswell's soul revolted at the sight of John Branner's bloodless face in the chill white dawn, and the feel of his clammy flesh. The gray fog wrapped wispy tentacles about their feet as they carried their grisly burden across the lawn.

2. The Snake's Brother

Again the shadows were lengthening over the pinelands, and again two men came bumping along the old road in a car with a New England license plate.

Buckner was driving. Griswell's nerves were too shattered for him to trust himself at the wheel. He looked gaunt and haggard, and his face was still pallid. The strain of the day spent at the county-seat was added to the horror that still rode his soul like the shadow of a black-winged vulture. He had not slept, had not tasted what he had eaten.

"I told you I'd tell you about the Blassenvilles," said Buckner. "They were proud folks, haughty, and pretty damn ruthless when they wanted their way. They didn't treat their niggers as well as the other planters did—got their ideas in the West Indies, I reckon. There was a streak of cruelty in them—especially Miss Celia, the last one of the family to come to these parts. That was long after the slaves had been freed, but she used to whip her mulatto maid just like she was a slave, the old folks say . . . The niggers said when a Blassenville died, the devil was always waitin' for him out in the black pines.

"Well, after the Civil War they died off pretty fast, livin' in poverty, on the plantation which was allowed to go to ruin. Finally only four girls were left, sisters, livin' in the old house and ekin' out a bare livin', with a few niggers livin' in the old slave huts and workin' the fields on the share. They kept to themselves, bein' proud, and ashamed of their poverty. Folks wouldn't see them for months at a time. When they needed supplies they sent a nigger to town after them.

"But folks knew about it when Miss Celia came to live with them. She came from somewhere in the West Indies, where the whole family originally had its roots—a fine, handsome woman, they say, in the early thirties. But she didn't mix with folks any more than the girls did. She brought a mulatto maid with her, and the Blassenville cruelty cropped out in her treatment of this maid. I knew an old nigger, years ago, who swore he saw Miss Celia tie this girl up to a tree, stark naked, and whip her with a horsewhip. Nobody was surprised when she disappeared. Everybody figured she'd run away, of course.

"Well, one day in the spring of 1890 Miss Elizabeth, the youngest girl, came in to town for the first time in maybe a year. She came after supplies. Said the niggers had all left the place. Talked a little more, too, a bit wild. Said Miss Celia had gone, without leaving any word. Said her sisters thought she'd gone back to the West Indies, but she believed her aunt was *still in the house*. She didn't say what she meant. Just got her supplies and pulled out for the Manor.

"A month went past, and a nigger came into town and said that Miss Elizabeth was livin' at the Manor alone. Said her three sisters weren't there any more, that they'd left one by one without givin' any word or explanation. She didn't know where they'd gone, and was afraid to stay there alone, but didn't know where else to go. She'd never known anything but the Manor, and had neither relatives nor friends. But she was in mortal terror of *something*. The nigger said she locked herself in her room at night and kept candles burnin' all night . . .

"It was a stormy spring night when Miss Elizabeth came tearin' into town on the one horse she owned, nearly dead from fright. She fell from her horse in the square; when she could talk she said she'd found a secret room in the Manor that had been forgotten for a hundred years. And she said that there she found her three sisters, dead, and hangin' by their necks from the ceilin'. She said *something* chased her and nearly brained her with an ax as she ran out the front door, but somehow she got to the horse and got away. She was nearly crazy with fear, and didn't know what it was that chased her—said it looked like a woman with a yellow face.

"About a hundred men rode out there, right away. They searched the house from top to bottom, but they didn't find any secret room, or the remains of the sisters. But they did find a hatchet stickin' in the doorjamb downstairs, with some of Miss Elizabeth's hairs stuck on it, just as she'd said. She wouldn't go back there and show them how to find the secret door; almost went crazy when they suggested it.

"When she was able to travel, the people made up some money and loaned it to her—she was still too proud to accept charity—and she went to California. She never came back, but later it was learned, when she went back to repay the money they'd loaned her, that she'd married out there.

"Nobody ever bought the house. It stood there just as she'd left it, and as the years passed folks stole all the furnishings out of it, poor white trash, I reckon. A nigger wouldn't go about it. But they came after sun-up and left long before sundown."

"What did the people think about Miss Elizabeth's story?" asked Griswell.

"Well, most folks thought she'd gone a little crazy livin' in that old house alone. But some people believed that mulatto girl, Joan, didn't run away, after all. They believed she'd hidden in the woods, and glutted her hatred of the Blassenvilles by murderin' Miss Celia and the three girls. They beat up the woods with bloodhounds, but never found a trace of her. If there was a secret room in the house, she might have been hidin' there—if there was anything to that theory."

"She couldn't have been hiding there all these

years," muttered Griswell. "Anyway, the thing in the house now isn't human."

Buckner wrenched the wheel around and turned into a dim trace that left the main road and meandered off through the pines.

"Where are you going?"

"There's an old nigger that lives off this way a few miles. I want to talk to him. We're up against something that takes more than white man's sense. The black people know more than we do about some things. This old man is nearly a hundred years old. His master educated him when he was a boy, and after he was freed he traveled more extensively than most white men do. They say he's a voodoo man."

Griswell shivered at the phrase, staring uneasily at the green forest walls that shut them in. The scent of the pines was mingled with the odors of the unfamiliar plants and blossoms. But underlying all was a reek of rot and decay. Again a sick abhorrence of these dark mysterious woodlands almost overpowered him.

"Voodoo!" he muttered. "I'd forgotten about that—I never could think of black magic in connection with the South. To me witchcraft was always associated with old crooked streets in waterfront towns, ovehhung by gabled roofs that were old when they were hanging witches in Salem; dark musty alleys where black cats and other things might steal at night. Witchcraft always meant the old towns of New England, to me—but all this is more terrible than any New England legend—these somber pines, old deserted houses, lost plantations, mysterious black people, old tales of madness and horror—God, what frightful, ancient terrors there are on this continent fools call 'young'!"

"Here's old Jacob's hut," announced Buckner, bringing the automobile to a halt.

Griswell saw a clearing and a small cabin squatting

under the shadows of the huge trees. There pines gave way to oaks and cypresses, bearded with gray trailing moss, and behind the cabin lay the edge of a swamp that ran away under the dimness of the trees, choked with rank vegetation. A thin wisp of blue smoke curled up from the stick-and-mud chimney.

He followed Buckner to the tiny stoop, where the sheriff pushed open the leather-hinged door and strode in. Griswell blinked in the comparative dimness of the interior. A single small window let in a little daylight. An old negro crouched beside the hearth, watching a pot stew over the open fire. He looked up as they entered, but did not rise. He seemed incredibly old. His face was a mass of wrinkles, and his eyes, dark and vital, were filmed momentarily at times as if his mind wandered.

Buckner motioned Griswell to sit down in a string-bottomed chair, and himself took a rudely-made bench near the hearth, facing the old man.

"Jacob," he said bluntly, "The time's come for you to talk. I know you know the secret of Blassenville Manor. I've never questioned you about it, because it wasn't in my line. But a man was murdered there last night, and this man here may hang for it, unless you tell me what haunts that old house of the Blassenvilles."

The old man's eyes gleamed, then grew misty as if clouds of extreme age drifted across his brittle mind.

"The Blassenvilles," he murmured, and his voice was mellow and rich, his speech not the patois of the piny woods darky. "They were proud people, sirs—proud and cruel. Some died in the war, some were killed in duels—the menfolks, sirs. Some died in the Manor—the old Manor——" His voice trailed off into unintelligible mumblings.

"What of the Manor?" asked Buckner patiently.

"Miss Celia was the proudest of them all," the old man muttered. "The proudest and the cruelest. The black people hated her; Joan most of all. Joan had white blood in her, and she was proud, too. Miss Celia whipped her like a slave."

"What is the secret of Blassenville Manor?" persisted Buckner.

The film faded from the old man's eyes; they were dark as moonlit wells.

"What secret, sir? I do not understand."

"Yes, you do. For years that old house has stood there with its mystery. You know the key to its riddle."

The old man stirred the stew. He seemed perfectly rational now.

"Sir, life is sweet, even to an old black man."

"You mean somebody would kill you if you told me?"

But the old man was mumbling again, his eyes clouded.

"Not somebody. No human. No human being. The black gods of the swamps. My secret is inviolate, guarded by the Big Serpent, the god above all gods. He would send a little brother to kiss me with his cold lips—a little brother with a white crescent moon on his head. I sold my soul to the Big Serpent when he made me maker of *zuvembies*——"

Buckner stiffened.

"I heard that word once before," he said softly, "from the lips of a dying black man, when I was a child. What does it mean?"

Fear filled the eyes of old Jacob.

"What have I said? No—no! I said nothing."

"*Zuvembies*," prompted Buckner.

"*Zuvembies*," mechanically repeated the old man, his eyes vacant. "A *zuvembie* was once a woman—on the Slave Coast they know of them. The drums that whisper by night in the hills of Haiti tell of them. The makers of *zuvembies* are honored of the people of Damballah. It is death to speak of it to a white man—it is one of the Snake God's forbidden secrets."

"You speak of the *zuvembies*," said Buckner softly.

"I must not speak of it," mumbled the old man, and Griswell realized that he was thinking aloud, too far gone in his dotage to be aware that he was speaking at all. "No white man must know that I danced in the Black Ceremony of the voodoo, and was made a maker of *zombies*—and *zuvembies*. The Big Snake punishes loose tongues with death."

"A *zuvembie* is a woman?" prompted Buckner.

"*Was* a woman," the old negro muttered. "*She* knew I was a maker of *zuvembies*—she came and stood in my hut and asked for the awful brew—the brew of ground snake-bones, and the blood of vampire bats, and the dew from a nighthawk's wings, and other elements unnamable. She had danced in the Black Ceremony—she was ripe to become a *zuvembie* —the Black Brew was all that was needed—the other was beautiful—I could not refuse her."

"Who?" demanded Buckner tensely, but the old man's head was sunk on his withered breast, and he did not reply. He seemed to slumber as he sat. Buckner shook him. "You gave a brew to make a woman a *zuvembie*—what is a *zuvembie*?"

The old man stirred resentfully and muttered drowsily.

"A *zuvembie* is no longer human. It knows neither relatives nor friends. It is one with the people of the Black World. It commands the natural demons—owls, bats, snakes and werewolves, and can fetch darkness to blot out a little light. It can be slain by lead or steel, but unless it is slain thus, it lives forever, and it eats no such food as humans eat. It dwells like a bat in a cave or an old house. Time means naught to the *zuvembie*; an hour, a day, a year, all is one. It cannot speak human words, nor think as a human thinks, but it can hypnotize the living by the sound of its voice, and when it slays a man, it can command his lifeless body until the flesh is cold. As long as the blood flows, the corpse is its slave. Its pleasure lies in the slaughter of human beings."

"And why should one become a *zuvembie?*" asked Buckner softly.

"Hate," whispered the old man. "Hate," whispered the old man. "Hate! Revenge!"

"Was her name Joan?" murmured Buckner.

It was as if the name penetrated the fogs of senility that clouded the voodoo-man's mind. He shook himself and the film faded from his eyes, leaving them hard and gleaming as wet black marble.

"Joan?" he said slowly. "I have not heard that name for the span of a generation. I seem to have been sleeping, gentlemen; I do not remember—I ask your pardon. Old men fall asleep before the fire, like old dogs. You asked me of Blassenville Manor? Sir, if I were to tell you why I cannot answer you, you would deem it mere superstition. Yet the white man's God be my witness——"

As he spoke he was reaching across the hearth for a piece of firewood, groping among the heaps of sticks there. And his voice broke in a scream, as he jerked back his arm convulsively. And a horrible, thrashing, trailing *thing* came with it. Around the voodoo-man's arm a mottled length of that shape was wrapped and a wicked wedge-shaped head struck again in silent fury.

The old man fell on the hearth, screaming, upsetting the simmering pot and scattering the embers, and then Buckner caught up a billet of firewood and crushed that flat head. Cursing, he kicked aside the knotting, twisting trunk, glaring briefly at the mangled head. Old Jacob had ceased screaming and writhing; he lay still, staring glassily upward.

"Dead?" whispered Griswell.

"Dead as Judas Iscariot," snapped Buckner, frowning at the twitching reptile. "That infernal snake crammed enough poison into his veins to kill a dozen men his age. But I think it was the shock and fright that killed him."

"What shall we do?" asked Griswell, shivering.

"Leave the body on that bunk. Nothin' can hurt it, if we bolt the door so the wild hogs can't get in, or any cat. We'll carry it into town tomorrow. We've got work to do tonight. Let's get goin'."

Griswell shrank from touching the corpse, but he helped Buckner lift it on the rude bunk, and then stumbled hastily out of the hut. The sun was hovering above the horizon, visible in dazzling red flame through the black stems of the trees.

They climbed into the car in silence, and went bumping back along the stumpy train.

"He said the Big Snake would send one of his brothers," muttered Griswell.

"Nonsense!" snorted Buckner. "Snakes like warmth, and that swamp is full of them. It crawled in and coiled up among that firewood. Old Jacob disturbed it, and it bit him. Nothin' supernatural about that." After a short silence he said, in a different voice, "That was the first time I ever saw a rattle strike without singin'; and the first time I ever saw a snake *with a white crescent moon on its head.*"

They were turning it to the main road before either spoke again.

"You think that the mulatto Joan has skulked in the house all these years?" Griswell asked.

"You heard what old Jacob said," answered Buckner grimly. "Time means nothin' to a *zuvembie.*"

As they made the last turn in the road, Griswell braced himself against the sight of Blassenville Manor looming black against the red sunset. When it came into view he bit his lip to keep from shrieking. The suggestion of cryptic horror came back in all its power.

"Look!" he whispered from dry lips as they came to a halt beside the road. Buckner grunted.

From the balustrades of the gallery rose a whirling cloud of pigeons that swept away into the sunset black against the lurid glare.

3. The Call of Zuvembie

Both men sat rigid for a few moments after the pigeons had flown.

"Well, I've seen them at last," muttered Buckner.

"Only the doomed see them, perhaps," whispered Griswell. "That tramp saw them——"

"Well, we'll see," returned the Southerner tranquilly, as he climbed out of the car, but Griswell noticed him unconsciously hitch forward his scabbarded gun.

The oaken door sagged on broken hinges. Their feet echoed on the broken brick walk. The blind windows reflected the sunset in sheets of flame. As they came into the broad hall Griswell saw the string of black marks that ran across the floor and into the chamber, marking the path of a dead man.

Buckner had brought blankets out of the automobile. He spread them before the fireplace.

"I'll lie next to the door," he said. "You lie where you did last night."

"Shall we light a fire in the grate?" asked Griswell, dreading the thought of the blackness that would cloak the woods when the brief twilight had died.

"No. You've got a flashlight and so have I. We'll lie here in the dark and see what happens. Can you use that gun I gave you?"

"I suppose so. I never fired a revolver, but I know how it's done."

"Well, leave the shootin' to me, if possible." The sheriff seated himself cross-legged on his blankets and emptied the cylinder of his big blue Colt, inspecting each cartridge with a critical eye before he replaced it.

Griswell prowled nervously back and forth, begrudging the slow fading of the light as a miser begrudges the waning of his gold. He leaned with one hand against the mantelpiece, staring down into the dust-covered ashes. The fire that produced those ashes must have been builded by Elizabeth Blassenville, more than forty years before. The thought was depressing. Idly he stirred the dusty ashes with his toe. Something came to view among the charred debris—a bit of paper, stained and yellowed. Still idly he bent and drew it out of the ashes. It was a note-book with moldering cardboard backs.

"What have you found?" asked Buckner, squinting down the gleaming barrel of his gun.

"Nothing but an old note-book. Looks like a diary. The pages are covered with writing—but the ink is so faded, and the paper is in such a state of decay that I can't tell much about it. How do you suppose it came in the fireplace, without being burned up?"

"Thrown in long after the fire was out," surmised Buckner. "Probably found and tossed in the fireplace by somebody who was in here stealin' furniture. Likely somebody who couldn't read."

Griswell fluttered the crumbling leaves listlessly, straining his eyes in the fading light over the yellowed scrawls. Then he stiffened.

"Here's an entry that's legible! Listen!" He read:

" 'I know someone is in the house besides myself. I can hear someone prowling about at night when the sun has set and the pines are black outside. Often in the night I hear *it* fumbling at my door. *Who* is it? Is it one of my sisters? Is it Aunt Celia? If it is either of these, why does she steal so subtly about the house? Why does she tug at my door, and glide away when I call to her? No, no! I dare not! I am afraid. Oh God, what shall I do? I dare not stay here—but where am I to go?' "

"By God!" ejaculated Buckner. "That must be Elizabeth Blassenville's diary! Go on!"

"I can't make out the rest of the pages," answered Griswell. "But a few pages further on I can make out some lines." He read:

" 'Why did the negroes all run away when Aunt Celia disappeared? My sisters are dead. I know they are dead. I seem to sense that they died horribly, in fear and agony. But why? *Why?* If someone murdered Aunt Celia, why should that person murder my poor sisters? They were always kind to the black people. Joan———' " He paused, scowling futilely.

"A piece of the page is torn out. Here's another entry under another date—at least I judge it's a date; I can't make it out for sure.

" '———the awful thing that the old negress hinted at? She named Jacob Blount, and Joan, but she would not speak plainly; perhaps she feared to———' Part of it gone here; then: 'No, no! How can it be? *She* is dead—or gone away. Yet—she was born and raised in the West Indies, and from hints she let fall in the past, I know she delved into the mysteries of the voodoo. I believe she even danced in one of their horrible ceremonies—how could she have been such a beast? And this—this horror. God, can such things be? I know not what to think. If it is *she* who roams the house at night, who fumbles at my door, who *whistles* so weirdly and sweetly—no, no, I must be going mad. If I stay here alone I shall die as hideously as my sisters must have died. Of that I am convinced.' "

The incoherent chronicle ended as abruptly as it had begun. Griswell was so engrossed in deciphering the scraps that he was not aware that darkness had stolen upon them, hardly aware that Buckner was holding his electric torch for him to read by. Waking from his abstraction he started and darted a quick glance at the black hallway.

"What do you make of it?"

"What I've suspected all the time," answered Buckner. "That mulatto maid Joan turned *zuvembie* to avenge herself on Miss Celia. Probably hated the whole family as much as she did her mistress. She'd taken part in voodoo ceremonies on her native island until she was 'ripe,' as old Jacob said. All she needed was the Black Brew—he supplied that. She killed Miss Celia and the three older girls, and would have gotten Elizabeth but for chance. She's been lurkin' in this old house all these years, like a snake in a ruin."

"But why should she murder a stranger?"

"You heard what old Jacob said," reminded Buckner. "A *zuvembie* finds satisfaction in the slaughter of humans. She called Branner up the stair and split his head and stuck the hatchet in his hand, and sent him downstairs to murder you. No court will ever believe that, but if we can produce her body, that will be evidence enough to prove your innocence. My word will be taken, that she murdered Branner. Jacob said a *zuvembie* could be killed . . . in reporting this affair I don't have to be too accurate in detail."

"She came and peered over the balustrade of the stair at us," muttered Griswell. "But why didn't we find her tracks on the stair?"

"Maybe you dreamed it. Maybe a *zuvembie* can project her spirit—hell! Why try to rationalize something that's outside the bounds of rationality? Let's begin our watch."

"Don't turn out the light!" exclaimed Griswell involuntarily. Then he added: "Of course. Turn it out. We must be in the dark as"—he gagged a bit—"as Branner and I were."

But fear like a physical sickness assailed him when the room was plunged in darkness. He lay trembling and his heart beat so heavily he felt as if he would suffocate.

"The West Indies must be the plague spot of the world," muttered Buckner, a blur on his blankets. "I've heard of *zombies*. Never knew before what a *zuvembie* was. Evidently some drug concocted by the voodoo-men to induce madness in women. That doesn't explain the other things, though: the hypnotic powers, the abnormal longevity, the ability to control corpses—no, a *zuvembie* can't be merely a madwoman. It's a monster, something more and less than a human being, created by the magic that spawns in black swamps and jungles—well, we'll see."

His voice ceased, and in the silence Griswell heard the pounding of his own heart. Outside in the black woods a wolf howled eerily, and owls hooted. Then silence fell again like a black fog.

Griswell forced himself to lie still on his blankets. Time seemed at a standstill. He felt as if he were choking. The suspense was growing unendurable; the effort he made to control his crumbling nerves bathed his limbs in sweat. He clenched his teeth until his jaws ached and almost locked, and the nails of his fingers bit deeply into his palms.

He did not know what he was expecting. The fiend would strike again—but how? Would it be a horrible, sweet whistling, bare feet stealing down the creaking steps, or a sudden hatchet stroke in the dark? Would it choose him or Buckner? *Was Buckner already dead?* He could see nothing in the blackness, but he heard the man's steady breathing. The Southerner must have nerves of steel. Or was that Buckner breathing beside him, separated by a narrow strip of darkness? Had the fiend already struck in silence, and taken the sheriff's place, there to lie in ghoulish glee until it was ready to strike?—a thousand hideous fancies assailed Griswell tooth and claw.

He began to feel that he would go mad if he did

not leap to his feet, screaming, and burst frenziedly out of that accursed house—not even the fear of the gallows could keep him lying there in the darkness any longer—the rhythm of Buckner's breathing was suddenly broken, and Griswell felt as if a bucket of ice-water had been poured over him. From somewhere above them rose a sound of weird, sweet whistling. . . .

Griswell's control snapped, plunging his brain into darkness deeper than the physical blackness which engulfed him. There was a period of absolute blankness, in which a realization of *motion* was his first sensation of awakening consciousness. He was running, madly, stumbling over an incredibly rough road. All was darkness about him, and he ran blindly. Vaguely he realized that he must have bolted from the house, and fled for perhaps miles before his overwrought brain begun to function. He did not care; dying on the gallows for a murder he never committed did not terrify him half as much as the thought of returning to that house of horror. He was overpowered by the urge to run—run—run as he was running now, blindly, until he reached the end of his endurance. The mist had not yet fully lifted from his brain, but he was aware of a dull wonder that he could not see the stars through the black branches. He wished vaguely that he could see where he was going. He believed he must be climbing a hill, and that was strange, for he knew there were no hills within miles of the Manor. Then above and ahead of him a dim glow began.

He scrambled toward it, over the ledge-like projections that were more and more and more taking on a disquieting symmetry. Then he was horror-stricken to realize that a sound was impacting on his ears—*a weird mocking whistle*. The sound swept the mists away. Why, what was this? *Where was he?* Awakening and realization came like the stunning stroke of a butcher's maul. He was not fleeing along a road, or climbing a hill; he was mounting a stair. He was still in Blassenville Manor! *And he was climbing the stair!*

An inhuman scream burst from his lips. Above it the mad whistling rose in a ghoulish piping of demoniac triumph. He tried to stop—to turn back—even to fling himself over the balustrade. His shrieking rang unbearably in his own ears. But his will-power was shattered to bits. It did not exist. He had no will. He had dropped his flashlight, and he had forgotten the gun in his pocket. He could not command his own body. His legs, moving stiffly, worked like pieces of mechanism detached from his brain, obeying an outside will. Clumping methodically they carried him shrieking up the stair toward the witch-fire glow shimmering above him.

"Buckner!" he screamed. "Buckner! Help, for God's sake!"

His voice strangled in his throat. He had reached the upper landing. He was tottering down the hallway. The whistling sank and ceased, but its impulsion still drove him on. He could not see from what source the dim glow came. It seemed to emanate from no central focus. But he saw a vague figure shambling toward him. It looked like a woman, but no human woman ever walked with that skulking gait, and no human woman ever had that face of horror, that leering yellow blur of lunacy—he tried to scream at the sight of that face, at the glint of keen steel in the uplifted claw-like hand—but his tongue was frozen.

Then something crashed deafeningly behind him, the shadows were split by a tongue of flame which lit a hideous figure falling backward. Hard on the heels of the report rang an inhuman squawk.

In the darkness that followed the flash Griswell fell to his knees and covered his face with his hands. He did not hear Buckner's voice. The Southerner's hand on his shoulder shook him out of his swoon.

A light in his eyes blinded him. He blinked, shaded his eyes, looked up into Buckner's face, bending at the rim of the circle of light. The sheriff was pale.

"Are you hurt? God, man, are you hurt? There's a butcher knife there on the floor——"

"I'm not hurt," mumbled Griswell. "You fired just in time—the fiend! Where is it? Where did it go?"

"Listen!"

Somewhere in the house there sounded a sickening flopping and flapping as of something that thrashed and struggled in its death convulsions.

"Jacob was right," said Buckner grimly. "Lead can kill them. I hit her, all right. Didn't dare use my flashlight, but there was enough light. When that whistlin' started you almost walked over me gettin' out. I knew you were hypnotized, or whatever it is. I followed you up to the stairs. I was right behind you, but crouchin' low so she wouldn't see me, and maybe get away again. I almost waited too long before I fired—but the sight of her almost paralyzed me. Look!"

He flashed his light down the hall, and now it shone bright and clear. And it shone on an aperture gaping in the wall where no door had showed before.

"The secret panel Miss Elizabeth found!" Buckner snapped. "Come on!"

He ran across the hallway and Griswell followed him dazedly. The flopping and thrashing came from beyond that mysterious door, and now the sounds had ceased.

The light revealed a narrow, tunnel-like corridor that evidently led through one of the thick walls. Buckner plunged into it without hesitation.

"Maybe it couldn't think like a human," he muttered, shining his light ahead of him. "But it had sense enough to erase its tracks last night so we couldn't trail it to that point in the wall and maybe find the secret panel. There's a room ahead—the secret room of the Blassenvilles!"

And Griswell cried out: "My God! It's the windowless chamber I saw in my dream, with the three bodies hanging—ahhhhh!"

Buckner's light playing about the circular chamber became suddenly motionless. In that wide ring of light three figures appeared, three dried, shriveled, mummy-like shapes, still clad in the moldering garments of the last century. Their slippers were clear of the floor as they hung by their withered necks from chains suspended from the ceiling.

"The three Blassenville sisters!" muttered Buckner. "Miss Elizabeth wasn't crazy, after all."

"Look!" Griswell could barely make his voice intelligible. "There—over there in the corner!"

The light moved, halted.

"Was that thing a woman once?" whispered Griswell. "God, look at that face, even in death. Look at those claw-like hands, with black talons like those of a beast. Yes, it was human, though—even the rags of an old ballroom gown. Why should a mulatto maid wear such a dress, I wonder?"

"This has been her lair for over forty years," muttered Buckner, brooding over the grinning grisly thing sprawling in the corner. "This clears you, Griswell—a crazy woman with a hatchet—that's all the authorities need to know. God, what a revenge! —what a foul revenge! Yet what a bestial nature she must have had, in the beginnin', to delve into voodoo as she must have done——"

"The mulatto woman?" whispered Griswell, dimly sensing a horror that overshadowed all the rest of the terror.

Buckner shook his head. "We misunderstood old Jacob's maunderin's, and the things Miss Elizabeth wrote—*she* must have known, but family pride sealed her lips. Griswell, I understand now; the mulatto woman had her revenge, but not as we'd supposed. She didn't drink the Black Brew old Jacob fixed for her. It was for somebody else, to be given secretly in her food, or coffee, no doubt. Then Joan ran away, leavin' the seeds of the hell she'd sowed to grow."

"That—that's not the mulatto woman?" whispered Griswell.

"When I saw her out there in the hallway I knew she was no mulatto. And those distorted features still reflect a family likeness. I've seen her portrait, and I can't be mistaken. There lies the creature that once was Celia Blassenville."

AN OPEN WINDOW

Behind the Veil, what gulfs of Time and Space?
What blinking mowing Shapes to blast the sight?
I shrink before a vague colossal Face
Born in the mad immensities of Night.

ROGER ZELAZNY
DREAM WEAVER

"Zelazny, telling of gods and wizards, uses magical words as if he were himself a wizard. He reaches into the subconscious and invokes archetypes to make the hair rise on the back of your neck. Yet these archetypes are transmuted into a science fiction world that is as believable—and as awe-inspiring—as the world you now live in." —**Philip José Farmer**

Wizard World
Infant exile, wizard's son, Pol Detson spent his formative years in total ignorance of his heritage, trapped in the most mundane of environments: Earth. But now has come the day when his banishers must beg him to return as their savior, lest their magic kingdom become no better than Earth itself. Previously published in parts as *Changeling* and *Madwand*.
69842-7 * $3.95

The Black Throne with Fred Saberhagen
One of the most remarkable exercises in the art and craft of fantasy fiction in the last decade.... As children they met and built sand castles on a beach out of space and time: Edgar Perry, little Annie, and Edgar Allan Poe.... Fifteen years later Edgar Perry has grown to manhood—and as the result of a trip through a maelstrom, he's leading a life of romantic adventure. But his alter ego, Edgar Allan, is stranded in a strange and unfriendly world where he can only write about the wonderful and mysterious reality he has lost forever....
72013-9 * $4.95

The Mask of Loki with Thomas T. Thomas
It started in the 12th century when their avatars first joined in battle. On that occasion the sorcerous Hasan al Sabah, the first Assassin, won handily against Thomas Amnet, Knight Templar. There have been many duels since then, and in each the undying Arab has ended the life of Loki's avatar. The wizard thinks he's in control. The gods think that's funny.... A new novel of demigods who walk the Earth, in the tradition of *Lord of Light*.
72021-X * $4.95

This Immortal
After the Three Days of War, and decades of Vegan occupation, Earth isn't doing too well. But Conrad Nimikos, if he could stop jet-setting for a minute, might just be Earth's redemption.... This, Zelazny's first novel, tied with *Dune* for the Hugo Award.
69848-6 * $4.99 _____

The Dream Master
When Charles Render, engineer-physician, agrees to help a blind woman learn to "see"—at least in her dreams—he is drawn into a web of powerful primal imagery. And once Render becomes one with the Dreamer, he must enter irrevocably the realm of nightmare....
69874-5 * $3.50 _____

Isle of the Dead
Francis Sandow was the only non-Pei'an to complete the religious rites that allowed him to become a World-builder—and to assume the Name and Aspect of one of the Pei'an gods. And now he's one of the richest men in the galaxy. A man like that makes a lot of enemies....
72011-2 * $3.50 _____

Four for Tomorrow
Featuring the Hugo winner "A Rose for Ecclesiastes" and the Nebula winner "The Doors of His Face, the Lamps of His Mouth."
72051-1 * $3.95 _____

ROBERT A. HEINLEIN

"Heinlein knows more about blending provocative scientific thinking with strong human stories than any dozen other contemporary science fiction writers."
—*Chicago Sun-Times*

"Robert A. Heinlein wears imagination as though it were his private suit of clothes. What makes his work so rich is that he combines his lively, creative sense with an approach that is at once literate, informed, and exciting."
—*New York Times*

Seven of Robert A. Heinlein's best-loved titles are now available in superbly packaged new Baen editions, with series-look covers by artist John Melo. Collect them all by sending in the order form below: